PRAISE FOR LANCI

C000108322

Heart Pounding from Start to Finish!

A unique plot and strong, believable characters, who you
find yourself rooting for right from the start

This Book Will Leave You Breathless

Oh boy what a way to finish a series, this book takes you
high then drops you down. You think it's all over but has
Lance got more up his sleeve? I can't wait to see.

Best series ever, must read!

Love this series! It seemed like this book went so fast as I
finished it in a little over a day and can't wait until the next
book. Hurry with the next book. It says finale but I think there
is room for one more book. Some loose ends need to be
tightened up.

On the Edge of Your Seat Read

Oh boy Lance can certainly write in this book. He is up
against the undead as well as having his brain and other
organs sliced up to see how he can keep from getting killed
by the undead. Fast moving with lots of blood and gore great
I can't wait for book six.

Lance Winkless was born in Sutton Coldfield, England, brought up in Plymouth, Devon and now lives in Staffordshire with his partner and daughter.

Lance is a member of the Society of Authors

For more information on Lance Winkless and future writing see his website.

www.LanceWinkless.com

By Lance Winkless

FOUNDATION DAY

CAPITAL FALLING - THE SERIES

&

THE Z SEASON – TRILOGY

KILL TONE
VOODOO SUN
CRUEL FIX

Visit Amazon Author Pages

Amazon US- Amazon.com/author/lancewinkless
Amazon UK- Amazon.co.uk/Lance-Winkless/e/B07QJV2LR3

Why Not Follow

Facebook LanceWinklessAuthor
Twitter   @LanceWinkless
Instagram @LanceWinkless
BookBub www.bookbub.com/authors/lance-winkless

FOUNDATION DAY

LANCE WINKLESS

This book is a work of fiction, any resemblance to actual persons, living or dead, organisations, places, incidents and events are coincidental.

Copyright © 2022 Lance Winkless

All rights reserved.

No part of this book may be reproduced, transmitted in any form or by any means, photocopying, electronic, mechanical or otherwise without the express written permission of the copyright holder.

ISBN 9798785897458

Published by Lance Winkless

www.LanceWinkless.com

Barbara Mary Winkless, Mum

7th April 1947 to 17th June 2022

Chapter 1

Behind him, the doors of the bus creak closed. Merle hates the bus, loathes it. He much prefers travelling by train, but no trains run to his neighbourhood, Billingham, in the east of the city. Underground or overground. Low rent and low-rise living aren't deemed high priorities by the city planners, they never have been.

Perhaps one day he might manage to save enough from his meagre wages to think about buying a car. There are no illusions in Merle's mind about the type of car he might manage to afford to rescue him from the bus. One that belches out more smoke than this goddam bus is the best he can hope for. No gleaming wheel trims or bucket racing seats for him. Much less a car that would plug into the electrical grid, even if Billingham had more than a handful of charging points on offer. Eco-warriors are few and far between on the streets of this neighbourhood. The only warriors that frequent the streets in the east carry knives and, commonly, handguns.

Turning, in the hope of locating a seat for his tortured journey, the faces of the great unwashed packed onto the bus stare back at him suspiciously. Merle doesn't know why but he has always felt destined for greater things than the cretins staring back at him. He knows how hopeless each of

1

them feels, nevertheless. Slaves to the system, a system that is impossibly stacked against each and every one of them. Low wages don't prevent the government from rinsing every penny of tax they possibly can from their flimsy pay packets.

Pulling his raincoat tighter around himself, and his bag closer to him, Merle steps away from the bus driver just as he releases the handbrake and staring eyes dart away from his direction when he moves. Suddenly everyone pretends they haven't seen the new interloper who, God forbid, might stand or sit next to them, invading their space.

Thankfully, seats are available, even if he will have to sit next to another unlucky passenger. The young woman occupying the seat next to the window doesn't glance away from the rain-spattered glass when Merle claims the seat next to her. She doesn't notice his eyes travelling over her legs and up her profile as he 'innocently' takes his seat.

The woman recoils in her seat, only the side of the bus stopping her from inching further away from the new passenger who has rudely invaded her personal space. The touch of his thigh against hers sends a chill down her spine. She wishes she had chosen the long dress and not the short one that is exposing her legs to the leering eyes that burn into her skin.

Transfixed by the sheen of the soft young skin under the overhead lights, Merle holds the bag carrying his precious cargo tightly on his lap. He notices the young woman glance in his direction; she has noticed him peering down. Her legs squirm under his inspection but he doesn't relent and look away. He doesn't release her from her turmoil. Instead, he leans forward slightly, his eyes wide, studying.

"Excuse me," the young woman says suddenly, just as his eyes settle on the white sandals she is wearing and her red painted toenails.

Hardly suitable shoes to be wearing on such a wet day, Merle decides, but he is glad she chose them.

He doesn't move for a moment, trapping her in the confined space between himself and the side of the bus. He takes one last look at the woman's bare legs before he finally swivels in his seat to allow her to squeeze past.

She doesn't thank him as she leaves, pressing the closest 'STOP' button as she barges through. The 'ding' of the 'STOP' bell is hardly heard. Merle's concentration is fixed, and he leers as she makes her exit from his trap. His eyes wander as the woman moves out of his view to the front of the bus, next to the driver. The bus stops and he finds himself peering at a stern older woman sitting on the other side of the bus. The woman peers back at him with a knowing expression of distaste but Merle simply smirks in reply, wondering if she would prefer his attention. *Obviously not*, he thinks, as the woman quickly pulls her eyes away from his, her expression rapidly changing to one of uneasy concern.

As the doors of the bus close behind the escaping young woman, Merle quickly shifts across to the window seat. Rain spoils his view, but he manages to catch one last look at the young woman as the bus rejoins the flow of traffic. She stands motionless in the fading light, watching him anxiously through the window, rain pouring over her, soaking her hair. *I hope we meet again*, Merle thinks, knowing that this was not the woman's intended stop.

With the feminine distraction gone Merle settles back into his seat to concentrate on the evening ahead. His unsuspecting fellow passengers believe him to be one of them: poor, sad and hard done by. That may have been true once, but things have changed. He has a purpose now, he is part of something bigger, something important.

Unable to help himself, his hands move to the zip of the bag sitting on his lap, his right hand slowly pulling the zip open. Merle looks over his shoulder to ensure nobody is prying before his fingers open the bag to let him see inside.

For months now, he has been conversing with his newfound friend, Janus18, on the dark web. The chatroom where they discovered each other is perfectly secure, a safe place where they can chat freely about their shared interests, and they soon discovered that they had many. In the beginning, the chat and files they shared were centred around frivolous subjects. Many of which other 'closed-minded' people might find perverse or unacceptable. That was their problem. He has no time for prudish, do-gooders who want to interfere in his life rather than worrying about their own.

Recently, his conversations with Janus18 have become more serious and intriguing, however. The frivolous discussions that accompanied the blossoming of their friendship, whilst not completely forgotten, have certainly begun to take a backseat in preference to more enlightened matters.

Janus18 is certainly not the normal gutter rat that often frequents clandestine chatrooms, seeking sexual gratification or searching for illicit commodities. Merle rapidly came to understand that. Janus18 has an agenda, a vision, which Merle slowly began to understand and share.

After their very first conversation on the dark web, Merle knew that there was something different about his new friend. His interest resulted in him researching his new acquaintance's online handle, Janus18 with interest, to try and gain more insight.

In ancient Rome, Janus was a god, the god of beginnings and passages who was depicted as a two-faced deity who could see both the past and future. Janus symbolised change or transition, and he represented time. The month of January, the change to a new year is named after Janus, and Janus18 seeks change.

Merle has questioned what the number eighteen represents in Janus18's handle but his question is always rebuffed. Perhaps the number eighteen was chosen at random, but Merle doesn't think anything Janus18 does is random. Could the number have personal significance for Janus? Merle doubts that also. He thinks that would be too self-indulgent. The number must have a deeper meaning and be a statement to others. In most countries, eighteen is the age when children come of age and are considered adults. Is that it? That would represent the passing of time, but again it's a flimsy theory. The theory of Merle's which has the greatest significance is also a sinister and exciting one. Could eighteen represent the devil? 666 is the number of the beast and eighteen is the sum of the digits that make up that number.

Merle's eyes focus into the darkness of his carry bag, immediately seeing the glint of the unmarked silver aerosol canister waiting inside. The bus bounces over a bump in the road, startling him, and he quickly zips the bag back up, looking around to check that nobody is watching him. *Act casually*, he tells himself, *blend in, don't draw attention to yourself.*

Merle does his best to play it cool. He sits back in his seat, relaxes and lets his gaze wander out of the window. Lights hovering high up in the falling darkness show Merle his destination: the city. He estimates that it will be around another fifteen minutes until the bus reaches the end of the bus route, which is where he will get off. This is the second time in as many evenings that he has rode the bus into the city, straight after work. He hasn't even gone home or grabbed something to eat. He went straight to the bus stop as soon as he clocked off.

When he'd arrived home after last night's event, at around ten-thirty, he was surprised by his neighbour once more. Dear old Mrs Wallace had appeared from inside her apartment the moment Merle's key touched the lock of his apartment's door. Mrs Wallace was muttering a complaint about being disturbed again by the delivery man as she offered Merle the parcel that had been left with her for him. Merle hadn't heard any of her complaints in the surprised excitement caused by the fact that another parcel had arrived for him. He hopes that he had apologised as he retrieved his package from her grasp. But because of his excitement, he can't be sure. He isn't sure if he said a single word to the old lady.

Inside the package was another canister, together with a vial of liquid and his latest instructions printed on an A4 sheet of paper. Merle made sure he'd absorbed and understood his instructions before destroying the sheet of paper by fire. The liquid had tasted bitter as he swigged it back. He had ensured he swallowed every drop, despite the liquid's assault on his tongue.

Still struggling to believe his luck that he is out on another mission so soon after the last, Merle goes over Janus's instructions once more in his mind. The very last thing he wants to do is make a mistake and let Janus18 down. The mission is too important to be making mistakes.

Satisfied that he knows what he must do, Merle finds himself going over last night's events in his head. *You learn*

6

by your mistakes, Merle tells himself. *Did I make any last night? Is there anything that can be improved upon?*

Merle takes himself back in time to yesterday evening when, as it will tonight, the bus reached the end of its journey. He hadn't rushed to disembark; he'd waited his turn as the passengers in front of him made their way off. The bus terminal was busy with commuters rushing to make their way home after work, moving around the terminal like ants. Security in the bus terminal was minimal and of little concern to Merle as he casually made his way to the exit to enter the city.

The instructions he received yesterday had been to find a specific type of subject. A white male in his thirties or forties was the requirement. Beggars or vagrants, either of which Merle could easily find, would not be suitable. A fit and healthy subject was required. The subject must also be watched and recorded once the trial was underway to enable him to give an account of the test to Janus.

It had taken some time to find a suitable subject. Merle remembers walking the streets of the city, urgently searching. There were plenty of suitable candidates, but there were also too many other people around to allow him to make his observations without being disturbed. Eventually, he found himself in the financial district, where things were quieter. He'd also decided to change tack and find a secluded area in which to wait for the candidate to come to him. He didn't have to wait long.

"Excuse me, have you got the time?" Merle asked the smartly dressed businessman who approached his location.

"Six twenty-five," the well-heeled man replied, taking his hand out of his pocket to see his watch.

"Thank you. Oh, wait. I think you've dropped something," Merle improvised, before stooping down to act

7

as though he was picking something off the ground. "Is this yours?"

In his hand, Merle grasped the thin canister Janus18 had sent him and held it out to the businessman, his hand covering the majority of the silver casing, his finger poised on the release valve. Thankfully, the businessman stopped immediately and turned toward Merle, suddenly worried he was missing something.

"What is it?" the businessman asked, unable to see properly what Merle was holding.

"I don't know," Merle had replied innocently, tempting his prey to move closer to get a better look.

"I don't think..." the businessman muttered, as he came in close for a look at what was in Merle's hand.

The moment his prey was in range Merle sprung his trap. His hand flipped over, and he pointed the nozzle of the canister into the face of the unsuspecting businessman. Before his quarry could react, Merle's finger had already pressed the nozzle down hard and a short burst of vaporised liquid hissed out of the canister. Almost instantly, the aerosol canister emptied its contents directly into the businessman's face.

Initially, Merle's prey stepped back in shock, confused by what had just happened. As he moved his hands to his face to wipe away the wetness with a reflex action, he released his briefcase, which bashed to the ground with a thud. But then Merle could see the rage in his eyes as his hands lowered to wipe away the liquid on his suit jacket.

"What the hell do you think...?"

"Don't fight it," Merle had responded. "Let it happen."

The businessman didn't just let it happen and Merle had to act quickly to avoid the fist that came his way. Another fist came, but this time it was laboured and Merle caught the flailing arm, taking the businessman into his control, the man already succumbing to his fate.

"I have children," Merle's test subject coughed and spluttered.

"Don't worry about them now. You are helping with something very important," Merle assured him, as he positioned himself under the arm of the businessman, as if the man was drunk. At least that is what Merle hoped it looked like to any prying members of the public.

"But... my... wife..."

"She will understand," Merle replied, as he kicked the man's briefcase into the side street next to them. "Come on, let's find you somewhere to relax," he added, as he steadied and guided his test subject.

Relieved to move out of the light and into the relative darkness of the side street, Merle replied with words of reassurance as the businessman stuttered complaints about feeling unwell.

"This looks like a good spot," Merle said, as he eased the businessman down onto the ground next to a pile of black rubbish bags and rested him against the wall.

Standing back, Merle began to record events on his phone just in time. His phone's camera found its focus just as the subject began to convulse. Merle watched eagerly when the businessman's stomach began to contort, pulling his upper body momentarily forward off the wall, his entire body shaking. Zooming in as the subject's face began to twist with strain, he ensured the camera caught his eyes rolling back into their sockets. Merle felt bile in his own

9

stomach bubble as the subject's face turned white the moment before a stream of vomit erupted out of the businessman's gaping mouth. Putrid liquid flowed down from his mouth, covering his immaculately tailored suit for an impossibly long time. Merle was beginning to think that the stream would never end, that the subject would die through lack of oxygen, when suddenly the stream of brown liquid cut off and his subject gasped for breath.

Gulping in air didn't come easily for the stricken man. Vomit was pulled back into his greedy lungs, causing a coughing fit of epic proportions. Blood pumped into his face; pressure built. His eyes bulged almost to the point when they might have popped out of his skull. Deep rasping coughing continued for an age, forcing the vomit back out of his lungs, together with mucus and blood. The ejected matter drooled out of his mouth in long sticky trains.

Merle continued to record as the coughing finally began to abate, replaced by moans carried on shallow breaths. Blood retreated from his subject's face, disappearing to who knows where. Below, the ground darkened as more unwanted matter flowed out of the man, soaking through the suit's expensive material. A foul odour rose to assault Merle's nostrils as the pool of faeces, urine and, possibly, the subject's innards spread out, staining the surrounding area. Merle was careful the vile liquid didn't flow so far as to tarnish his shoes.

Inaudible words of desperation mumbled out of the businessman. Merle guessed he was begging for mercy and help. He was forced to admit he felt a small pang of sympathy for his test subject. He had wondered where and to whom the man was travelling after he had finished work, before his unfortunate meeting in the streets outside his office. In the midst of his recounting, Merle makes a mental note not to allow his personal feelings to interfere with tonight's trial. Whatever his feelings, his task is too important for him to become side-tracked and lose concentration. His mental note filed, Merle continues to remember the businessman's final disturbing demise.

Janus18's agent, the one that he had administered to the subject, had taken effect almost immediately. Within seconds, the subject had become delirious and then, in no more than a couple of minutes, his bodily functions had begun to react to the agent, with horrific results. Eventually, life had been drawn from the subject. The businessman's head had flopped back against the wall in a futile bid to draw breath from the heavens above. His eyes were wide, full of fear, as he fought to draw precious oxygen into his lungs, but his lungs were failing. As each breath grew shallower, a rattle began to rasp out of his gaping mouth and, with each fading breath, a shade of colour visibly drained from the subject's complexion. The skin covering the businessman's face appeared to retract and to suck in around his face, turning grey, until the man's features were almost unrecognisable.

Merle had felt a pang of relief when the death rattle sounding from his subject's lungs had finally ceased. That was when he knew the test was complete and his subject had succumbed. The businessman was dead within a few minutes of the agent being administered.

Calmly, Merle had tapped his phone's screen to end the recording and had then put the phone away. He then carefully used the adjacent black bags full of refuse to cover his subject's body, knowing full well it would be discovered. That was fine, providing he had left the area and was on his way home when the grisly discovery was made.

He had made it home without incident and now he found himself strolling out of the bus station again. This time, however, he uses a different exit, one that will take him out into another part of the city.

11

Janus's instructions for tonight's trial are very different from last nights. There will be no lonely soul to find or discrete side streets to utilise. Merle's task this evening is going to be far riskier and will be carried out in full public view.

Chapter 2

Merle finds himself with an inner calmness as he exits the bus station, one that he hadn't expected. Tonight is a big night, he has been feeling anxious about it all day at work, constantly going over the different permutations of the evening ahead. Now that he is mingling in the throng of people bustling through the city those nerves have evaporated. Maybe that says more about his mind-numbing job than anything else. Until only recently his life had seemed like a never-ending dark tunnel of drudgery separated every five days by two days of wasted oblivion. Janus18 has given him a light at the end of that tunnel, one that Merle will go to any length to reach. There is no way he will let Janus down or fail him.

Merle hadn't counted on the city being so lively. Last night the city was calm; busy, but calm. Tonight, however, there is a different atmosphere and more people. People drinking and dressed for a night out are more prevalent, weaving their way through commuters to find the next bar.

Merle isn't used to visiting the city at night, especially on a weekday, and he wonders what the difference is between last night and this evening. It's only Thursday, it isn't the weekend yet, so why are so many people out and about, as if the weekend was already here? Perhaps there is a special occasion this evening that he doesn't know about. Are Thursdays in the city always like this? Did Janus plan it this way? Merle knows deep down that tonight is exactly as Janus planned it. He wants a public show and knew tonight would be the perfect scenario to have one. Putting his questions to one side, and trusting in his mentor, Merle decides which way to head.

Chinatown will be the perfect area for tonight's trial, Merle thinks, as he turns to follow two women in high heels who seem to be going in that direction. He can never fathom how women can walk any distance in such tall shoes, but he enjoys the view as he follows them. He is grateful that the rain has stopped and he can only imagine that the two women are even more pleased than he is. Now there is only the challenge of dodging multiple puddles that the rain has left behind.

Nice view or not, Merle finds himself overtaking the two women as they totter along. He has more important business tonight. Chinatown is approaching and he must concentrate. He allows himself one last look at the two women as he passes them, and they giggle as he does so. He wonders if they are going for drinks in Trinity Square, where he is heading. If they are, he doubts they will be giggling for much longer.

Merle sees the first Chinese lantern hanging off a building above the heads of the people walking in front of him. Nerves fizzle in his stomach and blood rushes to his head, causing him to lose his bearings. Merle isn't that familiar with the Chinese quarter of the city and his excitement isn't helping him find his destination. For a moment he simply follows the people in front of him while his brain rushes to remember his route.

14

Most of the pedestrians ahead turn a corner to the left and Merle follows suit, hoping that the new street will be familiar, and it is. An army of Chinese lanterns dance in the breeze, on each side of the wide road, hanging off every building. Merle knows exactly where he is now: he has found the main drag from the city centre into Chinatown.

Merle relaxes somewhat now that he knows where he is and is sure where he's going. Trinity Square is at the end of the road and that is where everyone is heading. He walks steadily along with his fellow pedestrians, blending in. Others stop to check menus mounted outside the plethora of suitably themed restaurants lining the road or go into a bar, but Merle doesn't delay, doesn't even pause to look at the lines of gold waving cats in the trinket stores.

As the traffic on the road filters away to the right, a Chinese arch welcomes pedestrians into Trinity Square. Merle files into the square with everyone else but, as he crosses the threshold, he steps to the side to allow himself to take in his surroundings. Trinity Square is the focal point of Chinatown and is bustling with people. Mounted in the centre of the square is a tall, slim Chinese pagoda. Members of the public look up, admiring the ornate tiered structure, or circle it to reach their desired food outlet or bar, and there are plenty to choose from.

Janus18 wanted a public trial of the agent he is carrying in his bag and, Merle thinks, *he's certainly going to get that here.*

"Mind out of the way, moron," a male voice barks, in unison with Merle's shoulder being bashed from behind.

Merle staggers under the assault but catches himself. Suddenly, he's afraid that the authorities have somehow discovered his encounter with the businessman last night and have arrived to arrest him. He reaches for his bag in a

15

panic. He must release Janus18's agent, even if not as planned. *Infecting any bystander or policeman will do*, Merle decides. He can't let Janus down. He won't. Merle would rather die than do that.

The heavyset man who had barged into him laughs along with his equally large male counterpart as Merle grips his bag, ready to open it. The two men keep walking into the square, not bothering to look back at Merle, and he relaxes his hold on the bag.

These men aren't the authorities, Merle realises, *they're just two boozed-up buffoons who think it's funny to barge him out of the way. Let's see how long they laugh for*, Merle rages and takes off after the two men.

With angry eyes fixed on the two lumbering bodies in front of him, Merle follows his assailants deeper into the square. The two men have obviously been drinking and Merle isn't the only person they rudely disturb as they walk. If they don't barge into the innocent people in their way, their loud and obnoxious manner certainly causes people to turn and look with nervous expressions.

This is one of the things that is wrong with this world, Merle decides, as he follows the two men. Having a good drink is one thing, but then acting like a Neanderthal with anyone who happens to be in the way is quite another. If you can't handle your drink then don't drink. It's simple. There is no excuse to go around physically and verbally assaulting people for no other reason than that you've had a drink or two. The two cretins in front of him definitely can't handle their drink, but Merle doubts that their behaviour would be much better even if a drop of alcohol hadn't passed their lips. Some people have no manners, either when inebriated or sober.

Having intentionally kept his distance from the two men as they steamroll their way around the central pagoda and through Trinity Square, Merle pauses and watches. His quarries stride straight toward a lavishly neon-lit bar, but their entry is unexpectedly blocked. Two heavyset, black-clad doormen step into their path, arms crossed over the lower part of their chests and with stern expressions fixed on their faces. Merle cannot hear what is being said between the four bulky men, but he can imagine. The shaking of heads by the two doormen confirms that the two inebriated Neanderthals have been refused entry to the bar. Merle watches eagerly to see how the two cocky men will react to their wings being clipped.

Just as he suspected the two drunken bullies back down from the two doormen, turn and walk away from the bar's entrance. *Typical,* Merle thinks, *as soon as somebody of equal size stands up to them they turn tail and slope away.*

Merle doesn't let the men out of his sight, however. He has a score to settle. As they move back into the main square, Merle begins to follow them again. The two men's temperaments have completely changed, Merle notices, as he follows. Now, they try to blend into the crowd. Gone are the bullying tactics used to deal with anyone in their way. Instead, they skirt around people and avoid confrontation. Merle even thinks he hears one of the men say 'Excuse me' as they move across to the other side of the square, no doubt to attempt entry into one of the bars positioned there.

This should be interesting, Merle thinks, as he watches the two men approach one of the bars. The bar they go for is called Vision; it is quieter and not so lavishly decorated as the one they were turned away from. A single man of smaller stature stands guarding the entry. His black attire is the only thing suggesting that he's working the door. Merle isn't surprised when the two new customers walk

17

straight in and are barely given a second glance by the outmatched doorman.

When the two men have disappeared inside the bar, Merle waits a moment to gather himself before he makes his attempt to enter Vision.

"Sorry, not tonight," the doorman announces to Merle, not moving from his position at the side of the door but suddenly finding some confidence.

"But I'm meeting friends inside," Merle pleads.

This turn of events doesn't surprise Merle. He isn't built for, or has the fashion sense for, nights out on the town, and neither does he have the inclination for that matter.

"Not dressed like that you're not," the doorman replies, eyeing Merle's well-worn raincoat.

"Just let me go and find them then. Ten minutes at the most," Merle counters.

"Can't do it, my friend. I'm just following orders; you know how it is. Phone them and tell them you're outside. Now move on please," the doorman replies, without malice.

"I've tried but there can't be any signal inside. I won't be long," Merle says, knowing it will do no good, but the twenty he produces from his pocket and discreetly offers to the doorman should.

"Quickly then. If you're not out in ten, I'm coming in to find you," the doorman warns, curling his fingers around the banknote before expertly sliding it into his front pocket.

"You won't have to come and find me," Merle informs the doorman slyly, as he moves toward the door.

Merle can ill afford the cost of his entry. Times are as hard as ever. He knew there was the possibility there would be costs attached to his participation in Janus18's plans. Costs that he is more than willing to pay so long as they don't become unmanageable. Nothing worthwhile in this life comes for free, after all. For a moment, he deliberates on enquiring about his expenses with Janus but quickly puts the thought out of his mind. He doesn't want Janus to think that he isn't equipped for the challenges ahead. Merle would be mortified if Janus lost confidence in him and decided to drop him from proceedings.

Loud music assaults Merle's ears as he pushes through the second set of doors and into the bar. He keeps his head down and casually pulls up the hood of his raincoat. The high tempo of the beat tells Merle it is dance music coming through the sound system. A genre of music that he hates. Music without a soul is not for him. He wants to feel emotion when listening to music. He doesn't listen to music to get high and dance around like a deranged monkey.

He ignores the music and moves away from the door so as not to draw more attention than he is already getting from the bar's patrons. Having his hood up inside is weird, but he is sure that CCTV cameras will be watching inside the bar, in case of any trouble. There will be trouble tonight and Merle would like to stay out of any CCTV recordings if he possibly can.

The bar is far from busy. Only desperados have arrived this early in the evening to ensure they have enough time to drink their fill, which some appear to have already achieved.

For a moment, Merle doesn't see the two men he followed into the seedy bar. They aren't ahead of him ordering more liquid fuel. Perhaps they went straight into the

19

Gents to drain the booze they have already taken on-board, ready for the next round. Merle's eyes follow the bar down to the left, looking for a sign the two men might have followed to find their destination, when a loud clattering noise on his right diverts his attention. His head turns toward the sound of the pool table regurgitating balls from its innards and the whereabouts of the two men is solved.

Two tall glasses of beer, which Merle is forced to admit look tempting, sit on a shelf adjacent to the green-baize table positioned in an enclave off the main bar area. The two men Merle was seeking are buzzing around the pool table, chalking cues and retrieving coloured balls from the table's belly.

This is it, Merle's nerves tell him. The two men who accosted him are in an ideal position for him to administer their therapy. Before he moves in to deliver his retribution, Merle considers where he will position himself to observe the trial and establish an emergency escape route, should one be required.

Inner tension threatens to paralyse Merle. A swarm of butterflies circle his stomach as he decides the time has come to approach his waiting quarries. He finds his hands shaking as he fumbles with the zip on his bag to retrieve Janus18's gift to him. Taking a breath, and keeping his head down, he steels himself as his hand closes around the canister lying in his bag and he pulls it free.

His head goes light, his legs go weak. It feels like a dream as he enters the enclave containing the pool table and the two men about to break off.

"Can I play the winner?" Merle hears his voice say, just as the oaf who barged into him is about to strike the cue ball.

"Piss off. We're playing, fuckwit," the other man, who is waiting behind, blurts out, taking a step forward.

"Yes, fuck off," the first man agrees, standing up from the table, his cue between his hands.

Both men are standing together now, giving Merle the best opportunity he is going to get. He moves forward.

"I think it's only right that you should let me play the winner after you barged into me outside," Merle insists, continuing to move forward, the canister gripped in his sweaty hand.

Merle's insistence and forceful manner take both men aback for a second. They were clearly expecting Merle to apologise and turn to leave after they verbally abused him. Each man glances at the other as Merle moves closer, doing exactly the opposite of what they had expected.

"Look, we don't want any trouble. We're playing a few frames and then we'll be leaving. You can play after," the friend of the man who barged into Merle offers, slightly rattled by Merle's demeanour.

"Yeah, you don't want to get hurt, bud. So just let us play," his assailant adds, less than confidently.

"Bud, is it now?" Merle's own confidence grows upon seeing the two men's caution. "You called me 'moron' when you almost knocked me over in the square."

"So? You were standing like a moron and in my way. Now I suggest you fuck off before I really knock you down," the man replies, regaining his unsavoury attitude.

"You know, it's bullies like you that make Janus's vision so important. You think you can go around assaulting and abusing people without repercussions, committing vile behaviour that goes unpunished. Well, things are going to change and I'm going to help make that happen. Your time has come," Merle insists, now no more than an arm's length away from the two men.

"What the fuck are you going on about, moron? If you don't fuck off now, I'm going to fuck you up," the man growls back at Merle, his hands moving on the pool cue threateningly.

"Go on then," Merle challenges, his eyes fixed on his adversary.

Again, the men glance at each other for a moment. This time it is to ensure they have each other's support before the man with the pool cue goes to attack.

Merle sees the man's knuckles whiten around the length of the varnished wood, even as his arms move to bring the pool cue into a swinging position. Merle's heart is pumping like a jackhammer as the pool cue rises into the air almost in slow motion. He bides his time as the man's face flushes red, his features contorting ready to attack, his friend poised for action next to him.

In a swift motion, as the pool cue reaches the peak of its arc, Merle makes his counterattack. Vapour hisses out of the canister's nozzle, spraying directly into the face of the man wielding the pool cue. His flared nostrils involuntarily drag the vapour into his lungs, his features immediately contorting. The pool cue hovers in mid-air, frozen above his head. Merle flicks the canister to the left, shooting vapour at the second man, who is too stunned to avoid the fine liquid squirting straight into his face.

Time appears to pause when the hiss of the canister stops, its contents exhausted. Merle watches breathlessly as the two men's features change from malice to surprise and disbelief.

22

A deep cough escapes the man wielding the pool cue, his arms slacken and his hands release his weapon, which clatters to the floor next to him. Merle takes a step back, waiting for the two men's reaction to the agent.

"What the hell was that?" the man behind begs, his eyes already bulging.

"Your comeuppance," Merle replies simply.

"I'm going to kill you," Merle's assailant insists through another savage cough. His face is red with anger, or is his new colour caused by the agent he has inhaled?

Merle takes another step back, his hand reaching into his pocket for his phone. Within another step, Merle is recording the two men. They fill his phone's screen, the timer indicating steady progress.

"Are you fucking recording us?" the man behind demands, as he also begins to cough. He tries to move to approach Merle, but his legs begin to fail him. He staggers, ending up stooping over the pool table to steady himself.

Merle keeps backing away, ensuring his phone remains fixed upon the two men, who both now cling to the pool table for support. The volume of the music increases as Merle moves into the main bar. He's careful not to back into anyone as he keeps going, putting distance between himself and his test subjects.

Nobody in the bar has noticed what has happened in the enclave where the pool table is situated. They are oblivious to anything apart from their drinks and the people immediately around them. They haven't a care for the two men, who are succumbing to an unknown toxin that is currently ripping through their bodies. Unaware that two of their fellow patrons have crumpled onto the pool table and then slid onto the floor. Even the barman hasn't noticed that two of his customers are having a medical emergency. All he is worried about is pouring the next round before moving on to serve the next waiting customer.

Merle takes up a position at the very end of the bar, where he zooms the camera of his phone in on his subjects. A door that he noticed when he entered is next to the end of the bar. A sign above the door indicates that this is where the Ladies and Gents are situated. Merle is positive that there will also be an escape route through the door. A fire escape or rear entry is sure to be there if required.

People move across Merle's line of sight, sometimes blocking it completely, but he adjusts his position to compensate. He keeps his phone at chest height so as not to attract too much attention while he films. He wishes that someone would cut off the incessant sound system, which seems to be banging out the same track over and over again on a loop. The music overrides any other sound, but he keeps his camera fixed on his targets and begins to get some good results, interesting results.

Both men on his screen have collapsed to the ground around the feet at the rear of the pool table. Merle is pleased with the position he caught them in at the back of the room because it keeps the two men out of immediate view and allows the agent to take its course. Luckily, both men's heads are unobstructed by the pool table and are in the direct line of sight of his camera.

The men squirm on the ground, obviously in distress, even the loud music cannot hide that. Their bodies twist one way and then the other, shaking as they try and fend off the transformation that is taking hold of them. Suddenly, almost in unison, both bodies whip out as straight as boards. The men's backs stiffen against the ground. Merle sees pain etched on the men's faces and their mouths gape open as screams of agony escape them. The screams shrill out, piercing through the music, and some people turn to see where the distressed human screams are coming from.

Only the influence of alcohol prevents the people in the bar from taking the normal course of action and going to see if the men need help. Most just stand and stare with slack jaws, wondering if they've had more to drink than they thought, and then it happens.

Fountains of vomit erupt from the men, spraying into the air and across the floor. Merle ensures he is catching every frame of the performance on his phone as the people in the bar recoil from the disgusting show. Nobody approaches the two men. Not with puke spreading across the floor and raining down onto the green cloth stretched across the pool table.

"Bloody hell! I'm not paid enough for this," Merle hears from behind the bar, as the man working there realises what is happening in the pool area.

Merle ignores the barman's whining. Instead, he concentrates on keeping his phone's camera fixed so that he doesn't miss anything. Judging from what he witnessed last night with the businessman, Merle expects that the show is about to come to an end. The businessman didn't last long after retching his guts up and the two men he is filming have stopped moving. Merle zooms the phone in tighter to see if he can tell if the men are still breathing. He manages to catch both men's faces in the same shot and, as far as he can tell, neither of them is breathing. Wanting to be sure that the procedure is over before he makes his getaway, Merle continues to record, even though both men are motionless.

"Ha, ha. What a state to get in! Had too much to drink, boys?" a man who is well oiled himself laughs. He takes a step toward the pool area and into Merle's camera shot, continuing to jibe at the forlorn men with each step.

Merle debates. *Is that it?* he asks himself, *is now the time to make my escape?* He definitely wants to have evacuated the area by the time the emergency services arrive but he must ensure he has documented the whole thing for Janus.

Suddenly, the music is cut off and a second later the barman storms out from behind the bar. *That will do*, Merle tells himself, his finger moving toward his phone's screen to end the recording, but something stops him. He keeps recording as the barman approaches the grim scene around the pool table.

Merle sees movement from one of the men. It's only slight, but the head of the man who had wielded the pool cue certainly moved an inch or two. Merle feels nervous excitement in his belly at this turn of events. Has the man survived the toxin? Is this what Janus has been striving for? Is it what he had expected and therefore why he had insisted on a public place? Merle steadies his hand and waits.

"I've called an ambulance… and the police," the barman states, as he reluctantly nears the men and their squalid mess.

The barman is unfazed when a head begins to turn in his direction. He doesn't feel excitement and anticipation like Merle does at the movement. The barman doesn't realise the significance of what he's witnessing. Amazingly, one of the men has survived the trial and Merle cannot wait to see what happens next.

Merle is unable to move; his eyes are fixed on the man's face as it turns, coming into full view on his phone's screen. The hair on the back of Merle's neck bristles, and his palms sweat as he comes face to face with an undead monster through his screen. He feels his eyes widen and his heart thump as he studies his and Janus's creation. Pure malicious evil is what Merle is staring at. The creature's piercing dead eyes are pools of blackness that threaten to drag him into hell with them. They are surrounded by fearsome features born from grey haggard skin that is stretched tight over the bones of the beast's face. The subject's transformation is both miraculous and bone-chilling at the same time. Merle is proud of his creation and his anticipation of sharing the amazing results with Janus is stifling.

Stony silence has fallen around Merle and he becomes conscious of it, pulling his eyes away from the chilling marvel displayed on his phone's screen. In front of him, the bar's customers look toward the pool area, not believing their eyes. Flabbergasted faces switch between the horror on display and the drinks in their hands, as if the booze will explain away what they are seeing.

Away to the right, the entrance door swings open and the doorman who'd been bribed by Merle appears. He looks straight at Merle, obviously annoyed that Merle hadn't kept his word and left the bar once he'd found his non-existent friends. Merle gives him a nonchalant glance for his troubles before discarding the doorman and returning to his more important business.

"Rodger! Help me over here," shouts the barman, who is looking to tackle the nightmare that is unfolding in his bar.

The doorman's anger toward Merle is instantly forgotten when he lays his eyes on the hideous incident in front of his colleague.

"What the fuck's happened?" Rodger, the doorman, exclaims.

"God knows. They've only just come in. It isn't anything we've done, they only ordered two beers," the barman defends.

"I know they've only just come in. I saw them. We'd better call an ambulance," Rodger replies.

"I already have. There's something seriously wrong with them. Look at them! They look evil, like zombies," the barman observes.

Merle settles back into position, recording events. His excitement grows as he repositions himself to get a better view and he sees not only that the first man is trying to get to his feet, but that the second is also showing signs of reincarnation.

"Are you okay, buddy?" the barman asks, as the man nearest to him pulls himself up, using the pool table for leverage.

Neither the barman nor Rodger the doorman seem willing to approach their distressed customers, Merle notices, and he doesn't blame them. Wading through pools of vomit to help a customer is one thing but attempting to tackle two customers who look like demons is quite another.

Both members of staff recoil when the first creature manages to get to his feet and releases its grip on the pool table. The beast stands motionless for a moment, with its head down staring at the floor, gaining its balance. Tension rises as customers and staff alike wait with bated breath to see what happens next.

Behind the first creature, the second beast has clawed itself upright and steadies itself on the left flank of the first. Merle's breathing has become shallow with anticipation. Something fearsome is about to happen, he can feel it.

Ominously, the first creature's head gradually rises, its evil black eyes piercing, leading the way. Sharp intakes of breath are audible from the bar's customers, some of whom begin to back away toward Merle. The two members of staff who are closest to the threat look at each other in fear, unsure how to react.

All of them are too slow to react and, without further warning, the first creature releases a deafening high-pitched scream from out of its gaping, cavernous mouth and surges forward. The beast's speed is awesome and within three steps it launches itself into the air, on a direct trajectory to the two closest victims.

The barman is the quickest to react. He dives left, managing to escape the oncoming onslaught. His quick reaction leaves the doorman, who is frozen in panic, exposed. The creature slams into the doorman, knocking him clean off his feet to crash into the floor behind, where a frenzied attack takes place.

The creature's right arm streaks through the air, its hand swiping across the doorman's face. Merle seems to feel the nails of the beast dig into the doorman's face as the doorman's head whips to the side, pieces of skin and blood flying into the air. The strike leaves the doorman stunned and completely defenceless for the creature's next attack. In a flash, the creature's head descends, aiming for the doorman's exposed neck, its grim mouth impossibly wide. Merle feels no guilt watching the doorman receive his vengeance. It was worth the cost of the bribe to witness this.

Even as the beast's head rises, pieces of bloody meat entangled between its teeth, the second creature has made its move.

The customers who were stunned in front of Merle now begin to panic, despite the alcohol in their systems.

Somehow, the barman has once again managed to scramble out of the line of fire. The second creature bypasses him and directs its attack at an easier target. The woman's drink flies out of her hand, tumbling through the air. The glass smashes to the floor only a second before her back hits the ground, taking the wind out of her and cutting her scream of terror off dead. Her fate is sealed: the second creature's teeth slice into her tender flesh before her terror has a chance to return.

Merle witnesses a stream of blood spurt into the air from the woman. The creature must have severed one of her main arteries. He congratulates himself on not missing the shot. *The gory performance will look even better in slow motion*, he thinks, as a customer barges past him, heading for the door behind him.

Other customers rush to follow the first one out of the rear entrance. Each of them has expressions of panic and disbelief fixed on their faces as they go. Merle would bet that they have all seen a bar fight before, but never one like this. This is slaughter and his two creations are only just getting started.

Merle adjusts his position again to allow the lucky customers to escape. It is not up to him who lives and who dies. As Darwin theorised, only the fittest will survive. The weak will succumb to their fate and be exterminated. Janus18 may have taken the name of a god, but he made it very clear to Merle that he is not one. He describes himself as a social engineer for a better future. He envisages a more productive and balanced future, both for humankind and, more importantly, for the planet. Janus has no intention of eradicating humans from the planet, he just wants to thin the pack. After all, as Janus asserts, a planet without sentient beings is doomed to be lost in the annals of time. Whether that be in a million or a billion years' time, if there is no one around to record history, will it have even happened?

Merle has no illusions that he is one of the fittest. Far from it. In the end, he will succumb. He is willing to sacrifice his meaningless life to aid Janus to realise his vision. Merle will at least have had a hand in creating a brighter future for his fellow humans. Maybe his part will be recorded in the pages of history or maybe Janus will protect him and find a place where he can be useful in the new world order.

Merle is willing to sacrifice himself, but not today. He must live in order to help bring Janus's plan to fruition. He doesn't move far from the door that the others have used to escape the onslaught. The door will be his escape route when the virgin species closes in. They will grant him no favours as their creator. He keeps filming while the fearsome creatures play their part and do their work until it's time to escape.

Neither of the beasts dwells on their prey. They slaughter those of the bar's customers who are too slow, or too drunk to evade them. Slain bodies gush blood into the already soiled carpet, which is more accustomed to receiving spilt beer and vomit. Screams of terror or attempts to fight back are futile against the awesome power of the creatures, which rip through the customers as if they were defenceless lambs. The bodies they leave behind twitch in the last throes of death or lie stiff with expressions of sheer terror forever fixed on their faces.

Just as Merle makes the decision that it's time to move to use the door behind him and make his escape, before he becomes one of the creature's victims, movement at the other end of the bar makes him pause. Out of nowhere the barman, who miraculously avoided the initial attack, bursts across the room, and he's not alone. A woman follows in his wake as he scrambles for the main door.

Impressed with the barman's fight for survival, Merle finds himself rooting for him to succeed and escape. Merle is almost positive that the woman behind will be cut down by the beasts, but the barman stands a chance. He is witnessing Janus18 and Darwin's theory play out in front of his eyes: survival of the fittest.

The camera on Merle's phone moves with the action. At first, the creatures don't react to the attempted escape. Both are distracted by other victims squirming under their grip. The barman's arm reaches for the door as the first creature sees the movement and whips around on top of the body below it. The woman is in no-man's-land when the creature leaps into the air at unbelievable speed.

Mid-stride, the creature crashes into the woman with incredible force, knocking her completely off her feet. In the same instant, the second creature joins in the new attack, but this one aims for the barman, who is halfway out of the main door. Merle wills the barman to make his escape but, as the door swings closed behind him, the creature smashes clean through it. Through the thick-glass sidewall of the entrance, Merle sees the creature crash into the barman, forcing them both halfway through the next door before they both disappear downwards, and out of his view.

All at once, excitement rushes through Merle's entire body. The main doors are open, and the creatures can reach the square outside. Tonight's experiment and excitement may only just be beginning.

Chapter 3

A distant scream echoes into the bar from the square beyond the main door. The slaughter is about to escalate but Merle, to his frustration, daren't move from his position to get a better filming angle. The second creature is still in the bar, sinking its teeth into its latest kill, and it could easily attack Merle if he approached it.

Suddenly, a shadow appears through the glass enclosing the entrance. Merle is in no doubt about what is casting the shadow even before his ears are assaulted by the high-pitched screech the creature emits once it is on its feet. The second creature's head whips up from the body of the woman it is chewing on, the bottom half of its face dripping with glistening dark-red blood.

Another screech rings out and the second creature immediately answers the call of its fellow hunter. Without delay, it springs off the woman's corpse and darts toward the main entrance to join its brethren and move out into the fertile new feeding ground.

Merle moves immediately, phone in hand to follow proceedings. He maintains his distance from the main entrance, and the danger, and finds a suitable relatively safe spot in which to capture the ongoing raw footage.

Multiple screams, both male and female, rise as the two creatures leave the bar, as if they were leaving their lair to go on the hunt. Merle quickly realises that that is exactly what they are doing, having all but exhausted the live prey with pumping blood streams in the bar. Why would they remain cooped up inside when there is so much on offer in the great expanse of the square? The opportunity is too good for the fledgling creatures to turn down.

The moment the first creature leads the other one out, Merle rushes across the bar, to gain a vantage point to record the imminent carnage.

He finds a perfect spot next to the main entrance where he can continue to film through a large plate-glass window without having to venture out. Going outside would not only put him in harm's way but there would also be too many witnesses, who may be able to identify him later. As proficient as his fearsome creatures are, surely there are too many people in the square for them to leave no witnesses? It is also only a matter of time before the authorities are in attendance if they're not already. The barman has already called an ambulance, he said as much, and you can be sure the police won't be far behind.

The action has already begun by the time Merle has positioned himself and he eagerly points his phone's camera to peer through the window. The two creatures steadily stalk out into the bustling square, deliberately at first. Merle presumes they are getting their bearings, or perhaps they are overwrought by the embarrassment of riches they find themselves in the midst of.

Whatever their reasons for moving away from the bar cautiously at first, their reserve doesn't last for long. Crowds of people mill around or stand chatting in groups across the expanse of the square. Only the people in the immediate vicinity of the bar see the demons stalking them. Whilst more screams ring out from the closest people who see the bloodied beasts approaching, others stand nonchalantly, watching their approach. Maybe they mistakenly believe two revellers have dressed up in fancy dress for the evening? The people's confused looks tell them that it's not Halloween.

One man, who has surely been enjoying more than a couple of drinks, stands laughing and pointing at the two creatures. He even slaps his friend across the chest with the back of his hand to ensure he looks at the freaks in fancy dress. His laughter fades the closer the creatures get to him. It fades to a forced smile that is rapidly replaced by a grimace, despite his inebriation. His friend's expression instantly twists into one of horror upon seeing the heinous monsters. Merle can tell that the man wants to turn and flee and that only his pride is holding that reaction at bay.

You should have swallowed your pride and run, my friend, Merle thinks, as the first creature bolts straight at the two friends, closely followed by the other beast. Any thought of fleeing is overwhelmed by fear and paralysis. Merle sees the total shock that has turned both men's brains to mush as the creatures, almost in unison, attack and take down their prey.

People in the vicinity of the two men see the brutal attack and mindlessly scatter for their lives. Men and women alike flee in desperation to get away from the vicious onslaught. Their panic results in chaos, which spreads throughout the square like a wave. Merle keeps his phone's camera on wide view with the creature's attack taking centre stage to ensure that Janus will be able to see and take everything in. Janus must see it all. It will be vital for his future plans.

Across the square, confusion and hysteria erupt. Those who haven't seen the ferocious attack taking place on the two men feed off the panic of those who have, joining in the free-for-all to escape the danger. A stampede threatens to break out as those nearest to the slaughter see the two creatures already rising from their slain, blood-spattered victims, ready to strike again.

For the most part, the men are better equipped in the fight to escape. The women's shoes and, in many cases, tight skirts and dresses hamper their progress. It is a fact of life that, as a rule, men are also physically stronger, and they use their strength to their advantage. This means it is mostly the backs of women that are exposed and in the line of fire when the next strike comes.

Screams of terror vibrate through the glass in front of Merle as the creatures burst toward the mass of the crowd. He sees the next victim to be taken down: a woman in high heels. She turns her head in the second before she is struck. Her face gawps in despair and panic, her teeth clenched in preparation for the inevitable. She is slammed into with unholy force from behind. Her arms reach out in front of her, in a futile attempt to break her fall, but the beast is too powerful. She crashes into the ground, her arms buckling and breaking in the second before her head smashes into the concrete. Merle is sure that she is at least knocked unconscious and doesn't feel the flesh on her exposed shoulder being ripped into with unforgiving teeth. *Small mercies*, Merle thinks, before his concentration is taken elsewhere.

The other creature also chooses its next target and, like the first, it attacks the easiest it can find. Another woman, dressed to the nines, has fallen behind the main pack of surging people. Her stunning outfit and long blonde hair have brought her attention tonight. Unwanted attention. Fatal attention. The creature flies at her across the square, its hands reaching for her like claws, its greedy mouth prising open, preparing to feed. Separated from the crowd, the woman sees the fearsome creature close in and falters. Her high-heeled shoes threaten to give way underneath her. She becomes more isolated, ready for the taking.

Merle's heart skips a beat when, suddenly, from out of nowhere, the creature is slammed into from the side, a split second before it envelops the beautiful woman. It takes a moment for Merle to realise what is happening. He doesn't believe his eyes. A colossal man has tackled the creature to the ground. His technique suggests to Merle that the man, bristling with muscles and with the courage to match, is a professional sports player. Merle has seen such tackles on television, on both the rugby field and in American football. The stunning woman doesn't pause to consider whether the man plays sport. She grabs her chance of survival and totters off into the crowd as fast as her shoes will allow.

Slamming the creature into the ground with tremendous force, the muscle-bound hero presses home his advantage. Positioning himself on top of the stunned creature, the man rains punches down from above onto the beast, which is expertly pinned down by the hero's legs. At first, the creature is overwhelmed by the barrage. Punches crash into its face from both arms of the man above it but, just as it appears the creature is beaten, it suddenly goes berserk, as if it had 10,000 volts of electricity charging through its body.

Now the man's arms fly into the air as if he were on a bucking bronco, as he tries to keep his balance and not be thrown off his enemy. Impressively, he does manage to keep his balance, taking the opportunity to grab hold of the beast's shoulders in an effort to pin it down again. For a second, his strength succeeds but the victory is short-lived. He hasn't taken into account one vital thing: the creature's ally.

As impressive as the man's bulging muscles are, and despite his bravery in saving the woman, the man's heroics come to a swift end. He doesn't see the other beast come for him as he uses all his determination to overpower his foe on the ground. Merle doesn't know if the other creature has come to the aid of the pinned-down creature or whether it has simply seen its next prey. That is a question that cannot be answered in these uncontrolled conditions, and perhaps it is academic, but the result is the same.

From behind, the hero is pounced upon, the beast landing on its back. The man's fate is sealed as he is forced to fight on two fronts. In a panic, he releases the beast on the ground to try and fend off the sudden attack from the rear. As soon as he releases the creature it goes into a frenzy again to try and free itself, and this time it succeeds. Even as the man topples off the squirming creature, the other creature's head nestles into the side of his neck, and sinks its teeth in.

The fight is over. The man falls to the side, his body going limp as blood spills across the ground. No longer pinned down, the creature underneath scurries free, getting to its feet in an instant. As soon as it is upright, it turns its back on the man and, without offering thanks to the other creature for its assistance, it bolts forward toward the thinning crowd of people evacuating the square.

Panting with excitement, Merle follows the beast, keeping it centred on his phone's screen. *How much more of this excitement can I take?* he thinks, as he follows the creature. Janus is surely going to be massively impressed with his footage and the results of his work. *The night is going far better than either of us could have hoped*, Merle congratulates himself.

Keeping his enthusiasm in check, Merle prepares himself for the next bout of carnage. He rolls his shoulder in its socket to relieve the stiffness he is feeling from holding his phone in position. The stiffness is no more than a nuisance, however. It is quickly forgotten when the creature on the ground disentangles itself from the body of the heroic man and rises to its feet, ready to join the hunt once more.

Merle tracks the beast as it shoots across the square to follow its accomplice and find its next victim. Although the square has emptied considerably, there are still offerings remaining for the two wild beasts to stalk. Amazingly, some people still appear unaware of the danger. Perhaps they are too caught up in their own business to have noticed or too drunk to understand the severity of the threat.

The action is now some distance away from Merle's position and he finds it difficult to catch the drama with any clarity on his phone. Should he have anticipated such a problem and brought a camera more suitable for long-distance filming? As he debates his possible shortcomings, his eye is attracted by something sinister.

Reflecting off the windows and walls of buildings away on the far left of the square, blue lights begin to flash. Merle cannot see directly what is emitting the strobing blue lights. It could just be the ambulance the barman called when he believed that two of his customers had taken a turn for the worse or, then again, someone else could have called in the entire cavalry of the emergency services.

Merle knows instinctively that the horror that has transpired in Trinity Square will attract more than one solitary ambulance. The full force of the authorities will be bearing down on the square at any moment. Even if the flashing blue lights are coming from the ambulance that the barman called, it will not be alone: the police will be in attendance very quickly, and in large numbers.

Tonight has been productive, more productive than Merle could have possibly wished for. Not even Janus could have planned the events of this evening better. He has masses of footage to submit to Janus, along with his own testimony. The time has come for him to make his escape, to live to fight another day. His two creatures have already moved off into the distance and the picture he is getting of them on his phone is poor. There isn't, therefore, much more to be gained by hanging around. Nothing but having his details taken by the authorities, or worse, being taken in for questioning. Merle cannot allow that; Janus will need him 'in play' to continue his work.

Merle ends the recording on his phone before he turns and takes a few snapshots of the carnage that is spread across the floor of the bar. He suddenly has a chilling thought as he slides the phone into his pocket. What if the victims of his creatures have become infected after being bitten and turned into monsters themselves? He has been standing with his back to the slaughtered customers in the bar. He would have been defenceless if they had turned and attacked. That is how it works in zombie movies, isn't it? If bitten, you die and turn into an undead zombie yourself.

Merle laughs at himself as he picks his way through the corpses strewn across the floor of the bar. *This isn't the movies*, he chuckles to himself, *this is real life*. He is sure Janus would have warned him if there was a possibility of the infection spreading to new subjects so that he would have been aware of it and able to take appropriate precautions. Wouldn't he?

The question doesn't play on Merle's mind; he has other things to concern himself with. Like escaping the area before the authorities descend on Trinity Square and cordon it off.

The floor around Merle is gruesome. Twisted, mutilated corpses excreting pools of blood that are still spreading into the carpet need to be stepped around. As anxious as he is to leave the bar, he does pause for a moment next to one body and bends down. He reluctantly pushes his hand into the front jeans pocket of the doorman, where he feels the edge of the money he'd handed over to gain entry to the bar. He pulls the note free, stuffs it into his pocket as he rises and then heads for the door at the back of the bar, the one he'd started his filming next to. He is still not sure where it leads but is confident there will be a way out. If there isn't, where have the customers who managed to escape the carnage disappeared to?

He is aware that the wise thing to have done would have been to scope out the place he intended to use for the trial beforehand. Janus had surprised him with the delivery last night. He'd made it clear in his instructions that he wanted the trial to be carried out today, which left no opportunity for such precautions. Maybe he would get the opportunity with the next trial. *I shouldn't bank on it*, Merle decides. *There is an urgency to Janus's plans and I'll just have to go with the flow.*

In any event, tonight's proceedings couldn't have gone any better, Merle congratulates himself again. Janus's confidence in him will be unquestioned now and he looks forward with anticipation to his next assignment.

The creaking noise of hinges needing oil sounds as Merle pushes open the door at the back of the bar. He finds a narrow corridor leading away from him, with doors on either side. An uneasy silence greets Merle as he enters and the door swings shut behind him. He doesn't hang about, however, and makes his way along the corridor. A door on the left has a sign mounted on it telling Merle that it's the Gents, which he could do with using. He ignores it, though, wanting to get away from the area as soon as possible. At the end of the corridor, he turns right, where he is relieved to see an exit. The moment he cracks the door open he hears sirens wailing away in the near distance. *The authorities are coming*, he thinks urgently, as he moves out into the night.

The back of the bar is positioned on a narrow road which also has other establishments backing onto it. Merle is thankful that the road is empty, because that means there are no witnesses to him leaving. The police will know from the barman's call for an ambulance that the bar was where tonight's carnage began. Even if the call doesn't give that away, the slaughtered bodies strewn across the floor of the bar will certainly tell them that much. The bar will be the focal point of their investigation and, the less evidence that he was there, the better. Hopefully, his coat's hood, which he keeps up, for now, has hidden him from the bar's CCTV. He was also careful not to touch anything with his fingers, so as not to leave prints. The doorman got a good look at him as he entered, but he won't be saying anything to the police from beyond the grave. So, with any luck, he will get away without leaving any hard evidence that he was ever inside.

Luckily, the road remains deserted as Merle hurries along, head down. All the businesses backing onto it are shut up tight, eerily so, but at least he doesn't see a soul until he nears the end of the road.

He slows down as he approaches the junction at the end of the road, so as not to draw attention to himself. Nobody gives him a second look, however; everyone is too concerned with getting as far away from Trinity Square as possible. People dash from right to left at the junction, heading in the opposite direction to the square. All of them have worried expressions and keep looking behind themselves, fearing that the horror might be following them.

The fastest route back to the bus station is to turn right at the end of the road, where Merle stops to review his options. Above the crowd of people streaming along the road away to his right, the night sky flashes with a blue glow. The emergency services have arrived at Trinity Square in numbers, and Merle needs to avoid them at all costs. He will have to skirt around the area to get back to the bus station without bumping into anybody in uniform who might want to ask him some uncomfortable questions.

Carefully stepping out into the road to avoid bumping into anyone, Merle decides to go straight on at the junction. There is another back road opposite which should allow him to circle back toward the bus station while avoiding the Trinity Square area.

In the end, Merle manages to find a route back to the bus station that completely avoids the authorities and isn't much further than the route he took to reach Trinity Square. He sees numerous police cars and ambulances flashing their emergency lights and gunning their engines on his travels, but he arrives at the bus station without incident.

He isn't the only one who has decided to call it a night and catch one of the earlier buses home. The bus station is busy when he arrives, and many of the people waiting for their connections are upset or even distraught. There is a constant chatter of disbelief amongst the groups of people waiting and plenty of arms around shoulders to console friends and loved ones who have witnessed the evening's horrific events.

Merle has mixed feelings as he listens and watches while keeping a low profile. He is proud of tonight's trial. It was necessary to forge ahead with Janus's vision. There was carnage and death, which couldn't have been avoided. Merle admits to himself that he found the horror exciting, exhilarating even. He didn't want it to end. Hearing the trauma of the people waiting for buses doesn't quell that feeling in the slightest, in fact it amplifies it.

There will be more opportunities to hear people recounting their horror on the bus ride home, Merle thinks, as he sees his bus approaching. Surely it won't be long until Janus18 provides him with another opportunity to rekindle his excitement for real?

Chapter 4

The city's stink is engrained in every pore of Cal's skin. Exhaust fumes, cheap fast food, coffee and tobacco penetrate every fibre of his clothing, despite the fact that his unimpressive dark suit was put on fresh from the dry cleaners this morning. Cal can taste the city on his tongue and placing another cigarette into his mouth will only heighten the bitter taste. His lips curl around the stick, nevertheless. *Fuck it*, he thinks, as a flame flashes in front of his eyes against the darkness, and he brings it closer to light the orange embers, his cheeks drawn in.

Cal's arm saws at the steering wheel of the unmarked police car as he drags the first breath of cancerous smoke into his lungs. Only this morning, on the phone, he had promised his pregnant wife, Kim, that he had finished with this evil habit. That promise lasted until he had exited the store first thing this morning, his breakfast forgotten, replaced by a pack of Marlboro. Another broken promise that had fallen from his mouth. Kim has been living with her sister for nearly three months now, two of them since she discovered she was pregnant. Cal had relied on his wife's forgiving nature and devotion for too long. She saw through him and decided her future, and now the future of their unborn child will be best met elsewhere.

Poor Kim's frustration at their life had been obvious for Cal to see for a long time, despite her best attempts to hide it. He is certain that she didn't know what she was letting herself in for when she agreed to marry a copper, five years ago. Late nights and stony silences on the occasions when he managed to grace the dinner table are not on any woman's list of requirements for marital bliss. They are not on Cal's list either and he realised a long time ago that he also didn't know what he was letting himself in for when he decided to undertake a career in law enforcement. Only the household bills keep him trapped in his chosen career. Should he say to hell with it? Resign and let the house go? He only keeps paying the mortgage in the hope that Kim will return. But what would she return to? An absent husband and more silence?

"If you insist on smoking in the car, at least pass me one, Detective," Cal's partner and, to a certain degree, mentor, Mike, says from the passenger seat.

Cal grunts and offers the pack to the older man, who silently prises a cigarette out of it without taking it out of Cal's hand.

"Another day from hell," Mike says, through his first exhalation of smoke. "I can't wait to get home and flake out."

Cal grunts again, this time in agreement. Mike isn't wrong: the whole city seems to be intent on poisoning itself just lately. Hard drugs are rife and taking their usual toll, but even they don't explain the dark cloud hanging over the city recently.

Unexplained dead bodies keep turning up throughout the city. Over the last five days, seven corpses have been found discarded in the streets. Dead bodies are not uncommon in such a large city, but even the coroner is struggling to handle their business and offering no explanation for the worrying increase in trade.

Just this morning, Cal and Mike attended another grim find in a back alley of the financial district. The well-heeled victim had been found by refuse collectors, the body in amongst stuffed black binbags. Cal had found it difficult to inspect the male victim, who looked as if he had had the life sucked out of him. The man's skin was grey and drawn, appearing to be mummified. Cal was glad when the scenes of crime investigators had arrived to take over the body, freeing him and Mike to begin their investigations into the victim.

Their initial investigations told them that the man had been alive and well yesterday in his office at a stockbroking company not far from the back alley. Both of them should have been surprised to hear this evidence. The victim's appearance suggested that he had been dead for a long time, years even. However, neither Cal nor Mike were surprised when the several witnesses attested to the victim having been at work yesterday. Unfortunately, the body wasn't the first that has been found in such a state so soon after being seen alive. Wondering what the hell is going on, Cal takes another deep drag of his cigarette before changing his train of thought back to his estranged wife Kim.

He would have missed dinner yet again tonight. His plate would be sitting in an ever-cooling oven. He would at least have made it home before Kim had totally given up and gone to bed. She would have had plenty of time to throw him looks of disappointment and to nag his tired mind. Cal would take that in a heartbeat if it meant that Kim was home and not residing at her sister's.

Cal's thoughts of despair are suddenly eradicated from his mind as blue lights flash through his car's back window, moments before a marked police car thunders past them on the wrong side of the road.

The high-pitched two-tone siren forces Cal bolt upright as the car streaks past. The siren fades rapidly, only to be replaced by the sound of the police radio squawking urgently. It takes a moment for Cal to register the orders blaring at him through the speaker. A disturbance on Trinity... Chinatown... all available units...

Trinity is a square in the centre of Chinatown, packed full of bars, restaurants and nightclubs. Cal's foot hits the floor, adrenaline flooding his bloodstream as the car lurches forward. "Sierra 2 zero 8, responding," Mike barks into the receiver of the radio, immediately before he flicks the switch that bursts their car's hidden blues and twos into action. Ahead in the distance are the fading blue flashing lights of the marked police car that raced past him only moments before. Cal takes up the challenge of not letting the lights fade completely from their view and chases after them.

Maybe Kim would have been in bed after all.

Accelerating hard, Cal is now forced to cross over onto the wrong side of the road to overtake a slow-moving road user. *Get out of the way, Grandad!* his mind screams just as he draws level with the other car. *That's it, you're almost past*, Cal thinks too soon.

"Watch it!" Mike panics, as lights suddenly appear in front of them as another car pulls out into the road from a side road.

"Calm down, old-timer," Cal teases Mike, as tyres screech and he cuts back onto the correct side of the road just in time to miss both cars.

"You're not exactly a youngster yourself any more, you know," Mike retorts, through gritted teeth.

"I am compared to you," Cal insists, knowing that, having reached the age of thirty-four, Mike isn't wrong.

"I wonder what we're in for this time?" Mike says, as they approach Chinatown. His hand unconsciously pads his chest area to reassure himself that his Glock 19 sidearm hasn't miraculously vanished.

"Probably drunk revellers causing trouble," Cal offers.

"I don't think so, not for an all-units bulletin," Mike responds.

"Well, we'll find out soon enough," Cal says, the car charging forward.

Cal catches the first glimpse of the ornate, illuminated Chinese arch over the road ahead that will welcome them into the city's Chinese quarter. The blue lights of the marked police car he is chasing look as if they have already crossed the threshold. Trinity Square will be upon them quickly, the nervous tension in Cal's stomach confirms it.

"It could be all over by the time we arrive," Cal says, hopefully.

"Dream on, my friend, we're never that lucky. It will be in full swing, you can guarantee it," Mike counters.

They follow the police car ahead into Chinatown, Cal already watching for the turning onto Trinity Square. The car in front turns sharply, showing him the way, and Cal prepares to make his turn. Just as he goes to pull on the steering wheel to turn, figures dart out from the left and into the road.

Terrified pedestrians stream into the road, taking no heed of the threat of the speeding car. Cal is forced to slam his foot on the brake pedal to avoid ploughing into the people. Mike's hand slams into the dashboard to stop himself from shooting forward, his teeth clenched. His habit of keeping his seat belt slack will be his undoing one day, especially with Cal at the wheel.

"Fuck me, where did they come from?" Cal gasps, as the car grinds to a halt.

"Go through them," Mike orders, from his position back in his seat.

Cal looks out of the windscreen, searching for a gap in the crowd of people to edge the car through. People with expressions of shock and panic on their faces peer back at him and shout at them, urgently pointing toward Trinity.

"Move out the way," Mike shouts in frustration, waving his hand at the windscreen.

Cal edges forward to force his way through the civilians ahead of them. The blue flashing lights hidden in the grille of the unmarked police car reflect off sequined dresses and loud shirts which many of the revellers have worn especially for their night on the town. But with their night ruined by something still unknown to the two police officers, some of the crowd decide to evacuate the area under their own steam and Cal sees his chance.

He edges the car forward, his hand holding down the centre of the steering wheel. The horn adds a constant loud warning noise to the high-pitched siren that is already blaring and, thankfully, the gap remains for Cal to roll through.

"This is no good," Mike protests, as it becomes obvious that the constant stream of people emerging from Trinity Square and blocking their progress shows no sign of ending. "Stop over there," he insists. "We'll proceed on foot."

Cal does as he is told and stops the car in the middle of the road, just past the entrance to Trinity. As Cal kills the engine, Mike switches off the siren but leaves the blue lights flashing to warn others of the obstacle they have created.

"Move back," Cal orders the panicked members of the public, who are threatening to swamp the car as he opens his door. He rises to his feet, reaching under his cheap suit jacket to pull his sidearm from its holster. The weight of the Glock feels reassuring in his hand and he is not surprised to see that Mike's weapon is also out of its holster as his partner rounds the front of the car.

"Hurry, they are attacking people," a pretty young woman dressed in high heels and a small black dress gasps at Cal through teary eyes.

"Who is attacking people?" Cal questions the woman urgently, but she is already hurrying away as fast as her high heels will carry her.

What the hell is happening down there? Cal's mind reels as he looks at the entrance into Trinity that Mike is already approaching. Moving quickly to support Mike, Cal is forced to ignore other members of the public who approach him as he moves. Their information might be vital, but he cannot allow his partner to get away from him. Whatever the threat, they will face it together.

In the distance, gunfire coming from the direction of Trinity Square echoes into the night sky. Mike's head whips back as he moves to check where Cal is, a nervous expression fixed on his face. Cal nods, to confirm he is with him and to hopefully instil some reassurance into his partner. Cal is beginning to lack confidence himself as figures rush toward him, making their terrified exit from the square.

Mike stops at the corner of the junction, using the building there for cover, his gun pointed. Cal quickly moves to join him, his trepidation building. The rush of people evacuating Trinity Square begins to thin as Mike slowly turns the corner to get a view of the danger area.

"What's happening?" Cal asks anxiously at Mike's back.

Mike doesn't respond to Cal's question; he just stands motionless, peering down the sight of his gun into the

51

square ahead. Cal waits for Mike to report but his partner still remains worryingly silent.

Both Cal and Mike are all too familiar with Chinatown, especially its main focal point, Trinity. The square is a magnet for night-time revellers from across the city and beyond, drawn to its concentration of after-hours drinking establishments. The square and its surrounding streets, free flowing with alcohol, are renowned for drunken behaviour and the trouble that invariably accompanies the booze. Bright lights and loud music are accompanied by a spectrum of criminal activity, from organised crime to drunken louts who cannot handle their liquor. Cal and Mike are repeatedly called in to investigate Trinity's organised crime scene but also often attend crimes committed by perpetrators under the influence, which can be just as serious.

Growing concerned with Mike's lack of action, Cal warily edges around his partner to see the square for himself. Just as the bright Chinese-themed façade of Trinity Square begins to reveal itself to Cal, bursts of automatic gunfire erupt from close by. Cal doesn't allow himself to cower back behind Mike when the blasts hit his ears. He keeps moving forward, his Glock poised, ready to fire.

The marked police car he had chased after into Chinatown has pulled up a short distance into the square, the driver forced to halt its progress by the crowds of panicked revellers streaming out of the square. Using the vehicle as cover, two uniformed police officers are pointing automatic rifles over the top of the car. One uses the car's roof as a firing point, whilst the other uses the platform above the front wheel arch. A green Chinese dragon hovers ominously in the air above the two men.

Without warning, the officer next to the wheel arch releases another burst from his weapon. Cal ignores the assault of the blast on his eardrums, ducking in reflex, his concentration focused on searching for whatever the officer is firing at.

"Can you see what they are firing at?" Cal asks Mike, his view blocked by the police car.

"I saw it, but it's gone," Mike replies cryptically.

"What did you see?" Cal demands in frustration.

"It was... a creature," Mike stutters.

Mike is making no sense to Cal. He is acting strange and talking gibberish. Putting Mike's conduct down to stress and exhaustion, Cal decides to take matters into his own hands.

"Moving," Cal informs Mike, knowing that his partner will follow suit to back him up.

Cal immediately leaves the cover of the building. Staying low, he rushes into the square toward the police car and the floating dragon. He shouts, "Police officer," as he nears the two men with weapons, to let them know he is approaching. The officer positioned on the car's roof whips his head in Cal's direction as he arrives, a look of terror fixed on his face. Another volley of bullets bursts from the second officer's weapon as he maintains his concentration.

"What we got?" Cal shouts over the din of gunfire, his back against the police car's door.

"It's a slaughter," the terrified officer blurts in reply.

What the hell is going on? Cal's mind reels as Mike arrives next to him, still looking perplexed. *Is everyone losing their minds?* Deciding that there is only one way to solve this mystery, Cal's legs push him upright to take a position next to the officer on the roof. He is barely aware of the metallic noise caused by the butt of his gun knocking against the roof of the car. His eyes are wide as he takes in the scene ahead, his stomach in knots.

Neon lights illuminate the shocking scene laid out across the square in front of the police car. Cal struggles to process the carnage presented to him. Mutilated bodies litter the expanse of the square, the blood and guts extracted from ripped-apart torsos glistening in the artificial light. Wherever Cal's eyes move they meet horror. Twisted faces rest against the paved ground, their petrified lifeless eyes fixed open, staring at the last thing they saw. Blood pools around each corpse, spreading and merging with other pools of dark-red liquid draining from the next mangled body.

Stunned into silence, Cal's eyes wander from one horrendous image to the next. Even the copious amounts of spilt blood don't hide more sequined dresses and loud shirts adorning many of the dead bodies. Men and women who had congregated for a night of fun and frivolity in Trinity, only to be slaughtered and discarded on the ground, soaked in their own blood. Cal's heart hangs heavy at the sight of the lost souls in front of him. *How many of the victims' loved ones will be left bereft by whatever has transpired here?* Cal asks himself sadly.

Cal is glad when a burst of gunfire drags him out of his waking nightmare. The shots don't come from their immediate vicinity. The two officers next to him are as still as statues and Mike is still low down. Noise ricochets in, the shots echoing from an adjacent street. Other police units must have arrived from different directions, answering the call of the all-units bulletin.

At least we aren't alone, Cal tells himself reassuringly, his mind clearing. *But what has caused this carnage?* he asks himself, anxiously.

"There!" the officer mounted on the roof next to Cal says urgently, as the echo of gunfire subsides.

Cal's eyes dart, searching for whatever the officer has seen, and something catches his eye. A shadowy figure moves out of a darkened side street that adjoins the far side of the square from their position. Cal is confident that the figure is emerging from the same direction as the gunshots. Has the figure been forced to retreat from the gunfire? Is the figure the cause of the bloodbath?

Gingerly, the chilling figure moves further into the square, where light begins to be cast over it. Cal believes he is watching the figure move on the screen of a television for a moment. The motion of the figure appears strange and unreal. *This is no television programme*, he is forced to remind himself, as the figure moves further into the square, stepping in amongst the carnage. The hideous creature becomes clearer with every step it takes.

"What the fuck is that?" Cal utters, hoping someone will give him a reasonable answer, his anxiety increasing.

"A zombie," the officer next to Cal answers, as he focuses his aim, shredding Cal's nerves even further.

"Don't be ridiculous…" Cal begins to reply, but his words taper off.

The figure, with its head down, moves further into the square and closer to their position. Taking no heed of where it treads, its smart shoes splash into the pools of blood, leaving bloody footprints on the ground as it travels. Cal's wide eyes stare mesmerised at the shoes and the moist prints they press into the paving below. He finally blinks and his eyes begin to travel up the legs of the figure and the blood-soiled blue jeans covering them. Cal's eyes continue their journey, travelling up to the figure's torso, fixating on the shredded white shirt, which is ripped open. He sees bare grey skin stretched across the protruding bones of the figure's ribcage. Dark-red blood stains the leathery skin, but there is something else pockmarking the grim torso. Holes. Holes that could only have been caused by bullets peppering the upper section of the figure's body. *How can this person still be alive after such catastrophic bullet wounds?* Cal's mind begs. His subconscious already knows that the officer next to him has already given him the answer. Cal refuses to accept that answer and forces his eyes to continue their journey. The figure's face will surely confirm that this is no zombie, and instead just a person who has miraculously survived the carnage that they find themselves in.

With trepidation, Cal's eyes gradually rise further, away from the grisly, stained, pockmarked torso, his head becoming light, afraid of what he will see when he focuses on the figure's face. But the figure's head is still lowered, and the only thing his eyes meet is a mop of dark, matted hair. Part of him is relieved that the face is hidden, the part that knows the officer's assessment of the creature is accurate.

Gunfire erupts from next to Cal, the figure being in the officer's line of sight. Cal cannot tear his eyes away from the creature. He watches in morbid fascination as bullets rip into the already bullet-ridden torso. A deathly scream comes from the creature's hidden mouth as bullets blast into its chest, and then it happens. Suddenly the mop of matted hair is gone, replaced by the terrifying features of the creature's face.

Cal gasps in shock as he stares at the face of a terrifying zombie. Its screaming mouth gapes open, forming a dark hole, with yellow, bloodstained teeth surrounding the crevice. Fearsome blackened eyes stare directly at Cal through sunken sockets attached to a jutting-out forehead and ballooned cheeks. Cal nearly takes a step backwards to fall and cower down next to Mike. The blood draining from his brain almost makes his legs buckle. Bullets fill the body of the creature and it shudders under the bombardment, its evil features turned to rage.

Afraid that nothing can kill this beast, Cal gains enough of his wits to aim his Glock. He is sure that the beast will attack as soon as the rain of bullets ceases. It will take its chance and move in for the kill. But just as Cal panics that he will be paralysed by the zombie's evil stare, unable to defend himself when the attack comes, a bullet smashes into the creature's formidable forehead. Instantly, the beast collapses, falling into a pile on the ground.

Silence envelops Cal, only the ringing in his ears from the gunfire directly next to him reverberating in his head. He stares at the heap of torn flesh where the creature had stood, half expecting it to spring back to its feet. Gradually, Cal feels himself breathing. His senses begin to return and he realises the beast is dead.

"Cal... Cal," Mike's voice creeps into Cal's ear.

"It's dead," Cal says, turning to look at his partner, who has his back against the car, gun pointed outwards, protecting their rear.

"Was it the creature?" Mike asks, nervously.

"It was definitely a creature," Cal answers.

"Are you sure it's dead?" Mike persists.

"Pretty sure," Cal answers, not completely sure of anything anymore.

"There could be more of them," the police officer interjects, dismally.

"What? Why do you say that?" Cal asks, disparagingly.

"There's a lot of bodies out there for just one of those things to have killed," the officer replies, not taking his eyes off the square.

Chapter 5

Cal realises grimly that the officer isn't wrong. There are almost too many corpses to count, they are strewn right across the square. If there is more than one creature, how many are there? One more, two, three, more even? And where the hell are they?

"Okay," Cal says, trying to sound confident. "We need to get a closer look."

"A closer look, are you crazy?" Mike replies, from near Cal's legs. "We don't know what we're dealing with, anything could be out there. We need to wait for the backup to arrive."

"We can't afford to wait. People might need our help. Some of those out there could still be alive!" Cal insists.

"The cavalry will be here at any moment; I say we wait," Mike argues.

"We are the cavalry, Mike. If we wait, others might die," Cal tells his colleague.

"Jay, cover us with Mike while we go and check it out. Understood?" the officer next to Cal orders his partner, from the front of the police car.

"Understood," his partner confirms.

"Are you okay with that, Mike?" Cal asks.

Okay, fine, but I still think we should wait for backup," Mike replies.

"My name's Callum, or Cal," Cal tells the officer next to him, without taking his eyes off the square.

"I know who you are, Detective Chambers. I'm Matt Wright," the officer informs Cal.

"Thanks for volunteering, Matt. Are you ready?" Cal responds.

"As I'll ever be, Detective."

"Call me Cal, okay?"

"As you wish, Cal," Matt smiles, nervously.

"Good. Let's go," Cal instructs, as Mike takes his position on top of the car.

"Be careful. Don't take any risks," Mike says, as Cal begins to edge around the car.

"Watch our backs," Cal replies, as he goes.

"I got you," Mike assures.

Cal's police-issue Glock hovers out in front of him as he breaks cover from behind the police car. Matt is at his back, his rifle nestled into his shoulder, pointing. How Cal wishes he had an automatic rifle instead of his handgun. He has already seen how much firepower it requires to take out one of these creatures and they have no idea how many more there are out there.

His legs feel like jelly and his stomach burns with fear as he moves around the front of the police car and into the square. Blue flashing lights flicker on the other side of the square, telling Cal that other emergency services are in position, ready to help. Someone had already fired bullets into the creature that Matt finished off, giving Cal some confidence. Approaching sirens pierce the night sky, building his confidence further. The square will soon be crawling with first responders. Cal and Matt just need to hold out until then.

Any hope that survivors are clinging on to life in amongst the gruesome carnage of the square fades quickly. Cal peers down into the face of the first body he comes across. A young woman stares back at him through haunting eyes, fear frozen in time on her face. There is no doubt that the woman was once glamorous and attractive. Now she has a morbid look of death that Cal is all too familiar with. Below her blood-splattered face, the front of her neck horribly gapes open displaying moist red flesh, veins and tendons, her windpipe torn in two. There is no helping this victim, Cal knows, without having to check for a pulse.

"She's so young," Matt says, from beside Cal.

"She can't have been more than twenty-five, if that," Cal replies.

"It's a massacre. What the fuck's going on? What was that thing?" Matt asks.

"I don't know," Cal replies.

"Where did it come from?" Matt presses.

"I don't know that either. Those questions are for another time. All we can do now is see if anyone needs our help," Cal replies, not holding out much hope that anyone will.

"They're all dead," Matt says, thinking the same.

"Let's check anyway, just in case. You check that body there and I'll check that one," Cal replies, pointing.

Cal and Matt don't stray too far from each other as they move deeper into the graveyard of corpses. After checking only two more bodies, Cal finds himself next to the prime suspect of the slaughter. The body of the creature Matt filled with bullets is buckled over on the ground near his feet. He doesn't want to touch the body in case he contaminates any evidence, or because the corpse gives him the creeps. He must, however. This body needs to be checked for signs of life just like any other.

"Cover me," Cal tells Matt, who has arrived next to the same body.

"Are you sure you want to do this?" Matt asks. "It's dead."

"No, but I have to," Cal replies, not taking Matt up on his offer of an excuse to let sleeping dogs lie.

Remaining at arm's length, Cal bends down, leaning toward the body. His hand with the Glock in it reaches out toward the crumpled corpse, the muzzle of the gun closing in. As the muzzle reaches within a few inches of the corpse, Cal's arm juts forward, poking the gun solidly into the shoulder of the hunched-over body.

The moment Cal hits its shoulder, he rises, taking a step away. Matt's rifle is trained directly at the creature as it slowly topples to the side, away from the two men. Rolling over and flopping to the ground, gravity takes its body all the way over onto its back, revealing the full horror of the beast to Cal and Matt, who peer down at it in silence.

Dark, black holes riddle the creature's torso, catastrophic holes that seemed of little consequence to it. Only the final bullet to its head had finally put the beast down and Cal forces his eyes to travel to find the kill shot. The bullet hit the creature through its right cheekbone, leaving only a small, well-rounded entry hole.

Cal becomes transfixed by the monster's dead, shockingly grey face, its dark, bloodshot eyes staring back. He has come across other corpses with matching appearances lately, including the businessman only this morning. He knew there was a connection between all the dead bodies that have been turning up recently. That much was obvious, even if they haven't been able to identify what the connection is yet. Whatever it is, the connection has taken a sinister new direction. Lone dead bodies are one thing, but horrific undead creatures and mass slaughter are a disturbingly different thing.

"It's not natural," Matt says, pulling Cal out of his stupor.

"No, it's not," Cal agrees.

"You've got to admit it looks like a zombie," Matt observes.

"I don't know what it is, but it definitely looks like one," Cal concedes.

"And acts like one," Matt pushes.

"I can't argue with you there. But there's got to be a reasonable explanation," Cal argues.

"If it looks like shit and it smells like shit then it's shit, no matter how much you try to polish it," Matt announces grimly to make his point, a point that Cal cannot argue with either.

"Let's continue to check the other victims," Cal suggests, avoiding having to challenge Matt's assessment.

Matt nods in agreement, knowing that this is not the time to continue the speculation. Both men are happy to turn their backs on the ghastly dead remains on the ground in front of them. Cal glances back toward the police car, where he sees Mike and Matt's partner, Jay, in the same position, covering them. He considers giving them a thumbs up but doesn't. There's nothing okay about this situation.

Turning to look over the square, ready to move on, Cal's heart sinks. The dead creature is grim but so is the task ahead. There are still many bodies for him and Matt to check. Too many.

"Movement, 11 o'clock!" Matt suddenly barks.

Cal turns in panic, in no particular direction, and he loses his bearings, his brain struggling to find Matt's 11 o'clock. Something catches his eye away to his left and his eyes focus in, trying to see the fast-moving apparition.

Matt is already aiming to fire by the time it has sunk in with Cal what he is looking at. The creature moves in the same manner as the one Matt shot dead, but this one is moving at speed, as if it is being chased. Matt's rifle tracks the beast as it rushes across the opposite side of the square, disappearing behind the central pagoda monument for a moment.

"Hold your fire!" Cal shouts when he suddenly sees figures bursting through an entrance into the square behind the creature.

Matt checks his aim as he also sees the team of crack firearms officers enter the square, dressed in grey camouflage, looking as if they're ready for combat. The team fan out as they arrive in the square in a well-drilled action before bringing the fast-moving creature into their sights.

Waiting for the burst of bullets to erupt from the team, Cal prepares himself for the onslaught, but nothing happens. The creature is almost past them before he understands what is happening. Nobody in the team has seen anything like this beast before. They're unsure if it is a threat or simply a crazed member of the public traumatised by the shocking carnage they have witnessed in the square. The creature bears no weapons and they cannot shoot unless there is imminent danger to themselves or the public.

"Take it down!" Cal shouts across the square at the team.

Cal sees one of the team, probably the commander, looking in his direction, but the team still takes no action. In frustration, Cal rushes forward in the direction of the team, avoiding the scattered dead bodies as he does. He must explain the situation to the team's commander.

"Hold your position!" orders the team member that had looked at Cal.

Stopping immediately, Cal finds himself in no-man's-land, halfway between the team of firearms officers and Matt, with only his Glock for company. Ahead and on his right, the creature also stops, but only momentarily. Its head whips around and looks directly at him, its hunger burning. In an instant, the body of the fearsome zombie turns and it bolts forward, directly at Cal.

"Shoot it!" Cal pleads at the top of his voice to anyone who is listening, whilst at the same moment aiming his sidearm.

Gunfire cracks from behind Cal, coming from the direction of the police car. Multiple shots ring out from both men positioned there. Cal knows how desperate Mike will be to protect his partner and, in his head, he also thanks the other man, Jay, for trying to assist. No bullets rip into the rapidly moving creature and, as Cal takes aim with his Glock, he realises that he is standing directly in the firing line between Matt and the beast.

Knowing Matt can't help him, and that Mike and Jay are too far away to get an accurate shot away, a sudden calmness floods over Cal. He is on his own. Nobody can or will help him, not even the crack firearms team. He aims directly at the oncoming zombie and waits.

There are plenty of bullets loaded into the Glock but, as Cal has discovered, there is only one shot that will take the beast down, a head shot. His enemy surges at him, closing in fast. The creature's head bobs this way and that through the air as it comes, the target constantly seesawing in his aim.

Evil, bloodthirsty eyes are fixed on Cal and he locks onto them in return. He follows them, becoming at one with their motion and with the motion of the head they are sunk into. The target gets closer, bigger. The barrel of the Glock sways in unison with its target, the mouth of which begins to widen, ready to feed.

With the target no more than two metres away, Cal's trigger finger depresses the trigger and the Glock explodes in his hand, recoiling backwards. The first bullet misses its target, but Cal catches the gun's recoil and fires again instantly. The second bullet crashes into the side of the creature's skull. Flesh and bone erupt into the air, but the bullet doesn't do enough damage. The creature's head is knocked sideways but it keeps coming, the beast almost upon him.

Keeping his cool, Cal taps out two more shots in quick succession. Bullet three shoots past its target but bullet four slams home. Almost in slow motion, Cal watches the fourth bullet hit the raging zombie. The bullet disappears into the left eye socket of the creature, halting its attack instantly. More flesh and bone spray into the sky, but this time brain matter gushes out with it as the creature's head whips backwards. The bullet's force is awesome, but it doesn't carry enough power to knock the entire creature backwards, its forward motion continuing.

Cal rapidly steps out of the way as the creature's trajectory lets it tumble straight past him. Taking deep gulps of breath, Cal stares down at the twisted body on the ground, his Glock at full arm's length, aiming down at the threat. His entire being was calm under the attack but now his heart thumps in double time and his whole body trembles.

"I thought it had you. Nicely done, Detective," Matt's voice sounds from next to Cal, who is unable to speak and can only breathe.

Suddenly, Cal is aware of movement on his left flank. Another attack is coming. He suddenly panics, twisting his body to meet it. The blood pumping into his head causes his vision to blur as his trembling arms bring the Glock to bear on the new threat. *I will have to fire blind*, he panics, his finger reaching for the gun's trigger, ready to defend himself. Lining up the gun as best he can on the figure coming toward him at speed he prepares to fire when, out of nowhere, a weight pushes his arms down horribly. *No*, he cries inside, trying to fight the downward pressure.

"Stand down, Cal," he hears Matt's voice say. "It's the firearms team."

Slowly Matt's words sink in and Cal stops fighting to raise the Glock. His body goes limp and he gulps down more air. Eventually, Cal's vision begins to clear as his heart rate slows. He is aware of a figure dressed in camouflage bending over the beast he has just taken out.

"He's dead," the man says, turning toward Cal and Matt.

"That wasn't a person," Matt informs the formidable-looking man, who is wearing a helmet and has the bottom half of his face covered in black material.

"Why didn't you kill it when you had the chance?" Cal demands, still breathing hard.

"We don't fire on unarmed civilians," Cal is told in reply.

"Does that thing look like a civilian?" Cal demands again.

The firearms officer, who Cal can see from the insignia on his sleeve is a police sergeant, turns to look again at the body he has turned over.

"He doesn't look normal; I'll give you that. But we can't shoot all the freaks we happen to see," the sergeant tells Cal.

"What, you have to wait until it rips my throat out? That isn't a freak, it's a fucking zombie or something," Cal insists. "Have you seen all the slaughtered bodies around here?"

"I don't know what's happened here. But I think you're delusional if you think zombies are the cause," the sergeant says, plainly.

"Delusional? Are you for real? Is he for real?" Cal barks, looking at Matt.

"Let's all calm down," Matt suggests. "The sergeant hasn't seen what we've seen, Detective. He wasn't to know what these things are."

"Well, he'd better get to know because I'll tell you one thing for sure. This won't be the last we see of them," Cal insists.

"Listen," the sergeant says, compromising. "My team is clearing the area. Once that's done, we can let the specialist teams in to find out what's happened. Let's take it from there, okay?"

"Whatever, Sergeant," Cal replies, raising his hands in surrender and turning to see Mike and Jay approaching.

"Are you okay?" Mike asks, as he arrives.

"Yes, I'm okay," Cal tells his partner. "No thanks to the cavalry though."

The sergeant ignores Cal's dig at him and instead moves off to join his team in clearing the area.

Matt suggests that they all continue to check the bodies while the firearms team does its work. Mike joins Cal as they stay in pairs and move around the square, doing just as Matt suggested.

Gradually, as the bodies are checked, the square is cleared and more police officers filter into the area. As confidence grows, medical services are permitted to rush in to see if they can utilise their skills to help any of the victims. Cal watches them swarm in despondently, knowing they will find nothing but death certificates to issue. Not even the best medic, with state-of-the-art equipment, is going to be able to use their skill to revive any of the poor souls scattered around him.

Cal and Mike look on as realisation sinks in with the medical teams. Their enthusiasm to help is quickly replaced by morbid horror and they surrender to the fact that there is nothing they can do to help the victims. Too soon they come to understand that the only item they are going to need from their arsenal of medical equipment is body bags. Cal has an urge to tell them all that there was nothing they could have done, as he sees their helplessness, but they will come to that conclusion themselves on their journeys home.

Chapter 6

Unsurprisingly, the last members of the emergency services to enter the square, once everything is totally secure of course, are the ones in authority. Cal recognises the police commissioner immediately in the group of dignitaries. Commissioner Jackson walks in with a look of horror on her face, one that has become all too common this evening. Her mouth hangs open in shock as she surveys the scene. Next to her, Cal suddenly recognises the city's mayor. He bears the same expression as Commissioner Jackson and, judging by the tuxedo he is wearing, he has just come from another official event.

Bringing up the rear of the group, Cal catches sight of his direct superior, Chief Arnold. Her presence suggests that Commissioner Jackson has put Arnold in charge of the investigation into what has transpired at Trinity Square, and that wouldn't surprise Cal in the slightest. Arnold is probably the commissioner's most trusted chief and, if she is in charge, the onus will be on him and Mike to get her some answers.

"Detectives," a voice disturbs Cal's concentration, "you'd better see this."

Switching his view from the group of dignitaries to the voice, Cal sees another firearms officer standing waiting.

Cal looks at Mike for a second, who tells the officer to lead the way.

They follow the grey camouflage-clad man across the square toward its outskirts and to one of the bars nestled on the edge of the square. Another armed officer stands guarding the door of the bar named Vision as they are led inside.

As they walk into Vision bar, the firearms officer steps to the side to let them see the full horror waiting for them inside. Twisted, mutilated corpses are strewn across the bar's carpeted floor like discarded pieces of meat. Blood-splattered, deranged, dead faces, their eyes fixed open in terror, stare up, begging for mercy. The only mercy any of these poor souls received was to have their throats torn out, which from what Cal can see happened to almost all of them. The ones who didn't have their own stories to tell and their catastrophic injuries do more than enough to tell those stories.

Below him, Cal can hear and feel the carpet squelch beneath his feet. The many discarded drinks glasses might suggest that it is booze that has soaked into the carpet. Whilst that might be true, he knows from the torn-apart bodies that the carpet is soaked with pints of blood as well as pints of beer. Everywhere he looks there is another body. He counts eight in quick succession, men and women alike. No quarter was offered to either sex.

Across the bar from Cal, he sees the firearms sergeant standing. His mouth is moving but Cal doesn't register what he is saying. He is too shocked to hear.

"Sorry, what did you say, Sergeant?" Cal eventually says, regaining some composure.

"I said, this looks like where the massacre began. None of the other bars have any victims inside," the sergeant repeats himself.

"What, this is the only one?" Mike asks.

"Yes, all of the other victims are outside, in the square," the sergeant confirms.

"Okay. I don't need to say it, but nobody touches anything," Mike orders. "In fact, everybody out. We can't risk contaminating the scene before forensics have combed this place," Mike demands.

Without question, the sergeant and the other firearms officer carefully exit the bar, leaving Cal and Mike alone inside.

"What do you think?" Cal asks Mike, before they evacuate.

"Christ knows. I've never seen anything like it. Not even close. All I do know is we're going to have our work cut out finding out," Mike answers.

"Yes, we're going to be in the box seat on this one. So much for trying to sort out my marriage," Cal says, immediately feeling guilty for his selfishness in the face of such sorrow.

"Kim will understand when she sees this on the news. Won't she?" Mike offers.

"Oh, yes. This will definitely put her mind at rest," Cal replies, sarcastically.

"Fair point," Mike concedes, as he turns to leave the bar. "At least you'll have something to take your mind off it," he adds, trying to be funny.

"Yeah, great. Zombies and dozens of mutilated dead victims. Marvellous. I will sleep soundly tonight," Cal replies, following Mike out.

"Who said you're getting any sleep tonight?" Mike questions.

Cal hasn't the energy to answer Mike as they return outside, where the view is just as grim but at least there's fresh air.

The square is now busy with emergency services, mainly police officers. Cal assumes that the medical teams are beginning to pronounce all the victims deceased and are starting to leave. Some will remain in case they are needed but the majority will go back to their normal duties. The body bags that Cal thought about earlier won't be used tonight, not until forensics have finished with each victim. He can see the forensics teams gearing up to begin their grim work across the square. Some are stepping into white bodysuits, so as not to contaminate the scene, whilst others are setting up equipment. Cal and Mike aren't the only ones who are going to be in for a long night. The forensics teams have got a mountain to climb with the number of victims they are facing in such a large area. Cal wouldn't be surprised if they are forced to call in help from other police departments in nearby areas to assist them on this crime scene.

"Detectives," a female voice calls.

Chief Arnold's assistant, a youngish woman called Tilly, is making her way across the square. Cal almost doesn't recognise her dressed in civilian clothing. He has only ever seen her in uniform. She must have been urgently called in from home, Cal suspects, as was Chief Arnold herself.

"Chief Arnold has asked to see you. Please follow me," Tilly requests, courteously.

"Lead on," Mike answers.

Tilly skirts the edge of the square, keeping well clear of the carnage as she leads them toward Arnold. Officers in white bodysuits that rise to cover their heads and who have also put masks over their faces have begun to move in amongst the dead bodies. Cal assumes that Tilly is keeping clear of the crime scene for forensic reasons, and not because she is squeamish, but he can't be sure.

Chief Arnold is nursing a small paper cup of coffee as they approach her. She is positioned next to the major incident vehicle, which has made its way into the square. The large white truck will be the focus of the investigation in the square. Other detectives very familiar to Cal and Mike are already making use of the vehicle and greetings are nodded between them all as they arrive with Arnold.

"I understand that you were first on the scene. Give me your report on the incident," Chief Arnold asks, without ceremony.

Cal would estimate that Arnold is in her early forties. She is a career police officer, who joined the police force as soon as her education was finished. Her father was quite a well-renowned policeman who had gained a high rank by the time he retired. Some might assume that Arnold's rapid rise through the ranks was because she is a woman, or that perhaps some nepotism was involved on account of her father, but those people would be sorely mistaken. Arnold is the most intelligent operator that Cal has ever come across and with that intelligence, together with her drive and determination, it was inevitable that she would take the fast road to promotion. Another thing Cal knows for sure is that it wasn't her humour or small talk that got her where she is. She is a plain-looking woman who doesn't suffer fools easily, or bullshit for that matter, which she can smell a mile off.

"Cal," Mike says, deferring to him to report.

"Ma'am. After responding to the all-units call, we arrived in the area to find the public evacuating Trinity Square urgently and en masse. A marked police car was already on the scene, with two armed officers in attendance, who we teamed up with.

"We found the massacre you have seen in the square upon arrival, with no indication of what had transpired. One of the officers that we had teamed up with informed us that they had seen a creature of some description in the square that they believed was the perpetrator of the massacre. The officer described the creature as a zombie, Ma'am, and they had already fired on it."

"A zombie, Detective?" Arnold questions, showing no emotion.

"If I may, Ma'am?" Cal asks.

"Yes, please continue," Arnold concedes.

"We assumed a position behind the police car to survey the situation and decide on the best course of action. While we were behind the car, the creature presented itself, appearing from one of the side streets. The creature then approached our position and, the closer it got, the more it did look like the officer had described. A zombie.

"The creature then moved to attack our position, at which point the two officers, who both had automatic weapons, opened fire on it. Ma'am, they shot the creature multiple times in the body, but it didn't go down. Quite the opposite: it still attacked. It wasn't until the creature was shot in the head that it went down and was killed."

"One moment please, Detective," Arnold interjects, before she turns to her assistant, Tilly. "Get me a phone number for disease control. I don't know which department you need exactly but find out, Tilly. Understood?"

Tilly nods, turns and rushes toward the major incident vehicle.

"Continue, Detective," Arnold says, looking back at Cal.

"Ma'am, once the creature or zombie was eliminated, me and one of the uniform officers, Officer Matt Wright, decided that we should move into the square to see if we could help any of the victims, while Mike and the other officer stayed in position to cover us.

"Unfortunately, we found all the victims deceased, Ma'am, with catastrophic injuries. All the injuries appeared to have been caused by teeth. The victims had been bitten, usually in the throat.

"While we were checking the victims, another creature presented itself, moving at speed. At almost the same time the specialist firearms team arrived in the square, but they were unaware of the threat and what was happening. The second creature saw me and Officer Wright, changed direction and moved to attack us. I was ahead of Officer Wright and was forced to engage the creature with deadly force. I shot it in the head. Ma'am."

"I see, Detective. And that is when the square was secured?" Arnold asks, still not showing any surprise or emotion at Cal's account.

"Yes, Ma'am, that is correct. You arrived shortly after that," Cal tells her.

"Ma'am," Mike interjects. "The firearms team have also discovered multiple bodies in a bar on the other side of the square. That is where we have just come from. It appears that the bar could be where the incident started. We cleared the bar to prevent cross-contamination of the scene. Forensics need to get in there, Ma'am. Their results could be vital in finding some answers."

"Thank you for bringing that to my attention, Detective," Arnold replies.

"We have a strong suspicion that this incident is directly connected to the unexplained corpses we have been investigating, Ma'am. Including the victim we attended this morning," Cal reports.

"Has a cause of death been established for those victims yet?" Arnold questions.

"No, Ma'am. The toxicology reports are still coming back as inconclusive," Mike answers.

"Perhaps you could see if you could get more help on that when you speak to disease control, Ma'am?" Cal suggests.

"We will get the help we need from every government department after this, Detective. I can assure you of that," Arnold states.

"About time," Mike adds.

"Indeed," Arnold agrees.

"What are your orders, Ma'am?" Cal asks.

"This is a major incident and the scene is now in the hands of forensics. Two more forensics teams are on their way from neighbouring departments to assist in gathering evidence and so, for now, the scene is off-limits to us.

"Officers are already taking statements from members of the public who witnessed the incident, those who haven't already left the area. I have also instructed another team of detectives to gather every piece of digital evidence we can find. CCTV from the scene and routes into the city, web chatter, etcetera. Other officers are on their way to the bus and train stations to gather the same. Taxi companies will be questioned. So there isn't much more you can do tonight here.

"I have been ordered to make a preliminary report to the mayor and commissioner at 9 am tomorrow, so I will need your statements completed. Go back to headquarters and get your statements done, while events are fresh in your mind. We will also need statements from Officer Wright and his partner. I will leave you to instruct them.

"I will be holding an initial major incident meeting first thing tomorrow morning and you will both be integral to the meeting, and the investigation. Understood?"

"Ma'am," both Cal and Mike confirm.

"When your statements are complete, get some rest," Arnold orders. "I'm going to need you fresh tomorrow, gentlemen. Evidence will be arriving in large quantities. You will need to be on your A-game. Is that clear?"

"Ma'am," both men confirm again.

"Be back in the office before 7 am," Arnold instructs them. "The meeting will be in the major incident room, at 7 am sharp. We will have a full team of officers at our disposal. In fact, the whole department will be at our disposal. I want your investigation so far into the other unexplained victims correlated and ready to be integrated into this investigation. You will provide me with an interim report at eight-thirty. Is that clear?"

Cal and Mike confirm they understand, at which point Arnold tells them to "Carry on". As soon as she is finished with them, she turns toward the major incident vehicle behind, climbs the steps and goes inside. Cal watches her as she walks straight over to Tilly. He wonders if Tilly has found the relevant phone number Arnold asked for. He would like to hear the conversation Arnold has with disease control, but he has his orders. The first of which is for him to find Officer Wright and his partner.

Thankfully, they find the two officers quickly. The two men are back with their vehicle, helping to secure the square and stopping the public from wandering into the crime scene.

"Thanks for backing me up before," Cal says, when he sees Matt.

"All in a day's work, Detective," Matt replies coolly, his automatic rifle positioned across his chest.

"I'm glad you think this is a normal day's work," Cal replies, dryly.

"Well, not quite, Sir, but you get my drift. Happy to help," Matt concedes.

"Good, then you can help us some more. Chief Arnold has given us some very clear instructions. We've been ordered to submit an initial incident report to her by eight-thirty tomorrow, so we're going to need your incident reports done tonight. Tell your sergeant to get other officers to replace you and then head back to get your statements done. I'm sure I don't need to tell you that every detail must be included in your reports, no matter how trivial they may seem to you. The devil is in the detail, gentlemen, and it seems like the devil has been at work here tonight so don't omit anything. Understood?" Cal finishes.

"Yes, Sir. Our incident reports will arrive in your inbox by the end of the night," Matt confirms.

"And inform your sergeant that you have both been seconded to this investigation. Report at 7 am tomorrow to the major incident room at police HQ, level six. We'll submit the relevant paperwork tomorrow. Understood?"

"Yes, Sir!" both officers confirm eagerly.

"Good. You did well tonight, Officer Wright. Keep it up," Mike says, as he and Cal leave to find their car.

"Nice parking," Mike jests, when they see the car parked askew in the road, exactly where they'd abandoned it, close by the square.

"It's a lot quieter than when we arrived," Cal points out, looking around.

Further up the road, they can see police manning other cordons cutting off the roads to normal traffic. Arnold obviously doesn't want the public anywhere near the scene. While traffic is relatively easy to divert, people on foot pose more of a problem. There are a myriad of ways to reach any part of the city on foot and Trinity Square is no different. It will take some manpower to keep the crime scene secure, but Cal knows Arnold has enough officers to call upon.

"They're going to be at it all night," Mike says.

"And the rest. It'll be a while until Trinity Square reopens," Cal replies.

"We're going to have a mountain of evidence to get through. Why did she have to choose us?" Mike jokes.

"Because we're the best she's got," Cal grins, as he presses the key fob to unlock the car. "Or we were in the wrong place at the wrong time."

"The latter, but I don't need this at my age," Mike says, seriously.

"There'll definitely be a commendation in this for us when we crack the case," Cal encourages.

"Stick your commendations. I just want an easy life," Mike retorts, opening his car door.

"Well, you chose the wrong profession for that," Cal tells him, as he gets behind the wheel.

"Don't get me wrong, I used to be eager when I was your age. Now I'm just tired," Mike replies.

"My eagerness is waning already," Cal confides. "But I'm going to get my teeth into this one. Whoever is responsible for that atrocity is going to burn, and we're the ones who are going to light the match."

"Big words," Mike says, seemingly unimpressed.

"Not big words," Cal presses, vehemently looking across the car at Mike. "That was just horrendous. Those poor people. Someone has gotta pay. If we don't find them, and find them fast, it will happen again, you can guarantee it. Who knows where it could end?"

"You're right," Mike agrees.

"I know I am. Are you with me, partner?" Cal asks, eagerly.

"You know I am. It's just been a long day," Mike assures. "Let's get back to HQ so that we can get some rest before tomorrow."

Chapter 7

At one fifty-five in the morning, Cal arrives home and finally shuts his front door on the day. The house is in complete darkness and deadly silent. He feels a deep sadness that the house is empty, that Kim hasn't left a light on for him and won't be upstairs in bed waiting for him. Before she left and moved to her sister's, she would always wake when he got into bed, no matter what the time. She would groggily ask him how his day had been and snuggle into him. How he misses her, especially on nights like tonight.

He doesn't bother switching a light on. Instead, he wearily climbs straight up the stairs in darkness. One thing he is looking forward to is brushing his teeth. He can still taste the rancid burger he'd eaten at his desk while writing the lengthy incident report. Mike was still writing his when he'd left. Cal isn't sure how fresh Chief Arnold expects them to be at seven in the morning tomorrow, with barely any sleep. He tells himself not to stress about it now, such is the life of a police detective. A life that has become too much for Kim.

His cold and empty bed is uninviting but welcome, nevertheless. As stressful and horrific as the day has been, the images of death and slaughter fail to keep Cal awake for too long. Even the sounds of the house creaking, threatening the presence of the undead, fade as sleep thankfully takes over his tired body and overworked mind.

In a flash, Cal's phone begins to vibrate on the nightstand. He is aware of it in his dream, but only the rising tone of the melodic alarm forces him to react. There is no option this morning to select snooze on the phone's screen to give him five minutes more to rouse himself properly. He has left himself barely enough time to get ready and go into the office as it is. A flick of his finger silences his phone before he drops back onto the bed, dog-tired and feeling sorry for himself.

Cal jolts back awake suddenly at the sound of his phone vibrating again. Disorientated and even more tired than he was when his alarm went off, he looks at his phone in confusion, unsure what day it is. Mike's name pulses on the screen as reality sinks in, and he realises he must have fallen back to sleep. His alarm went off fifteen minutes ago, for fuck's sake.

"Hello," Cal forces out of his dry mouth.

"Overslept again, have we, Detective?" Mike asks, knowingly.

"No, I'm just brushing my teeth," Cal improvises.

"Good. I've picked up breakfast, so see you shortly," Mike tells him.

"Leaving in five," Cal replies, and hangs up before scrambling out of bed.

Five minutes later, Cal is climbing into his car, having not had a shower and with stubble still clinging to his chin. At the first set of traffic lights, he stops and grabs his electric razor from the central console to tackle the stubble. He will have to sneak off for ten minutes at the first opportunity he gets to use the staff showers when he gets to work. *It won't be the first time*, he tells himself, as the low morning sun assaults his eyes.

Stealing a shower at work has become a more regular occurrence since he has become a reluctant bachelor. Kim is certainly a morning person. She loves mornings, which was marvellous for Cal. When he was due in the office at a reasonable time, she would rise before him to prepare a fresh breakfast, then come back into the bedroom to wake him. Seeing Kim's glowing smile first thing in the morning was wonderful; it made waking up worthwhile. She would do the same on their days off. She was always up early, unlike him. Sometimes, on those special mornings, breakfast would have to wait. Kim never protested when he dragged her back into bed, and she often took it upon herself to slide in next to him, sliding her soft skin over his.

His shave complete, Cal throws the razor back into the central console just as the news jingle sounds on the radio. Inevitably, there is only one story for the newscaster to begin the bulletin with and she barges straight into it. 'Twenty-eight people slaughtered... the massacre remains unexplained... the Chinese quarter is under police lockdown... the city's mayor and police commissioner will be making a statement at 11 am...'

In fact, no other news is reported; even the sports headlines are cut from the bulletin. Cal always has his car radio tuned in to a local station in case anything has happened in the city that night that he might need to know about. This morning, however, he is positive that every news programme in the country, local and national, will be bloated with the same reports, together with most radio stations across the entire planet.

As the trunk road, he has joined rises over the railway tracks and factories below, Cal sees the city spread out. In the centre, a cluster of skyscrapers rise into the morning sky. A short distance away to the left, a shorter building pokes up, police headquarters, his destination. Now he turns off the radio so he can concentrate and get down to business. For the remainder of the journey, Cal goes through last night's gruesome events and how they could possibly be linked to the other cases of corpses that have been discovered, if the two are connected at all.

"Morning," Cal announces, as he reaches his and Mike's small corner of the office.

"Cutting it fine, aren't we?" Mike asks, raising his eyebrows.

"It's only ten to," Cal argues, knowing that won't wash with Mike.

"Yes, and I want to be in the incident room before the chief," Mike protests.

"Yes, I know. Sorry, bud. It was a struggle getting up this morning. Not all of us can survive on as little sleep as you do," Cal concedes.

"Wait until you get to my age. You'll understand then that sleeping is just a waste of the valuable time you've still got remaining," Mike grins.

Cal knows he's talking out of the back of his head. Mike often takes great enjoyment in telling Cal how he's never needed much sleep. He especially enjoys rubbing it in when he sees Cal struggling due to a lack of it.

"Don't sweat it, partner," Mike continues. "Our statements are done and we have the two from the other officers. Everyone probably knows as much as we do at this stage, anyway."

"Okay," Cal agrees, knowing that Mike will take the lead as the senior detective when Chief Arnold calls on them.

"Now, get that down you before we go in," Mike suggests, pointing at a groovy paper bag, which will contain an overpriced Danish with a coffee next to it, both from Starbucks.

Cal devours the Danish whilst sipping lukewarm coffee. The coffee brings him round a bit more and he carries it with him while they make their way to the major incident room across from the main office.

Inside the largest incident room available, about a dozen plain-clothes detectives are waiting, together with an equal number of uniformed officers. Cal spots Officer Wright and his partner sitting toward the back of the room; both look raring to go. Unfortunately, Chief Arnold has already arrived, which is why the room is so quiet when they enter.

Arnold sits at the front of the room, like the headmistress of a school who has decided to sit in on a lesson. She looks at Mike and Cal sternly as they enter, before checking her watch. Cal sees thankfully from the large clock on the wall that they have just made it in time. The men quickly take the two empty seats at the front of the crowded seating area. The seats appear to have been reserved for them.

Arnold dispenses with any formal greeting and begins the briefing as she stands. She gets straight down to business. In a deadly serious tone, she calls Cal and Mike to the front to describe last night's events. They are on their feet again before they have even managed to get comfortable.

As the senior detective, Mike assumes the lead. He takes the room step by step through the horrendous events of last night, just in case anyone is not fully aware of the seriousness of what transpired.

Cal sees from the stern faces of those present that each of them knows how serious the situation is. Not one of them flinches when Mike describes the two creatures that they faced. Their expressions do not even change when he uses the word 'zombie' to describe them.

"Have you anything to add?" Mike asks, looking at Cal when he finishes his account.

"I'd just like to reiterate what it took to kill these creatures. The first was shot multiple times in the body using an automatic weapon. Those shots had little effect. It was only when the creature received a shot to the head that it was killed. This was like nothing I or any of the other officers present have seen before. So, take that on-board. I don't believe we are facing something that any of us has seen in the past. This incident is different," Cal hammers home his point.

"Thank you, Detective," Arnold says, when Cal has finished and both men have retaken their seats. Just as they do, Tilly, Arnold's assistant, enters the room silently, nods at Arnold and then simply stands against the wall next to the door.

Without saying a word, Arnold picks up a remote control from a nearby table. She walks over to the door where Tilly is standing and flicks the light switch positioned on the wall next to the door, sending the room into almost complete darkness.

A second later, the overhead projector bursts into life. Suddenly, moving images are being projected onto the screen mounted on the wall at the front of the incident room. No warning is given to the rows of police officers present about the horror they are about to be submitted to. Arnold is obviously attempting to instil a shock factor into every officer present. Trying to concentrate their minds, making them focus on their work.

Within a few seconds, Cal recognises the interior of the bar in Trinity Square where the concentration of slaughtered corpses was found. The CCTV pictures are grainy and have been taken through a camera that was mounted at the back of the bar. The wide-angled view shows the main entrance on the right of the screen, the pool-table area at the centre back and the actual bar on the left.

"Keep your eyes on the three men standing at the back next to the pool table," Arnold announces.

Cal's focus is already on the three men. He doesn't know why his eyes have been drawn to that position. The three men look innocent enough at the distance they are from the camera and with the unfavourable quality of the footage. They could easily be just three friends playing pool and drinking. Swiftly, one of the men raises his hand toward the other two, as if to show them something. He is definitely holding something in his hand.

After lowering his arm, that man turns and walks away, leaving just two men by the pool table. Cal concentrates as the man moves across the bar, closer to the area where the camera is positioned, trying to see if he can see the man's face. With frustration, Cal sees that the man deliberately keeps his hooded head down. The ominous figure jumps to the top of the whole room's 'person of interest' list.

"He is filming!" Cal suddenly announces out loud, as he sees the man turn his back to the camera, but he clearly sees him holding up a phone.

"I agree, Detective," Arnold replies. "Watch the two men at the back by the pool table."

On the grainy picture, Cal can see that the men have become distressed, so much so they both fall around the feet of the pool table. He knows instinctively that this is the start of the hideous incident. His eyes are glued to the screen, his heart pumping rapidly.

Movement on the right shows another man enter the bar through the main door. He approaches another man who is standing with his back to the camera, closest to the two men in distress, facing them. Cal is sure that the two men are working at the bar and are checking on the two distressed customers. Both men seem reluctant to approach the customers, however, despite their obvious distress.

From next to the pool table, there is more movement. One of the two distressed men is rising off the floor, using the pool table for leverage. Slowly the man gets to his feet while, behind him, the second man is also attempting to get up.

The stand-off between the bar staff and the two men by the pool table doesn't last long. Cal hears audible gasps in the room around him when suddenly the lead man by the pool table bursts forward to attack.

Even though Cal saw the results of the slaughter in the bar last night, he has a hard time believing the ferocity of the attack that follows. Many people scatter in panic, some rushing past the person of interest who is filming the unfolding carnage. Every officer in the incident room watches on in horror as the two creatures rip through those in the bar who are either too slow or too drunk to react quickly enough to the threat.

Cal is forced to admit to himself that he is deeply disturbed by the gruesome footage. He hears the screams of terror ring in his head, even though the footage has no sound accompanying it. As much as he wants to divert his eyes from the massacre, he forces himself to watch every second closely in case more vital evidence presents itself. He is also well aware that this will only be the first of numerous times he will have to watch the brutality. The footage will have to be reviewed over and over again.

Thankfully, the worst of the bloodshed ends when the two creatures chase a man, who looks like one of the two members of staff, out of the main entrance. This is when Cal expects the screening to finally end and Arnold to switch the lights back on. His relief is postponed though; the lights aren't switched back on and the images don't disappear from the screen.

Arnold keeps the footage rolling. She wants them all to see something else. Cal quickly understands why Chief Arnold doesn't relent. He watches with interest as the hooded figure moves across the room toward the main entrance. There, remaining inside the bar, he takes up a position at a large window. The man carried on recording the creatures even after they had moved out into the square. This man isn't just a person of interest, Cal realises. This sick fuck is their prime suspect.

A moment later, the CCTV footage does finally end, and the screen suddenly goes black, but Arnold doesn't turn to switch the lights on. Instead, she fiddles with the remote control in her hand, struggling to see its buttons in the darkness.

As fast as the screen had darkened, it suddenly bursts back into action as Arnold finds the button she was looking for. Now the screen is filled with the image of Trinity Square. The CCTV camera taking the new footage is positioned high above the square, capturing a bird's eye view of the bustling area.

The entire incident room is morbidly quiet as everyone witnesses the unfolding of the barbaric slaughter that took place in the square. Arnold forces them all to watch every person, one after another, suffer a brutal killing. She doesn't stop their torture until Cal is forced to watch himself shoot the second beast dead. Only then does Arnold turn off the footage and, thankfully, turn the lights back on.

"I'm sorry to have had to put you all through those horrific scenes," Arnold says, genuinely. "I know how hard it is to watch. I was shocked and sickened when I first saw it early this morning.

"Unfortunately, it was necessary. I need you all to be in no doubt about what we are dealing with and how serious this situation is. Be under no illusion that we are simply dealing with two unexplained but contained monsters that went on the rampage for one reason or another. We are not. Far from it, it would seem.

"As you all clearly saw in the footage, the two zombified creatures were undoubtedly fearsome and brutal and, yes, they were both eventually killed."

Cal continues to sip his coffee, which is now all but cold, as Arnold goes into greater detail regarding the initial evidence that has been discovered. She is positive that there are more suspects to find and new witnesses who will be able to help find those suspects. She tells the room how the local Disease Control Department has taken custody of the two creatures' bodies and will be performing autopsies under quarantine conditions, with preliminary results expected this morning.

Chief Arnold then begins to hand out assignments, splitting the officers present into teams to investigate different aspects of the case. Cal and Mike wait to see what they will be assigned by Arnold but, as work is handed out and senior detectives are assigned to manage each team, Cal and Mike seem to have been overlooked. Cal was hoping to be assigned to victim and witness investigation, he prefers dealing with people, but that aspect of the investigation is handed to one of his colleagues. Thankfully, digital evidence is also handed to another detective. Cal has done his time sitting in front of a screen trawling through hours and hours of CCTV footage. He doesn't want to go back there.

Arnold finishes handing out assignments, with Cal and Mike still left unassigned. The two men look at each other in confusion, wondering why they have been left on the side-lines.

"The mayor and Commissioner Jackson will be making a statement to the media at 11 this morning. I am sure they would like something positive to tell the public, as we all would, so let's see what we can find that they could use.

"They will also be making an appeal for new witnesses to come forward. There must be many more people who were in the Trinity Square area last night who ran before we could interview them. I expect these witnesses will come forward in numbers. They could hold vital information for this investigation. Every one of them will be interviewed and more officers will be assigned as needed.

"Detectives Mike Turner and Callum Chambers will be the senior investigators on this case. They will direct you and everything goes through them. Any insight into the incident or relevant evidence must be brought to their attention immediately. If you are unsure of the significance of even the smallest piece of information, consult with them and, if they can't give you an answer, then they will bring it to me. Is that understood?" Arnold demands.

"Yes, Ma'am," the entire room replies in unison.

"Very well. Let's get to work!" Arnold insists. "Mike, Callum, I need to talk to you in my office."

Chatter erupts and everyone rises from their chairs the moment Chief Arnold turns to leave the incident room.

"It looks like we're in the box seat on this one," Cal observes, as he and Mike set off to follow Arnold.

"Why am I not surprised?" Mike replies, rolling his eyes.

"Don't sound so happy about it," Cal jokes.

"Our workload is going to go through the roof," Mike tells him.

"You're not wrong there," Cal agrees, as they step out into the corridor.

Both men zip their lips as they move into the relative quietness of the corridor, following Arnold, who is chattering away to Tilly beside her. Tilly is professionally taking notes, continuing to do so even when she enters Arnold's office with her.

"Gentlemen, are you up for the challenge?" Arnold asks, standing behind her desk.

"Yes, Ma'am. We are eager to get to the bottom of this," Cal replies for both of them, before Mike has a chance to suggest the opposite.

"That's what I was hoping to hear, Detective," Arnold says, eyeing them before continuing. "I will deal with the commissioner and mayor. I have already begun to write up my initial assessment of the situation to allow them to make their statement to the media. In my opinion, the statement is secondary as far as we're concerned. The priority is for them to ask for witnesses, or anyone with information, to come forward.

"As I said in the briefing, I think there will be dozens, if not more. We need to be ready for that and, to that end, Tilly and I have already assigned officers in preparation. They will take the calls and arrange for witnesses to come in for their statements to be taken. They will flag any that they believe contain important information and bring them to you. It goes without saying that they will hold witnesses who have information that needs immediate further investigation.

"In the meantime, your top priority is to identify and bring into custody the hooded suspect who filmed the incident. At least one of the witnesses must have seen his face and can help us with a facial reconstruction. Somebody might know him and be able to identify him. It is possible, if unlikely, that he's a regular visitor to the area and known locally, in the bars and restaurants," Arnold insists.

"Absolutely, Ma'am," Mike agrees. "He is our top priority. We will instruct all teams to concentrate on finding him."

"If we can discover a facial image of the suspect, Ma'am, it must be added to the public appeal," Cal offers.

"Indeed, Detective, but time is against us. That might have to wait for the news bulletins," Arnold points out. "Take a team to Trinity Square with the best image we have uncovered so far and talk to the proprietors of the bars and restaurants. See if they can identify him. Speak to staff. Get home addresses of staff who aren't at work, which will be most of them with the square closed. Send officers to their home addresses to speak to them, whether they were working last night or not."

"Ma'am," both men confirm.

"This man holds the key. I can feel it. We must find him," Arnold presses.

"We will find him, Ma'am," Mike assures, as he and Cal leave Arnold's office.

Chapter 8

"I need to give Kim a call. I haven't spoken to her since yesterday morning," Cal tells Mike, as they make their way back to their department.

"No problem. You go and do that now while I assemble a team to take to the square and get some pictures printed of the suspect," Mike replies.

"Are you sure?" Cal asks.

"Yes, of course. As long as it's not too early for her," Mike enquires.

"She'll be up. No doubt about that," Cal tells him.

"Okay, it'll take twenty to thirty minutes to get everything ready, so there's plenty of time. There's no point getting to the square before nine anyway. They'll be nobody there, probably not before ten in fact," Mike surmises.

"Maybe I should have gone into the hospitality industry to get more sleep," Cal jokes.

"They work late though," Mike points out.

"And we don't?" Cal retorts.

"Fair point. I can't see you waiting tables though," Mike laughs.

"Me neither to be fair," Cal agrees, as he leaves Mike behind to make his call and to grab a quick sneaky shower.

The locker room is busy when Cal finishes dressing, after his shower, with officers both finishing their shifts and starting them. He needs to find somewhere more private to call Kim. As he leaves the locker room, he is panting for breath having rushed his shower. The locker room isn't far away from his desk, but he easily finds a private spot to make his call. He knows this level of police headquarters like the back of his hand.

"Morning, Cal," Kim's soothing voice answers his call.

"Good morning. H-h-how are you?" Cal stammers, not quite sure what to say. How has he become so nervous about making a phone call to his own wife?

"I'm as well as can be expected," Kim tells him. "And you?"

"I'm good, thanks. You know, busy at work as usual." He daren't tell her how tired he is after such little sleep last night. It would only confirm her misgivings about their marriage.

"I should think you are after last night's terrible killings in Chinatown. Are you involved in that investigation?" Kim asks.

"I'm afraid so. Me and Mike are two of the lead investigators," Cal confesses.

"Oh my God," Kim gasps. "Was it as horrible as it sounds?"

"It wasn't good," Cal tells her, not mentioning that he was attacked by and shot one of the creatures. The last thing he wants is to worry Kim unduly, especially in her condition.

"It must have been awful. You weren't in any danger, were you?" Kim asks, with genuine concern.

"No," Cal lies.

"Well, just be careful. Promise me," Kim insists.

"I will be, I promise. We have a good team on this and I'm sure it will be resolved quickly," Cal replies, taking comfort in Kim's concern for him, whether he is clutching at straws or not.

"Is it still going on? I thought they said on the news that the suspects were killed on sight?" Kim asks, the concern obvious in her voice.

"We think that there is more at play than just those two suspects," Cal confides. "But don't worry, we will handle it."

"Oh, God! Please be careful, Cal," Kim pleads.

"I didn't know you cared," Cal jokes, immediately regretting it.

"Of course I care, Callum!" Kim snaps. "This situation isn't my fault. You're the one who's given up on this marriage and it's time you realised it."

"I'm sorry, Kim. It was a silly joke. I know I'd become distant and work was getting on top of me. I didn't want that, and I don't want this. I love you and I'm working on a way to fix us. You do know that, don't you?" Cal pleads.

"I don't see much changing, Cal," Kim says. "What time did you get home last night?"

"It was late," Cal confesses.

"I know your work is important, Cal, but so is our marriage. Now more than ever," Kim insists.

"Believe me, I know that. I've just got to find an alternative that's going to provide for the three of us," Cal defends.

"Do you realise how long you've been saying that?" Kim asks.

"I know, but it's not easy. The bills keep dropping through the door," Cal answers.

"There's more to life than money and bills," Kim tells him.

"I know," Cal answers, wondering how she imagines they would keep the house without his salary.

"I've got to go," Kim says, the upset in her voice plain to hear.

"Can we meet for lunch or something? I'd love to see you," Cal asks, nervously. Kim is living with her sister, who has an upmarket apartment in the city's Arena District, not too far from police headquarters.

"Not yet, Cal. I need more time," Kim replies, disappointingly.

"Please think about meeting up," Cal pleads. "We don't have to talk about us. I just want to see you," Cal says.

"I will think about it," Kim agrees. "I really must go now. Just be careful. Okay?"

"I will. We'll speak soon," Cal replies, hopefully.

"Bye, Cal," Kim simply answers and ends the call.

Cal stands looking aimlessly at his phone, his emotions in turmoil. What can he do to be reconciled with Kim? She is of great importance to him, as is his unborn child. He knows that the answer she wants is for him to leave his career and move into a 'normal career', whatever that is. He has investigated that possibility, but options are limited. Cal only knows policing and those skills aren't easily transferable. Kim's suggestion of going into private security sounds promising until you actually look into the facts and figures. With the number of police officers leaving the force at present, all looking to go into the private sector, jobs are scarce and remuneration is poor. Cal knows he must do something if he wants to win Kim back, which he is desperate to do. In the end, he might have to bite the bullet and retrain for a totally different career, although where he'll find the time to do that remains to be seen.

Cal's phone suddenly buzzes in his hand and he zones back to reality to see Mike's name displayed.

"I'm just coming," Cal reassures his partner.

"Good. I thought you'd decided to clock off," Mike jokes.

"Sorry, bud. Women trouble. You know how it is," Cal replies.

"Do I ever," Mike concedes. "We're ready to go but we need to get moving."

"I'll be with you in less than a minute," Cal tells him, ending the call to rush back to the office.

Cal attempts to put the Kim conundrum out of his mind for the time being. He will win her back. He is sure of it. He just needs to figure out the finer details.

Mike is waiting by their desks, Cal sees, as he arrives back in the office. Close by are the two younger officers from last night, Matt and Jay. All three watch him enter and are ready for the off as he does.

"Everything okay?" Mike wonders, as he moves toward the other exit out of the office and the way off the floor and down to the carpool.

"Yep, thanks. Kim is worried about what she saw on the news, but I tried to settle her mind," Cal replies, as they leave.

Mike tells Cal that he isn't surprised Kim is worried. His own wife, Janet, was equally worried last night when Mike arrived home. Janet is a lovely woman and has been married to Mike for over two decades. Cal often uses their marriage as a way of motivating himself that there is a way to balance police work with family life, although Kim is always quick to remind him that she isn't Janet, despite the two women being quite close. Janet, for her part, has advised Cal to be patient because Kim's life has changed and become unbalanced since she became pregnant. 'Give her time,' Janet tells Cal, which he has, but it is becoming more and more apparent that Kim is indeed different to Janet.

Matt and Jay are silent on the ride down to the carpool, not saying a word, even as the metal doors open to let them out into the underground concrete parking lot.

"We'll see you there," Mike tells the two men, as they head toward the minibus that is waiting to take them and the other half-dozen officers to Trinity Square. "I will brief you on arrival," Mike adds, as they walk off.

Cal is behind the wheel of their patrol car as they lead the minibus up the ramp and through the exit gate. He turns right onto the street in the direction of Chinatown, which is about a ten-minute drive away, depending on traffic.

Perhaps unsurprisingly, the traffic becomes worse the nearer they get to Chinatown. The closure of roads leading to the quarter plays havoc with the normally congested flow of traffic. Cal is even glad to see the first police roadblock, despite the horrendous reason for it being there and the horrors it is protecting the public from.

Mike turns on the car's hidden flashing lights, to let the officers manning the roadblock know they are coming. The marked minibus has fallen behind in the traffic so cannot give the officers prior warning of the team's arrival.

Cal pulls up at the same entrance into Trinity Square that he did last night, only closer. He stops a short distance from the police tape cutting off the entrance and the officer stationed there and sees, in the rear-view mirror, that the minibus has stopped just behind.

"Let's go then," Mike says, as he opens the door, his voice sounding slightly nervous.

Cal can't blame Mike for sounding nervous. He can't say he's looking forward to returning to the sight of last night's horrific slaughter either.

Behind them, the minibus is emptying of police officers ready to go to work in and around Trinity Square. Cal and Mike make them wait for a moment while they go and talk to the policewoman who is guarding the entrance to the square.

"Morning," Mike says, as they approach.

"Good morning, Sir," the young officer replies.

"Have you been on duty here for long?" Cal questions.

"I took over at 6 am, Sir," Cal is told.

"What's been happening?" Mike asks.

"The scenes of crime and forensics officers have been busy in the square since I arrived, Sir. I think they are beginning to clear the square of evidence and bodies now, Sir, but it's difficult to tell from here," the young woman informs them.

"Have any of the owners or managers of the establishments in the square arrived this morning?" Cal questions.

"One or two, Sir. They were escorted to their buildings," the officer answers.

"Do you know if anyone from Vision bar has turned up?" Mike asks.

"I don't know, Sir."

"Okay, thank you," Mike says, before turning toward the waiting officers congregating around the minibus.

Mike proceeds to give his instructions to the team of officers, while Cal hands each officer one of the A4 prints of the suspect. The image on the piece of paper is poor, to say the least. The grainy picture shows little more than a man's chin. The rest of his face is hidden by his hood. It might nevertheless jog someone's memory so that they could give a description of the man or, possibly, even provide a name if they're lucky.

Mike prepares to send pairs of officers in different directions to cover as much ground as possible. He tells them to visit every bar, restaurant and store surrounding Trinity Square and to talk to anyone they can, either working or not. "Approach people in the street," he tells them. "Show them the picture and ask if they were in the area last night or have any information." All the officers nod their understanding and, when Mike has told them that he and Cal will be questioning whoever they can find inside the square, he sends them on their way. The only two officers he orders to remain behind are Matt and Jay. Those two officers follow Mike and Cal past the policewoman into Trinity Square.

Trinity Square is still a hive of activity. The major incident vehicle is still parked in the same position as last night, on the opposite side of the square. Sprouting up from the ground, the tall Chinese pagoda has been joined by several blue-and-white forensics tents. The tents are designed to protect crime scenes from the elements, as well as to keep prying eyes away from sensitive areas. Forensics scientists covered from head to toe in white protective suits wander in and out of tents, carrying out their work. The suits are worn to prevent the scientists from contaminating evidence.

Cal quickly notices that a good proportion of the dead bodies have already been removed from the square. Only their dried blood remains, staining the ground in large dark-red patches. Another, larger tent engulfs the entrance to Vision bar, where more white figures move in and out of its front flap and past a firearms officer who is guarding it.

Mike orders Matt and Jay to begin their enquiries on the opposite side of the square to Vision bar. He tells them to knock on the door of every establishment to search for witnesses. He reminds them that all of the businesses will have rear entrances that could have been used without the police necessarily knowing, so they must be persistent.

As Matt and Jay turn, Cal and Mike head straight for Vision bar. They walk around the perimeter of the square, keeping as far away from the central crime scene as they can. They pass a plethora of bars and restaurants as they go, all of which they will visit after they have visited Vision bar.

The firearms officer guarding the entrance to Vision bar watches them approach and Cal sees the man's body tense up the closer they get. He is almost standing to attention by the time he and Mike arrive.

"Have any staff members or management arrived on scene and tried to gain access to the bar?" Mike asks the officer.

"Not that I'm aware of, Sir," the officer replies.

"Has there been any communication from anyone?" Cal questions.

"I don't know, Sir. I've just been ordered to guard the entrance," Cal is told.

"Ordered by whom?" Cal presses.

"The team sergeant, Sir, but he's off-site now," the officer tells them.

"Okay, thanks. If anyone arrives, radio it in immediately. Tell them to relay the message to me, Detective Chambers," Cal orders.

"Yes, Sir," the officer responds.

"It was a long shot," Mike says, as they turn away. "The team back at base will find contact details of the owners and staff members."

"They will," Cal agrees. "Let's see if we can find anyone in the other businesses."

Mike is already turning to check out the business situated next to Vision bar, which appears to be another, smaller bar. Cal doesn't follow him; he instead carries on to the next establishment, which he is sure is a restaurant, before he looks through the window.

Inside the building, the ground floor is in darkness. That doesn't mean there isn't anyone there. The owner or manager could easily be in the kitchens or on the upper floor. Cal peers through the window, his hand above his eyes to try and block out the light from outside. He sees no movement inside the restaurant, it looks deserted, so he moves right to the main entrance, which is shut up tight.

"No one home in there either?" Mike asks, as he passes Cal, who is knocking fruitlessly on the restaurant's door, and makes his way to the next business.

"Nope, it's dead," Cal replies, instantly regretting his choice of words.

Mike has his notebook out, scribbling in it as he walks. Cal knows he's taking down the name of the restaurant for future reference, which saves him the job. Mike has taken down the names of several more businesses by the time they near the end of the block. Both men look at each other in disappointment as they draw a blank. *Nobody wants to be in this area today who doesn't have to be*, Cal thinks. Hence only the emergency services are present. They have no choice.

"What time you got?" Mike asks Cal.

"Ten fifty-four," Cal states.

"Get the news channel on your phone. Let's see what the bigwigs have to say in their statement," Mike insists.

Cal does as he's told, opening his preferred news app on his phone. The feed buffers for a couple of seconds before the live stream begins. The presenter is debating last night's events with unknown 'experts' in Trinity Square when the feed begins. Cal zones out of the feed for a moment to look over the square, where work seems to have halted. He and Mike aren't the only ones interested in what the city's mayor and police commissioner have to say. Every officer in the square is peering down at a phone, on the off-chance that either of the two officials may have some insight into what transpired in their immediate vicinity.

Unsurprisingly, they don't talk about anything that Cal and Mike don't already know. Their statement is vague and topped off with some heartfelt platitudes of concern for the victims and their families. Cal is just about to exit the new app when Police Commissioner Jackson surprisingly hands over to Chief Arnold, who appears from camera right. As she peers into the camera, her determination is apparent for anyone to see. Her scraped-back black hair, gripped into a ponytail, adds to her appearance of dedication and her conviction of the seriousness of the situation.

After also offering her condolences and ensuring the public that everything possible is being done to explain the terrible events of last night, Arnold changes tack. She begins to appeal for the public's help. She asks any members of the public who were in the Chinatown area last night to come forward, whether they believe they witnessed events or not. She tells them that they may have witnessed vital information that they are unaware of. She then asks anyone who did witness the incident to contact the police immediately to provide a statement. Finally, she implores people to search their memories to see if they may have any information that could shed light on what happened in Trinity Square. To search their souls and to bring any information they have to the police, even if it might incriminate close friends or family.

Arnold's appeal is sincere and heartfelt. Cal and Mike glance at each other as they watch with impressed expressions. They are both surprised when Arnold asks the public to study a picture that instantly pops up on the screen. Neither of them was expecting to be faced with a picture of their prime suspect at this stage. Especially the same poor one they hold in their hands as they watch.

"It could be almost anyone," Mike states. "It looks even worse on TV."

"Yes, it could," Cal agrees. "But it might jog someone's memory, or someone might even recognise him. She must have decided that we won't get a bigger audience than this and we can always update the picture if we discover a better one later."

"Let's hope it does the trick," Mike replies.

"We need some sort of break in the investigation, and quickly," Cal says, looking over the remnants of the square's carnage.

The forensics teams in the square are getting back to work as the news statement finishes. Cal idly wonders when the square will reopen and get back to normal. If it ever can after such horrific events.

Matt and Jay are making their way back around the square toward the entrance where they all arrived. Cal can see by the two officers' demeanours that they have had the same result as he and Mike.

"Let's find a coffee," Mike suggests, as they head to meet up with the two disappointed police officers.

Chapter 9

"We haven't got much to report back to Chief Arnold, have we?" Cal says, as they drive back to headquarters.

"The rest of the team could still have some luck," Mike replies, referring to the team they have left behind to continue their enquiries in Chinatown and beyond.

"You hold out more hope than me," Cal says. "This asshole is either very good or very lucky."

"He obviously took precautions. The raincoat and hood tell us that much. He will have made a mistake though, you can be sure of that. They always do," Mike states.

"Not always, partner. There are plenty of unsolved cases back at base if you don't believe me," Cal retorts.

"Not like this case," Mike replies. "This isn't a random act of violence. There is planning involved and nobody can plan for every eventuality. People invariably make mistakes, it's in our nature. We get overconfident, cut corners or simply fuck the plan up. Take my word for it, the evidence is somewhere, we just need to find it."

"Good pep talk, old-timer," Cal teases Mike, knowing that his partner is right.

"Call it what you will but it's true. As you say, I'm old enough to know," Mike responds, vehemently.

"I know you are and I do take these things on-board, my friend," Cal concedes.

"You'd better, because I'm not going to be around much longer to look after you, my young apprentice," Mike laughs.

Cal laughs along with Mike, who nearly misses his phone ringing amidst the laughter.

"It's Arnold," Mike states seriously, looking at his phone.

Cal's amusement is immediately curtailed and silence breaks out as Mike answers the chief's call.

"Ma'am," Mike says into his phone, as Cal listens in intently. "Is she sure?" Mike asks, Cal's frustration increasing at only hearing half of the conversation. "How long until she arrives?" Mike asks eagerly, before ending the call.

"Step on it. We need to get back to HQ," Mike barks at Cal.

"What is it?" Cal snaps, as he accelerates.

"A witness has called in. She says she saw the image of our man on the press briefing and has information," Mike answers, grasping the handgrip above his head as Cal's driving becomes more forceful.

"Does she know him? Has she got a name?" Cal questions, as he saws at the steering wheel.

"I don't know. The chief just said a car's been sent to bring her in," Mike answers.

"How long until she arrives?" Cal pushes.

"I don't know that either. Not long. Arnold wants us there when she arrives," Mike replies.

"But..." Cal's question is cut off.

"Concentrate on driving," Mike orders. "That's all I know."

Cal shuts up and does just that. Luckily, the morning traffic has thinned out and things improve the further they get from Chinatown and its newly enforced road restrictions.

In good time, Cal swings the car into police headquarters, braking hard at the barrier blocking the entrance into the parking lot. Thankfully, the attendant manning the barrier recognises Mike in the passenger seat and presses the button to lift the barrier without asking Mike for his identification. As soon as he can squeeze under the barrier, which is still rising, Cal depresses the accelerator. Gravity seems to vanish momentarily as the car speeds forward down the slope into the underground car lot. Tyres screech several times against concrete as the car turns sharply until Cal brakes hard as close to the building entrance as possible. The sound of slamming doors reverberates around the enclosed space as Cal and Mike rush toward the entry door, where Cal swipes his security card.

"I wonder what she knows?" Cal questions on the way up to level six.

"Who knows. She could be completely mistaken for all we know right now," Mike answers.

"Or this woman could be a crackpot," Cal observes.

"Arnold must be optimistic to call us back to base urgently," Mike points out.

"Let's hope she's right," Cal replies.

"She's not usually wrong," Mike points out.

"No, she's not," Cal agrees, his anticipation increasing.

Mike leads them straight back to their desks when they reach the seventh level of the building. The general office is a hive of activity. Their colleagues are hard at work trawling through the available evidence, with some of them on the phone trying to gather more information and identify possible suspects. Each suspect will have their criminal records analysed before a decision is made on whether to bring them in for questioning or not. The office is like the tip of the iceberg in regard to the investigation, however. Throughout the headquarters building, multiple other departments and officers are working to sift through the evidence.

On floor four, dozens of TV monitors will be alive with CCTV footage from last night. Captured throughout the city, the hours of footage might show vital evidence that requires further investigation. On other floors, physical evidence rescued from the scene and surrounding areas will be being picked through, including waste collected from public bins. That's not a task that officers volunteer for. It is a given that most of the officers assigned to that revolting task will be young and new to the force.

More diligent work will be underway in other buildings across the city, from the city mortuary to specialist forensics laboratories. The investigation will go house to house if that is where it leads.

"Ah, gentlemen. Good. You're back," Arnold's voice sounds from behind Cal, as he leans over his desk to check his computer's inbox for messages.

"Yes, Ma'am," Mike answers. "I'm afraid we came up empty-handed at the crime scene. We did compile a list of businesses in the square for reference and the team is still in the area continuing the investigation."

"Thank you for the update, Detective," Arnold replies.

"Tell us about the possible witness, Ma'am," Cal asks, impatiently.

"She is a young woman named Suzie Mercer. She claims to have had a disturbing encounter with a man matching the appearance of the man in the picture that is being circulated. The encounter took place on a bus yesterday at approximately five forty-five in the evening," Arnold replies.

"It fits our time frame," Mike says, hopefully.

"Indeed, Detective. But let's not get ahead of ourselves. Let's wait to see what she has to say," Arnold responds.

"Of course, Ma'am," Mike replies. "Did she phone in after seeing the picture on the television?"

"Yes, and apparently she was quite upset on the phone," Arnold tells them.

"When is she due to arrive?" Cal asks.

"Imminently. We need to tread carefully when she arrives. I will conduct the interview with you, Cal. Mike, I want you to oversee the interview from the observation room. Okay?"

"Yes, Ma'am," both men reply.

Tilly suddenly appears at Arnold's side to inform her that the witness has arrived in the building and is on her way up. Arnold tells Tilly to put the witness into the waiting room and offer her a drink.

"Ready, gentlemen?" Arnold asks, without expecting an answer as she turns.

Following their preparations, Mike heads into the observation room, which is adjacent to the interview room where the witness is now waiting. Cal follows Arnold through the door and into the interview room.

Already sitting behind the table is a very nervous-looking young woman. Suzie Mercer looks at Cal and Arnold anxiously as they move to take their seats on the other side of the table. Cal gives a reassuring smile to the young woman as he takes his seat, in an attempt to try to help settle her nerves.

"Thank you for coming in, Miss Mercer," Arnold begins, soothingly. "I am Chief Arnold and my colleague here is Detective Chambers. Is it alright if I call you Suzie?"

Suzie nods her agreement and Arnold then takes her through the procedure for the interview. Cal studies Suzie as Arnold talks. It is obvious how nervous Suzie is having found herself at police headquarters, being interviewed as a witness to such horrific events. She doesn't look down into her lap, instead she looks straight at Arnold as the procedure is explained. Cal estimates that Suzie is about 21 years old. She has attended the interview wearing no make-up, but she is a very pretty young woman, which in this case may have worked against her. As Arnold ends her explanation, Cal's interest in hearing her story increases.

"In your own words, Suzie, please tell us what happened," Arnold finally says.

"After college," Suzie starts after a short pause, her voice wavering, "I caught the bus to meet friends in the city for a drink. The bus was busy, but I had a seat to myself and I was just looking out of the window watching the world go by.

"Two stops after I'd got on, the bus stopped to pick up another passenger, a man. I glanced at him but didn't give him much thought. The next thing I knew, he was standing over me, next to the empty seat. I looked at him again and he was just standing there, staring at me. He wasn't even looking at my face, he was staring down at my legs. I was wearing a skirt. It wasn't that short a skirt, but the bottoms of my legs were showing. He stood there staring, even as the bus pulled off. He gave me the creeps and made me feel uncomfortable.

"I remember he was wearing an oversized raincoat," Suzie continues, her voice under control as she gains confidence. "The coat was just like in the picture on TV. The material was old and very worn, it was quite ragged. I could tell even though he was wearing a big coat that the man was overweight. His face was chubby and wet, probably from the rain mostly, but I'd bet he was sweating too. He looked like one of those men who sweat constantly."

"I know the type of man you mean," Arnold says, encouragingly. "What happened then?"

"Eventually, after having a good look at me, he sat down, right next to me. He sat extremely close, deliberately too close, so that his thigh was touching mine. It made me cringe. I tried to move away but I was stuck between him and the side of the bus. I was trapped." Suzie's voice cracks again, and now she does look down at her lap.

"How awful," Arnold consoles. "I should think you felt extremely threatened and uncomfortable."

"It was horrible. He smelled of BO. I admit I was frightened. I didn't know what to do. I couldn't move." Suzie sniffles slightly.

"How did you escape?" Arnold asks, as Suzie goes quiet.

"I knew the bus was approaching another stop and, without thinking, I barged my way out. He had a bag on his lap, and that didn't help, but I said, 'Excuse me', and just pushed myself out," Suzie says, looking back up at Arnold.

"You were very brave," Cal says, full of admiration for the young woman. "Did you get off the bus there?"

"Yes, I rang the bell and went straight to the front, next to the driver. I didn't know the area where the bus stopped. It was raining heavily but anything was better than being on that bus with him.

"For a minute, I was afraid that he would follow me off the bus. I forced myself to look back as I got off and, luckily, he was still sitting down," Suzie says with relief.

"What did you do then?" Arnold asks.

"I waited for the next bus and took that to meet my friends. I was late, but they waited for me," Suzie answers.

"I bet they were concerned when you told them about your ordeal," Cal says.

"I didn't tell them. By the time I got there I felt silly and ashamed," Suzie confesses.

"You have nothing to be ashamed about," Arnold says, vigorously. "You showed courage in the face of danger. You should be proud of yourself."

"Maybe," Suzie mumbles.

"Chief Arnold is right, Suzie," Cal confirms. "You have also come forward to tell us what you know, which shows have brave you really are."

"Do you think it's the same man?" Suzie asks.

"We can't know for sure until we find him, but I think it's a strong possibility," Arnold answers.

"Oh my God! I wish I had reported him at the time. Someone might have stopped him before he did those horrible things. All those poor people," Suzie says, becoming upset.

"Don't think like that," Arnold soothes. "It wouldn't have stopped him. You're doing all you can to bring him to justice now. There isn't anything else you could have done."

"Chief Arnold is right, Suzie. You should be proud of what you're doing," Cal adds.

"If you say so," Suzie responds, her sniffles subsiding.

"It's true," Arnold confirms. "Now would you mind if we go over a few things to get some more detail? It could be very important."

"I don't mind. I want to help you as much as I can. Anything to try and catch him," Suzie volunteers.

It is over an hour until Arnold and Cal finish questioning Suzie. They extract every detail they can from her. To her credit, Suzie remains calm and is more than willing to answer all the questions she is asked, as well as she can.

"Do you think I'm in danger?" Suzie asks, as Arnold brings the interview to an end.

"I don't believe so," Arnold replies. "From what you have told us, your encounter with the suspect was coincidental. He doesn't know your name, your home address or any other details apart from the bus you caught. He doesn't even know which stop you used to catch the bus.

"That said, Suzie, I think it would be prudent for you to refrain from using that bus route until we have identified the suspect and questioned him. Even if he isn't connected to the events in Trinity Square, he could be a threat to you, judging by his actions. We need to find him and question him."

"Don't worry. I have no plans to use that route any time soon," Suzie tells Arnold.

"Good. We will keep an eye on you as well as we can and keep you informed of any developments. Hopefully, we can bring this to a swift conclusion," Arnold says.

"Thank you," Suzie replies.

"No, thank you, Suzie. You have been most helpful to this investigation," Arnold tells her. "Now, if it's okay with you, I will get one of my colleagues to take you to get the facial reconstruction image done."

"Okay," Suzie agrees.

"And I will see you again after. How does that sound?" Arnold asks.

"I hope I do well with the reconstruction," Suzie worries.

"Don't worry, Suzie. Just tell the officers what you remember and they will do the rest for you. They are very good at it. You'll be amazed by the results," Cal offers.

"Or creeped out." Suzie smiles nervously. She is not looking forward to the idea of coming face to face with her assailant again, even if it is just in the form of a reconstruction.

A female officer arrives in the interview room to take Suzie off. Arnold and Cal thank her again for her help as she is led out and both of them then follow her. Arnold pauses outside in silence as Cal closes the door.

"I definitely think it's our man," Arnold says, once Suzie has disappeared.

"I agree," Cal confirms, as Mike appears from the observation room.

"It's him," Mike announces as he joins them, having not heard Arnold's assessment.

"We agree," Cal tells him, with Arnold already walking off to act as the brake in the case.

"So, we're not only looking for a deranged psychopath but also a pervert," Mike says, as they chase Arnold down the corridor.

"It would seem so. There's a good chance he's already in the system," Cal replies.

"A very good chance. The net is closing in," Mike agrees.

Arnold bursts into the main office with Cal and Mike hot on her heels. Neither man heads for his desk, they remain with Arnold in support as she takes up a position in front of a large map of the city stuck to the wall. Everyone in the office looks around at them before Arnold says a word. All of them see her urgency. Calls are cut short and conversations cut dead.

"Can I have everyone's attention?" Arnold bellows, despite her whole team already being on tenterhooks to hear what she has to say.

"We have just completed interviewing a vital witness to the case. She has identified a man who accosted her last evening on a bus travelling into the city. I am confident that the man who accosted her and the man who carried out the attack last night are one and the same."

A shallow buzz of surprise and excitement briefly travels through the entire office to accompany Arnold's revelation.

"The witness is currently carrying out facial reconstruction," Arnold continues, bringing silence back to her officers. "Unfortunately for her, she got an extremely good look at the perpetrator, but that is of course lucky for this investigation. We will have a reconstructed image of the man we are looking for in short order. We need to be ready to act as soon as it is in hand.

"Cal," Arnold finishes, giving him the floor for him to continue.

"The perpetrator is described as a white male with dark hair of average height and overweight, bordering on obese. He sexually accosted the witness, not seriously but disturbingly. He is a sexual deviant, a predator and my bet is that he is already in our system.

"He boarded the bus at the Watling Street stop in Billingham, east of the city," Cal announces, turning to the map behind him. He picks up a red magnetised round marker, quickly finds Watling Street and sticks the marker to the map to pinpoint the bus stop. "Does the perpetrator live nearby, or does he work there? What businesses are in the area where he could be employed? What community focal points are located in the area that he may visit? Shops, bars, takeaway food outlets, religious centres even. I want a list of the most prominent.

"Gill," Cal says, looking at one of his colleagues who is sitting close by. "I want you to oversee the cross-referencing of registered sex offenders who match the description. Give priority to the ones with registered addresses in the Billingham area.

"Have we received communications from any other witnesses who mention a man of the same or similar description? Let's double-check. Start with the statements provided by the public in the east of the city. Is the perpetrator known to any of us? There is a good chance one of us has dealt with him in the past. As soon as the reconstruction image is available, I want it communicated to every station and precinct in the city. Every serving officer needs eyes on that image as quickly as possible.

"Has anyone anything to add, or any questions?" Cal demands. The room remains hushed and Arnold steps forward again.

"There will be no announcement to the press at this time, and there will be no leaks. Is that understood?" Arnold orders forcefully. "I don't want the perpetrator getting wind that we're onto him and going to ground, not yet!

"We are going to descend on Billingham in force. Every available unit and officer from across the city will arrive in unison and lock that part of the city down. Officers will be swarming across Billingham. Nobody will leave the area until they have been cleared and questioned or until such time that the perpetrator is taken into custody. Surprise is of the essence. We cannot afford to give the game away before we are in place and let him escape the area. If indeed he is there. When we are in position then, and only then, do we release the image to the press.

"The operation will begin at 1500 hours. The timing is tight but that will give us enough time to get units prepared and into the area.

"I need not remind you of Billingham's reputation. Criminality is significant in that neighbourhood, so expect severe pushback from that section of the community. We will stand firm against that section, using as much force as required. But please remember, criminals are a minority in that community. I expect that, following the horrific events of last night, the general public, and perhaps even the criminals, will want to help us catch this man. So please, keep an open mind, whilst also keeping your guard up," Arnold orders.

Arnold ends her participation in the meeting there. She has other work to do. For an operation of this magnitude, Arnold doesn't carry the authority to set the wheels in motion. Cal knows as he watches her leave that her first port of call will be Commissioner Jackson. She will update the commissioner on the breakthrough in the case and then brief him on her plan to trap her quarry. Finally, Arnold will request that the commissioner signs off on her plan and furnishes her with the manpower and tools she requires.

Cal does not doubt that the commissioner will give her the green light to proceed. But perhaps Arnold has doubts, because she suddenly stops at the exit from the office.

"Mike," Arnold says, turning.

"Yes, Ma'am," he replies.

"Can you hold the fort here for a while, if Cal comes with me?" she asks.

"Of course, Ma'am," he tells her.

"Thank you, he won't be long. Detective Chambers, you're with me," Arnold orders.

Cal is surprised by this turn of events. Then, on reflection, he can't blame the chief for deciding that some backup in tackling the commissioner might be prudent.

"See you shortly, and good luck," Mike says, as Cal moves to follow Arnold.

Cal is lucky to have Mike as his partner. He shares his wealth of experience with Cal and has no ill feelings when Cal is given tasks that, as the senior officer, he might be expected to be given, for example, assisting with interviewing a vital witness or accompanying Chief Arnold now. Mike knows he is in the twilight of his career and that Cal is the next generation.

Mike has high hopes for Cal. That's if he can reconcile his career with his marriage, which at present is far from certain.

Chapter 10

A loud knock at the door wakes Merle from his sleep, sleep he must admit to himself was disturbed by last night's events. He brushes off the terrors that sleep has brought him and throws the covers back to answer the door. *Wait*, Merle shouts in his head as he puts on his slippers, realising that he has slept in after last night's hysteria. He must be cautious answering his door as there is no telling who could be knocking.

Outside the apartment door, a delivery man stands holding a rather large box. Merle is excited to see that the outer packaging on the box is familiar, even though the box is bigger than those Janus18 usually sends. *It looks like I'm in for a busy day again*, he thinks, as he signs for the delivery.

Janus had kept him in the chatroom until late last night. Merle had to convey every tiny detail of last night's events to his friend. They must have used some bandwidth talking over the internet for so long. Janus was ravenous for information. Merle had been happy to go over sections of his story multiple times for Janus, who constantly interrupted to garner extra detail. He would ask Merle questions or explain aspects of the events that seemed of little or no consequence. Merle did so without question and Janus deserved all the knowledge he wanted.

Janus wouldn't allow Merle to upload one second of the video footage he had taken until he was satisfied with Merle's eyewitness account. When Merle was given permission to begin uploading the video footage, a specialist computer program had to be used to enable the videos to be uploaded without having to cut them down into smaller-sized files.

Needless to say, once Janus had viewed the videos, it was like opening a Pandora's box of new questions. The questions kept coming and Merle answered them to the best of his ability. Janus is a stickler for detail and he wouldn't relent until he had extracted every possible piece of information from Merle.

When the interrogation finally came to an end, Merle was worn out and left with an aching head. Janus couldn't have been more impressed with Merle, however, which made all the hard work worthwhile. A short pause in their chat was called by Janus, who told Merle to take a breather and get some refreshments.

When they resumed, Janus thanked Merle profusely for his efforts and asked him if he wanted to continue helping with the project. Merle vehemently insisted he did. Janus was pleased with Merle's response. He told Merle to expect another package to be delivered in the morning and, when it arrived, they would speak again. When Merle tried to ask questions about his next task, Janus had insisted that he get some rest after such a busy day and that they would speak tomorrow.

Tomorrow has turned into today, Merle realises, as he puts the package down on the desk next to his computer's keyboard. He switches on the monitor with a sudden pang of panic when he sees that Janus18 is already in the chatroom's waiting room. In a fluster for keeping Janus waiting, Merle races to his bedroom to quickly pull some clothes on. He can't talk to Janus in just his underpants and a T-shirt.

"Hello, Janus, are you there?" Merle says into the microphone standing on his desk.

"Good morning, Merle," Janus's well-spoken voice sounds after a short pause. "I trust you slept well after yesterday's adventures."

"Yes, thank you. I slept very well. Too well in fact. I've only just woken up," Merle replies, slightly embarrassed by his tardiness.

"I should think you deserved a lie-in. You had a busy day yesterday, after all," Janus soothes.

"It was exhilarating and I'm looking forward to seeing what today brings," Merle replies.

"I'm pleased to hear it. Have you opened your package yet?" Janus asks.

"No, it's only this minute arrived."

"Very good. I was hoping we would be talking when you opened it. I'm excited for you to see what's inside. It's just like Christmas, wouldn't you say?" Janus gushes.

"Absolutely. Shall I open it now?" Merle asks.

"Of course. Let's get on with the excitement," Janus replies.

Very carefully, Merle picks the carpet knife off the desk, the same knife he's used opening each of Janus's packages, and begins to cut through the tape. Upon opening the box, he is greeted by bubble wrap as expected. His recycling bin is already overflowing with the stuff. Below, he is surprised to see clothing.

"There is a baseball cap, a high-vis tabard and a work bag," Merle says out loud for Janus to hear, as he takes the pieces of clothing out, his confusion mounting.

"It's a disguise," Janus answers, excitedly. "Keep going."

Below the clothing, Merle takes out the smaller box that is lying there and opens it.

"In the other box, I have a pair of glasses, what looks like a car's key fob, an envelope and another smaller box," Merle announces, as he places each item onto the desk beside him. The fourth item in the box with the strange appearance is now familiar to Merle. "And, of course, a bottle of antidote serum."

"Yes, yes. What fun. Isn't it, Merle? Don't open the envelope or small box. Not yet. I want the surprise to continue," Janus replies.

"I'm intrigued. I'll admit that," Merle says.

"All will be revealed, my friend. Not long now. Take out the last item," Janus instructs.

At the bottom of the box, Merle expects to find another gas canister like the others he has received. As he unwraps more bubble wrap, however, he is faced with a strange contraption that he is unfamiliar with. The contraption is approximately a foot long and appears to be made of black plastic.

"What is this last thing?" Merle asks.

"It is the pièce de résistance," Janus replies, his excitement obvious. "You are holding a remotely activated gas-release system, which has been specially designed for you, Merle."

"Wow. Really?" Merle replies. "I take it we are expanding the operation?"

"We are indeed, and you are going to be the catalyst, Merle," Janus tells him. "This is a very special day for both of us."

"I'm intrigued," Merle replies enthusiastically, despite his apprehension about what is in store. "Can you tell me more?"

"Certainly, Merle. We are a team and I will tell you everything I can," Janus assures. "Our operation thus far has, as expected, drawn the attention of the authorities. Attention that I can tell you has escalated vastly following the latest part of the operation in Trinity Square. I'm sure that this information doesn't come as a surprise to you, Merle, following your tremendous work yesterday."

"No, it doesn't," Merle confirms. "It's not a surprise."

"We have allies who work closely with the authorities, including with the police," Janus continues. "Our contacts have told us that the police are now focusing their entire resources on solving yesterday's events. They mean to stop our operation in its tracks. We cannot allow that to happen. Our work is too important. Wouldn't you agree, Merle?"

"Absolutely, Janus. What are we going to do about the police?" Merle asks.

"We are going to strike at the very heart of their operation!" Janus announces. "We cannot stop their investigation entirely, but we don't need to. The final solution is approaching. We just need to knock the investigation off track and buy a small amount of time."

"The next target is the police authorities. That is what the new release system is for," Merle surmises.

"You are as intelligent as you are diligent, Merle. We are so lucky to have found you to help us on this journey. Are you prepared to continue?" Janus asks.

"Until the end, Janus. Where is the target?" Merle replies eagerly.

"The target is police headquarters, Merle, and the day is today. You have everything you need to succeed right in front of you," Janus tells him. "The disguise is simple, but will be sufficient. Please open the small box now, Merle."

Merle picks up the slender box and flips open its top. He sees a flash of blue ribbon, which he takes hold of, freeing the contents from the box. In his hand is a lanyard and the blue ribbon has white words stitched into it. Those words read 'POLICE HEADQUARTERS'. Clipped to the end of the ribbon is a security pass with a picture of Merle mounted front and centre.

"I'm to take the release system right into police headquarters?" Merle asks, anxiously.

"You are, but it sounds worse than it is, I promise you," Janus replies. "You will be a software engineer. The security card will get you in and out without any questions. I guarantee it. You will have to take the bag through a metal detector with the release system inside, but the system is made almost entirely of plastic, so put some other items on top of it inside the bag. Like a pullover and some food items so that, even if anyone looks inside the bag, they will have no reason to be suspicious.

"All you have to do is take the release system up to level seven, enter the main investigations office and place it down in a quiet area. Once you have positioned the system, simply walk out, pressing the button on the fob as you leave.

"I suggest that you exit the building immediately before all hell breaks loose. You probably won't even need to take the antidote serum on this occasion, but I think it would be advisable as a precaution."

"How will I know where the main investigations office is?" Merle questions.

"As you exit the lift, turn right into the corridor and it's the second door along. The security card will gain you access. I expect the process to be quite straightforward," Janus encourages Merle.

"I am sure I will manage to succeed," Merle replies, confidently.

"I have full confidence in you, Merle. The envelope you received has money for you. I'm sure you've had expenses already and, for this operation, you will need to use a taxi service. Stay away from public transport going forward," Janus insists. "Okay?"

"That seems prudent from now on," Merle agrees, looking at the envelope, which appears to have a hefty wad of cash inside it.

"Are you prepared to do this, Merle? Have you any questions?"

"I will get myself ready immediately, Janus. I know what to do," Merle replies.

"Excellent. This will be your final task before the day we have all been waiting for, Foundation Day. We are close, my friend. All of this hard work will be blessed and will bring a new beginning for mankind and mother nature."

"Only the fittest will survive!" Merle bellows.

"Only the fittest will survive," Janus repeats. "Good luck. Contact me when it's done."

Merle logs out of the chatroom, his pulse racing, his palms sweating. He looks at the paraphernalia scattered around him, his tools for the day. He wonders if it really will be as easy as Janus had assured him. To walk into police headquarters unchallenged and plant what amounts to a weapon. His confidence grows as he reminds himself of Janus's power. Janus has provided everything he needs to succeed, right down to a security pass into headquarters. Janus obviously knows what he's doing, his plans are meticulous and he has powerful friends. He must have friends in high places to acquire a security pass for the heart of the city's law enforcement.

I must trust in Janus and his associates, Merle decides, as he rises from his chair to get something to eat before he prepares to go into action.

Unusually for Merle, he finds eating tough. His nerves have ruined his appetite, but at least he manages to get some food inside him. A bitter taste lingers in his mouth from the measure of antidote he swigged down before he ate. Even brushing his teeth has failed to extinguish the aftertaste entirely. Now he stands in front of the only decent mirror he possesses, the one fixed to the front of the bathroom cabinet. The orange high-vis tabard he is wearing glows as if he is radioactive and he doesn't think that the thick-rimmed glasses he has perched on his nose do him any justice. Pulling the baseball cap down over his eyes to finish off his disguise makes him smile. He barely recognises himself. He almost looks official. Janus has done it again. Perhaps it will be as easy as described.

Don't take anything for granted. Expect the unexpected, he tells himself, as he walks back through to pack the bag. He slides the release system into the bottom of the bag. The contraption fits into the bag like a glove, with enough space remaining at the top to cover it with other items. The black plastic makes the machine almost invisible in the darkness of the bag. *No detail has been overlooked, it would seem*, Merle thinks, his nerves easing slightly.

On top of the release system, Merle does as suggested and stuffs a pullover into the bag, spreading it out so that it entirely covers the black plastic. Then he adds a bottle of water and some food items, together with a few other smaller items for good measure. Finally, he takes off the high-vis tabard and puts it in the top of the bag before closing it. He doesn't put the high-vis in the bag to help hide the system. He does it so that he isn't wearing it when he leaves his building. He would be too conspicuous wearing the Day-Glo orange tabard. He has no desire to draw unwanted attention to himself before he has even begun.

On the desk next to the bag, his phone buzzes. A quick check shows him the message, which tells him that the taxi he has ordered has arrived. Merle peers down from his apartment window and, sure enough, there is a car idling next to the kerb by the building's main entrance.

This is it, Merle thinks, his hand visibly shaking as he reaches for his bag, his anxiety threatening to overwhelm him. His mouth becomes dry whilst his bladder loosens. *Pull yourself together*, he tells himself, as he rushes to the bathroom to relieve himself once more before he leaves.

Whilst the day may be overcast, Merle's eyes squint as he leaves the building, and he pulls the peak of the baseball cap lower to try and protect himself. Sometimes, he wonders if he has vampire blood running through his veins as it is not often he ventures out in broad daylight. Darkness is his friend, especially when he's on a mission. All the other operations he has carried out to progress the cause have been undertaken after the sun has disappeared. Shadows are usually his ally, the darker the better, but he will struggle to find shadows today to give him cover. He must rely on his disguise for this operation, such as it is.

"The museum, is it?" the taxi driver questions, even before Merle's backside has hit the back seat.

"Yes, please. The science museum," Merle replies.

Merle watches the main entrance to his building recede as the taxi pulls away. The science museum is one block away from his real destination, the police headquarters building. He decided that it was a reasonable precaution not to go directly to the target when he ordered the taxi. He has no intention of making it too easy for the police to find him.

"Should be about thirty minutes," the driver informs Merle. "The traffic is in chaos in the city today. Most of Chinatown's roads are still closed after yesterday's attack."

"Really?" Merle forces an answer.

"What the hell was all that about? Did you see it on the news?" the driver persists. "This city is fast going to the dogs. It's full of nutters. Believe me, I know in my line of work. I see the dross every day. Drug addicts and freaks are taking over."

"Really," Merle repeats, wishing the man would shut up so that he can concentrate on the task at hand.

"Only yesterday I had a fare spew up all over the floor back there. It took me over an hour to clean it up. I charged him though. Believe you me, I charged him good. I can't afford to lose an hour's work because he couldn't handle drinking during the day. Why should it cost me?" the driver questions.

"You're right. It shouldn't," Merle mutters, hoping the driver will lose interest.

"I lost plenty because of that attack. I was supposed to be on until 6 am but the city emptied. I knocked off at 1 am. I was wasting my time. I'd like to get my hands on whoever was responsible. I'd make them pay!" the driver insists.

"Oh, yes," Merle replies, his interest finally piqued by the annoying driver. "And what would you do to them?"

"Erm, well, you know, I'd show 'em," the driver replies, vaguely.

"Show them what, exactly?" Merle presses.

"I dunno, but they owe me for lost business!" the driver insists.

"What about the victims: have you thought of them?" Merle asks.

"Erm, yes, of course. A real shame," the driver replies, unconvincingly.

Merle ends the conversation there, and thankfully so does the driver. Merle looks at the back of the man's head for a moment, wishing he had been one of the victims in Trinity Square last night. The driver is a leech on the body of humanity, only ever considering himself. He is just the type of person who deserves to perish when Janus's plan comes to fruition. *If only I could see to him now*, Merle thinks, his disdain for the driver growing.

Drawing his eyes away from the back of the driver's head, Merle peers out of the window. He cannot afford to be distracted. He must concentrate and prepare himself for his approaching work. In the distance, he sees clusters of tall buildings of the city, one of which will be his target building, the police headquarters. The vista vaporises his thoughts of the taxi driver and Merle doesn't think of him again, not until he pulls the taxi up outside the science museum.

"Cash or card?" the driver asks at the journey's end.

Merle, not wanting to talk to the man, silently hands him cash. He doesn't wait for his change. Instead, he gets straight out of the taxi. It pains him to give the driver extra money, but he might lose his temper if he has to talk to him again. Besides, Merle finds himself cash-rich for once after Janus's generous gift, so at least he can afford it.

Slinging his bag over his shoulder, Merle waits until the taxi pulls off and disappears into the traffic before he moves. It's best if the driver believes that Merle went into the museum if by chance he is questioned by the authorities.

Chapter 11

The city streets are bustling with traffic and pedestrians. Commuters and residents alike don't appear to have been put off visiting the centre following last night's horrors. Perhaps they think that daylight will protect them from the undead monsters. Daylight will offer no protection when the time comes. *All will understand that by the day's end*, Merle thinks, as he turns in the direction of police headquarters.

After a short walk, Merle reaches the vicinity of his target, but he doesn't approach the building immediately. He pauses to scope it out on the opposite side of the street. Police officers in uniform come and go through the main entrance of the tall building, together with people dressed in civilian clothes. Merle imagines that many of those in civilian clothes are also police officers. The entrance is daunting. It is busy with so many police, all of whom Merle assumes are searching for him in one way or another. Janus has asked him to walk straight into the lion's den, and carrying damning evidence on his person to boot.

Fear begins to paralyse Merle and he begins to doubt if he can go through with his mission. *Surely Janus can find someone else to carry out this task*, Merle debates. *Someone who isn't already sitting atop the city's most-wanted list. Surely they would stand more chance of slipping through security to do Janus's bidding.*

Merle curses himself for his fear. Nobody said it would be easy, certainly not Janus. Hard choices need to be made and hard jobs need to be carried out if change is going to come. If everyone involved in Janus's vision passes the buck or fails in their task nothing will change. The world will keep being ravaged by overpopulation and overconsumption and there will never be an awe-inspiring paradise here on earth.

Putting his bag down in front of him, Merle pushes out of his mind any thoughts of backing out of his mission. He opens the bag and pulls out his bright-orange high-vis vest, determined to proceed.

With his disguise fully in place, Merle doesn't delay from fear that his courage may desert him completely. He steps out to cross the road the moment a break in the traffic presents itself. As soon as he reaches the other side of the road, he strides determinedly toward the main entrance, not pausing for anything.

At the entrance door, Merle follows another man straight inside and the man is polite enough to hold the door open for him. The main foyer is blocked off by a tall glass wall, the only way through it being via a walk-through metal detector. Two burly security guards man the detector, casing everyone who enters the building, including Merle. He tries to act casual, but what he sees positioned next to the metal detector causes his stomach to drop in terror. An airport-style scanning machine is positioned next to the detector and everyone in the entry queue is required to present their bags for scanning. Some arrivals in front of Merle flash their credentials and are waved straight through, not even pausing if the metal detector bleeps and flashes. Merle realises that they are police officers and that he will have to join the short queue of people waiting to have their bags scanned.

In a panic, Merle nearly turns to leave there and then. Janus didn't mention that the bag would be scanned on entry.

The queue moves quickly and, with each shuffle forward that Merle makes toward the scanning machine, the more the butterflies fluttering in his stomach swarm. The butterflies have risen to his throat, clogging it, by the time it is his turn to place his bag on the conveyor belt for inspection. The sinking feeling deep within his stomach forces bile up through his clogged throat which then seeps in a bitter stream to the sides of his mouth as Merle watches his bag being swallowed by the mouth of the scanner.

Behind the glass wall, sitting beside the scanner, a woman dressed in a security uniform concentrates. She peers directly at a screen, which must now be filled with an image of his bag. The bag is bombarded with X-rays, which penetrate its wafer-thin material to reveal its sinister hidden contents.

With fear getting the better of him, Merle takes a step backwards. There can be only one outcome of the bag being examined so closely. At any moment now the security guard will register Janus's release system nestling at the bottom of the bag and instantly raise the alarm. Whether she will fix Merle in her gaze and point to alert her two colleagues to grab him or whether she will press an alarm button, Merle doesn't know. All he knows is that, if he doesn't make a run for it and escape now, it will be the end for him, along with any notions he had for a meaningful future.

"Careful," a voice sounds from behind Merle, as he steps back.

In a daze, Merle turns to see that he has bumped into the man behind him in the queue for the scanner. The room closes in on him, as panic rises. Across from him, the woman at the scanner turns to look at the commotion, saying something to Merle. *This is it*, Merle thinks, *she is raising the alarm.* He forces himself to concentrate on what she is saying, fearing the worst.

"Proceed, Sir. You're holding up the queue," Merle hears miraculously, taking a second to register the words.

With a small shove from behind, the man he has barged into sets Merle on his way toward the metal detector. Behind the detector, the two burly security guards peer at Merle, wondering what he is doing. *Play it cool*, Merle hears his inner voice demand, as he stumbles forward, regathering himself.

Neither guard manning the detector utters a word as Merle walks through the arch. He waits for the detector to buzz and flash, but it doesn't. It remains inactive and, all at once, Merle is through security.

"Don't forget your bag, Sir," the woman at the scanner announces to a bewildered Merle.

With his head clearing, Merle even manages to thank the woman as he retrieves his bag from the conveyor and moves away from security. Ahead of him is a reception area and another security checkpoint. Merle is more confident as he approaches the second security check and he sees that only the credentials of people entering are being checked. Merle shouldn't have doubted Janus's preparations at the scanner. He should have trusted him.

Raising his lanyard to the security guard at the checkpoint, Merle is waved through with barely a second look. Finally through security, and not delaying, he strides over to the bank of lifts before anyone can change their mind and decide to challenge him again. Just as Merle reaches the first of the stainless-steel doors it slides open to receive him without him having to press a button. Stepping straight inside without breaking his stride, he has the feeling that someone is watching over him. *Perhaps the gods are with him*, he thinks, as he presses the button for level seven.

Thankfully the doors close before anyone else can join him for his trip up the building. This allows Merle to clear out the surplus items from his bag that he put in to cover the release system. He stuffs the bits and pieces into his pockets, intending to take them out of the building with him so as not to leave evidence behind. He ensures he puts the remote fob in the right pocket of his jeans, with his phone, for ease of access. The only thing he leaves inside the bag with the release system is his pullover, just in case anyone demands to look inside, even though that is now doubtful.

Merle's nerves return as moments later the lift glides to a stop and the doors open. He moves to get off but is forced to check his progress due to two people rushing to board the lift and not immediately seeing him. Merle guesses that the stern-looking woman and the younger man with her are police officers as they finally realise he is exiting.

"Sorry," the man says, looking directly at Merle as he moves aside to let him past.

"Thank you," Merle replies, as he steps past, still caught in the officer's gaze.

Dread fills Merle's stomach for a moment, as the officer watches him intently. Has the officer somehow realised who Merle is? Is his identity already known to the police and has he just walked into their clutches? *Act casual, keep moving*, Merle tells himself again, as he passes the officer, half expecting a hand to grab his shoulder.

No hand arrives to stop his progress. In fact, as soon as he passes the two officers, they turn from Merle to board the lift. Within a couple of seconds, they disappear inside the lift and the door slides closed.

Merle finds himself alone in a corridor and it takes a moment for him to get his bearings before he turns to the right to follow the directions given to him by Janus. Stopping at the second door along, Merle peers through a slim glass panel in the door. Beyond the panel, Merle sees a section of a busy office. Almost reluctantly, he raises his security lanyard toward the panel mounted next to the door.

A magnetic lock clicks and Merle slowly opens the door, apprehensive about what will greet him. A buzz of chatter is the first thing to hit him as the door opens. He forces himself to keep going and, as the opening widens, a large bustling office is presented. Men and women in police uniforms are predominate inside but he knows instinctively that everyone inside the office is a police officer.

Merle timidly steps inside the office, hoping that nobody notices him. He hears the lock re-engage behind him as he realises that nobody is taking any notice of his presence whatsoever. All the officers are too deep in concentration or too busy with the task at hand to wonder who the newcomer is who has appeared in their midst.

In front of him are multiple islands of desks, covered in paperwork, with telephones and computer screens on them. Officers are beavering away at the majority of the desks. Many are hanging onto telephone receivers for dear life, tapping on keyboards or rummaging through mountains of files and paperwork. Occasionally, an important piece of information will be shouted across the office, with most of these outbursts aimed at the other side of the office.

Merle's focus travels across the office in the direction that the shouts are being directed and there, standing in front of a large whiteboard attached to the wall, is an older-looking officer in plain clothes who watches over proceedings. Occasionally he will jot a piece of information down and turn to attach it to the board. Merle quickly realises that the whiteboard overlooking the office is where important evidence and information that has been uncovered is correlated for ease of access.

A feeling of wonder, but not amazement, that his actions have caused such an outpouring of focused determination from the officers gathered in the office takes hold of Merle. He is not surprised that the events of last night have thrown the police force into an unfettered frenzy, but to see it in action is quite astounding to him. He quickly realises that it won't be long until the police are onto him, if they aren't already.

Blood rushes to Merle's head as the board's purpose and the investigative frenzy sink in. If he has already been identified then that information will be attached to the board and possibly even a picture of him may have been pinned to the board for everyone to see. His head ducks slightly in the hope that his cap will hide his face as his concentration fixes on the board. He is too far away to read the information the board holds but he will certainly be able to identify a picture of himself, even at the distance he is from the other side of the room.

The board has pictures attached to it, pictures of the crime scene at Trinity Square and pictures of Merle's other victims, like the man he met in the business district the previous night. Relief washes over Merle when he sees that there is no picture of him attached to the board. His head rises again, his confidence returning. There is nothing to stop him from continuing with his mission. Only now does Merle realise why Janus attributed so much importance to the task he gave him. Janus is trying to protect him from the police investigation.

Venturing another step into the office, Merle sees an empty desk on the other side of the room. The position will be an ideal site to place the release system. The desk is fairly central to the office but also toward the business end, where the senior police officer is gathering information. He is obviously in charge and Merle wants to ensure he is in the target area.

Despite the desk being in the centre, and in full view of the bustling office, Merle decides it is the best position to place the release system. He wanders forward unassumingly, expecting to be challenged at any moment by one of the packed room of police officers. No challenge comes as he keeps moving forward, past frantic telephone conversations and hammering keyboards. He quickly reaches the desk, with barely a second look from anyone around him.

At the desk, he turns his back on the board and the ranking officer standing in front of it, placing the bag on the desk's chair. With the bag concealed from everyone around him, Merle casually opens it. He removes his pullover before rapidly pulling the release system free. In one swift motion, Merle calmly lifts the release system over the arm of the chair and places it on the floor beside it and in front of the desk.

Merle's heart is performing somersaults as he stuffs the pullover back in the bag and takes hold of the bag's handle. The noise and chatter of the office close in on him as he lifts the bag back off the chair and moves to walk back to the office's exit.

"Excuse me," a voice sounds from behind Merle, as he rounds the desk. He ignores the mature male voice, pretending not to hear. He keeps moving toward the exit. "Hey, you. What is this?" the voice sounds again, this time louder and more assertively.

As his fingers pull the remote fob free from his pocket, Merle risks a look behind. Standing over the release system, looking straight at Merle, is the senior officer who has moved away from the whiteboard to challenge him and to see what he has left behind.

"Stop that ma…" The officer's words are cut off when Merle presses the button on the remote fob gripped in his right hand.

A split second after Merle presses the remote's button, the release system is activated and it is the loud popping sound the system makes that cuts off the officer's words so abruptly. But as Merle turns at the sound, he sees that it is the cloud of vapour rising from below the desk to engulf the officer that keeps him in stunned silence.

The entire office is also plunged into silence by the sudden noise of the attack. Officers stare in bewilderment at the senior officer, who is standing at the centre of a rising cloud of toxic mist. Merle forces himself to turn away from the spectacle. He cannot afford to delay his escape, to stand and watch the cloud of toxin rise. He knows it will rise to hit the office's ceiling, where it will spread out to fall back down across the office.

The release system has worked perfectly. The toxin will spread across the office in moments. Unsuspecting officers of the law, the exact same ones who are searching for the instigator of the horror that engulfed Trinity Square, will be consumed by the very same horror. Some officers may escape being infected, the office is large after all, but they won't be the lucky ones. Far from it. Those who aren't infected by the toxin will also inevitably succumb to its horror. Their colleagues, morphed into terrifying zombie-like creatures, will turn on them. Those who escape being infected will be attacked by their infected colleagues and hideously slain.

Knowing that he may be immune to the toxin, Merle knows that he isn't immune from being attacked. Even as the toxin spreads and inhuman noises begin to rise from the office behind him, he moves to make his escape from the danger area. With the security card already in his hand, Merle closes in on the exit door.

"Stop right there!" a uniformed woman demands, suddenly appearing between Merle and the exit door.

She holds her hand up, palm out in front of her, the gesture meant to reinforce her demand for Merle to stop. Her other hand is at her side, reaching for something. Merle is unsure whether the officer is reaching for a gun or some other piece of equipment she means to use to subdue him. A baton or a pepper spray perhaps.

The young officer is small and pretty. Merle is impressed by the courage she is displaying in trying to stop him. Her courage is misguided, however. She has no idea what is about to happen. At any moment, her workplace will turn into a horrific slaughterhouse. She should turn and escape while she can, before it is too late, and use the door behind her, the one Merle intends to use. He would let her use it too, let her join him in his escape. Surely the courage she is showing deserves mercy, a chance to live? The new world order will need women just like this young female officer. She is determined, brave and attractive. More importantly, she is young and fertile. Imagine the offspring she would provide for the new beginning.

There is no pleasure for Merle, only regret, as he swipes his hand through the air. He tells himself that his actions are forced on him by the young woman reaching for a weapon. The regret doesn't temper Merle's strike. The flat of his hand smashes into the side of the young woman's head in a slapping motion and he makes sure he follows through with the blow.

Pain shoots through Merle's hand, travelling up his arm as he makes contact. He keeps his eyes on the woman's face as he hits her, her expression turning from shock to terror and then oblivion as her brain blacks out from the force of his blow. Her head shoots to the side, taking the rest of her body with it. Like a boxer receiving a knockout blow in the ring, the woman's body goes limp as she falls to the side, her feet almost lifting off the ground. Her arms don't rise to protect her head from the fall, they stay by her side as she crashes into the ground, unconscious.

Telling himself that he has done the young woman a favour, Merle steps over her feet and reaches for the door.

At least she will be unaware of her impending doom and not have to face the beast that will slaughter her.

Urgently Merle yanks at the exit door, but it doesn't budge, staying locked tightly shut. He scrambles to retrieve the security card dangling near his waist, searching for the panel next to the door to slap it onto. There is no panel and it takes a moment for him to register the large green button mounted in its place. Merle hits the button and feels the door release under his grip. He pulls it open urgently and moves through into the corridor beyond.

An ear-splitting scream rings out from the office, just as the door begins to close behind Merle. *It has begun*, he thinks, turning to watch the door close and to see what is visible through the glass panel mounted in it.

What he sees comes as no surprise to Merle, although he is surprised by how quickly the toxin is taking effect. He peers straight through the glass panel, directly toward the desk where the release system was activated. There, in full view for him to see, stands the zombified beast of the former senior police officer. The man caught directly in the cloud of toxin has metamorphosed rapidly, quicker than Merle has witnessed before.

Around the creature, shock and panic are erupting in the officers who are still standing. Some of their colleagues are on the ground, undergoing their own conversion into their undead form. Merle knows he should make good his escape, but he is transfixed and cannot pull his eyes away. He simply must see how the slaughter begins to unfold.

The toxic mist appears to have dissipated. Merle looks down through the glass panel to see if the young officer he hit is still unconscious. Merle is surprised to see that she is beginning to move though. He felt sure that she was out for the count. That would have been a blessing for her because Merle isn't the only one who has noticed her movement.

Across the room, the senior officer has completed his metamorphosis. The creature stands fearsomely, its eyes searching menacingly. Merle knows only too well what the new creature is searching for. An unfamiliar craving is burning inside the newly born beast. A newfound and overwhelming primal instinct is rising, urging the beast to feed.

Without warning, the beast surges forward, its contorted face twisting, fixed upon its prey. Below Merle, on the floor, the young female officer is dazed, but she is managing to push her body up off the floor. Again, Merle is impressed by her determination but, horribly, in this instance, that same determination is only making her an obvious target. Just as she manages to push herself into a sitting position, the beast strikes.

Merle's heart drops in sympathy and loss as the young officer is knocked back onto the ground. *Such a waste*, he thinks, as the beast pins her to the floor, its evil eyes fixed upon her, teeth primed, ready to bite into the young flesh.

Suddenly, Merle's view of the woman's slaughter is cut off. The glass panel he is peering through becomes blocked. A man's panic-stricken face appears in front of Merle, on the other side of the glass. The magnetic lock disengages and the door swings violently outwards, almost smacking Merle in the head. Luckily, the door hits Merle's foot as his head juts backwards, away from the oncoming door.

Loud screams of terror burst through the gap in the door. Merle's foot slips backwards, the man on the other side pushing with all his might to get the door open so that he can escape the horror escalating inside the incident room. Merle applies his weight onto the foot that is holding the door back, stalling its progress, panic rising inside him. He knows instantly that he should have made his escape the moment he left the room. Delaying to watch the beginning of the carnage has put himself in imminent danger. He looks right, toward the lifts, wishing he had been sensible and gone straight to them.

The door moves again, the pressure on it increasing. Merle looks back through the glass panel, coming face to face with the desperate man on the other side. The man's eyes are filled with fear, and they plead with Merle to release him from the horror. Merle has no sympathy for the man, however, and applies more weight to his foot against the door, stopping its progress.

In unison, a blood-curdling scream pierces through the gap in the door and the pressure against Merle's foot ceases. The man's face fills with blood, his veins filling to bursting point, his eyes threatening to pop out of their sockets. A shadow moves behind the petrified man, arms curling around his chest, a head moving toward the back of his neck.

Merle bolts to the right, taking the only chance he will get to make his escape. The instant he removes his foot from the door it swings open. He is aware of bodies falling through the open door but he daren't look back as he rushes toward the call button that will open the door that will allow him to escape. Merle slams his hand onto the button, willing the stainless-steel door to open, but nothing happens.

Chilling, inhuman sounds reverberate down the corridor. Sounds of death and ripping flesh burrow their way into Merle's delicate ears. In desperation, he presses the button constantly, his panicked mind unable to focus on the number displayed above the closed door. A figure moves toward him—he sees that much out of the corner of his eye—but he is too afraid to turn his head to see it more clearly. He curses himself for delaying and putting himself in danger. What would Janus say about his mistake?

Light appears in front of Merle. The door is open, he realises, as the figure moves closer. Merle almost falls

144

forward into the space that has opened up for him, somehow pressing one of the bottom buttons on the panel as he steps inside. He isn't sure if it is the button for the lobby, but any button will do. Anything to get the door closed and to take him away from this floor.

Another bone-chilling screech cries out from close by as Merle swivels round, ready to try and defend himself. A shadow closes in, but Merle only sees it for an instant. The corridor and the danger it contains disappear as the stainless-steel door slides shut. Below his feet, the floor drops away as a loud crash sounds against the outer door, but that noise only lasts a second as Merle is whisked downwards.

Chapter 12

Cal stands at Arnold's side in front of Police Commissioner Jackson. Jackson eyes them both intently as Arnold begins to brief him on the latest developments in the case. Arnold is keen to tell Jackson about the eyewitness who has come forward and about her hopes of bringing the case to a swift conclusion with the witness's help.

Jackson is encouraged by Arnold's report. He asks several questions, which Arnold answers concisely and honestly. Cal watches on, not feeling he needs to add anything to the proceedings as Arnold has every detail covered.

Cal almost feels like a spare wheel in the briefing. When his phone vibrates in his hand, he has no qualms about checking what has come through. As expected, the message is official police business. It is from the facial reconstruction team and Cal clicks on it eagerly. With any luck, it is the image of the prime suspect that the witness Suzie Mercer has helped construct.

His phone takes a moment to load the image and Cal looks up at Jackson for a second. Hopefully, he might be able to add something to the briefing after all. In the second that Cal's eyes were away from his phone, the image has loaded. A face stares at him from his screen. Cal studies the face carefully, his heartbeat increasing, dread rising in his stomach.

"We have a problem. He's in the building!" Cal blurts out urgently, cutting across Chief Arnold and Commissioner Jackson's discussions.

"Detective?" Arnold questions Cal in confusion.

"The suspect, he's in this building. I saw him downstairs on level seven. He got off the lift when we came up here. Look!" Cal barks at Arnold, jabbing his phone at her so that she can see the picture.

"Are you saying you've seen the man responsible for last night's attack here, inside police headquarters?" Commissioner Jackson demands, rising out of his chair.

"I am, Sir," Cal confirms.

"Why would he possibly come here...?" Jackson's words trail off as he guesses why, the awful realisation sinking in.

"He's going for the incident room. It can't be a coincidence he went to level seven," Arnold insists.

"Get down there!" Jackson shouts the order while reaching for his phone.

Cal is already hastily turning for the door, his mind in a spin. Commissioner Jackson's receptionist gasps in fright as he bursts out of Jackson's office, with Arnold close behind. They race across the reception area, aiming for the door that will take them back out into the corridor and to the bank of lifts.

Cal reaches the call buttons moments before Arnold and presses them frantically. *How has this man managed to get through security?* Cal questions himself urgently, willing the doors in front of him to slide open. Visions of his partner, Mike, and his other colleagues who were in the incident room play on Cal's mind. There can be only one reason the man's destination was the incident room. He means to attack it, to derail the investigation in its tracks.

"Come on!" Cal shouts at the stainless-steel doors in front of him, which refuse to open. "Fuck this!"

Cal bolts to the left, toward the stairwell, not caring if Arnold follows or if the lift finally arrives. His partner is in danger, and the stairs will probably be quicker anyway. He scolds himself for not having used them immediately.

The door to the stairwell flies open under his frantic force, banging loudly into the wall behind it, the sound echoing around the enclosed space of the stairwell. Cal doesn't even notice if Arnold is behind him as he races down the first flight of steps. Halfway down them, he jumps, his feet catching him easily at the bottom, his shoes squeaking against the blue-plastic-covered ground. His hand grabs onto the handrail to pull himself around, ready to descend the next flight of stairs. Each flight of stairs is taken in the same manner. Cal has descended rapidly and he reaches for the door handle as he lands below the sign reading 'SEVEN'.

Pulling the door open, Cal whips out his sidearm as he exits the stairwell. He raises the firearm in front of him, steadying it in both hands. Now he slows his progress; nobody will gain anything by him rushing in the face of danger.

Immediately, Cal sees that the incident room's door is jammed open, his heart dropping as he takes in the fact that there is a body on the ground holding the door open. *Mike!* his mind screams, fearing he is too late to help his partner and friend.

Movement on his right causes Cal to swivel in fright, his gun aiming straight at the threat, his trigger finger poised. Arnold moves out of the lift, her gun pointing in the direction of the incident room. She sees Cal's gun pointing at her out of the corner of her eye, but she ignores it, focusing her concentration on the open door.

Both Cal and Arnold know they should wait for backup to arrive, but neither of them suggests it. Cal moves over to the lift to take up a position next to Arnold, his weapon in line with hers, and they look at each other nervously before stepping forward in unison.

Disturbing noises begin to reach them as they step closer to the body on the floor and the door that it is holding open. Low-pitched grunts, combined with snaffling sounds reminiscent of pigs feeding at a trough, become audible. The gruesome noises give rise to horrific thoughts of torn, bloody flesh. Both Cal and Arnold understand the carnage waiting for them after the horror of Trinity Square.

Cal widens the gap between himself and Arnold. He moves close to the left side of the corridor to approach the incident room from a wider angle. Arnold nods her approval, knowing it will increase their coverage as they close in.

As he changes direction, Cal glances down at the motionless body. He can tell it is male, but the uniformed officer is lying face down, meaning Cal is unable to identify which of his colleagues it is. *At least it isn't Mike*, he thinks selfishly, regretting the thought immediately. Mike would take a very dim view of such thoughts. Cal knows all too well how selfless his partner is. Mike would do just about anything for just about anybody.

As they near the opening, Cal signals for Arnold to hold her position and cover him as he makes his approach. He has a better angle to see inside the incident room before he gets right on top of it. Arnold stops moving, her gun out in front of her, ready to fire. Cal sees the fear burning inside her, the same fear that burns his belly.

Gradually, Cal begins to get a view inside the incident room. Tables and chairs have been turned over and paperwork litters the office floor. Cal barely registers that the office has been turned upside down, that vital evidence is scattered like confetti across the room. With growing horror, his concentration is taken by the chilling figures nestled on the floor, in amongst the office debris.

Just inside the doorway, a pair of frozen legs stick out across the floor in Cal's field of view. Further into the room, another body lies on the floor. It is one that Cal doesn't want to focus on because there is another figure moving beside it, leaning over its midriff. There is other movement beyond, but Cal blinks slowly, forcing himself to look at the hideous sight directly in his line of vision. Bile rises into the back of his throat at the sight of a creature leaning over one of his fellow officers, feeding on his colleague's guts.

"What is it?" Arnold asks from across the corridor, having seen Cal's horrified look and green complexion.

"We're much too late. It's a bloodbath in there," Cal splutters through his bile.

"Are there any survivors?" Arnold presses.

"I can't see from here," Cal replies, regaining some composure. "Possibly. They could be hiding."

"Then we go in," Arnold states, without any argument from Cal.

Arnold is the first to move toward the door, not expecting Cal to do anything she isn't prepared to do. He tells her to hold her position, though, as he has the better angle to approach from. A fire builds in Cal's stomach to accompany his next step forward, which this time is directly at the door. He steps around the corpse blocking the door, not allowing his concentration to be taken by it. There will be plenty of time to identify the poor victim once the danger has been dealt with.

Close by, inside the incident room, Cal cannot avoid his gaze falling on the owner of the frozen legs. He must look in their direction in case anything threatening is waiting out of sight in that area. Sadness takes hold of him as he recognises the young female officer motionless on the ground. Cal doesn't think that he had ever seen her before this morning's incident briefing. She may indeed be a new recruit to the police force, but he certainly remembers her once-pretty face from various times earlier in the day.

Splatters of blood pepper the young woman's deceased face, which has an expression of terror fixed on it. Her petrified eyes stare lifelessly at the ceiling above. Below her chin is the source of the splattered blood. The front of her neck is ripped to shreds and almost entirely missing, consumed by whatever unnatural creature fed upon her tender meat. Gory tatters of flesh glisten with recently pumped blood, which was meant to travel up past her neck to her head.

Concentrate, Cal orders himself, as he closes in on the threshold of the incident room. Behind him, Arnold has moved onto his shoulder, ready to go into battle with him, her presence giving him the courage to continue inside.

"It's bad," Cal utters to Arnold, the words meant to try to prepare his superior for the horror she is about to meet.

Whether Arnold acknowledges his words as he crosses through the doorway, Cal doesn't know. A deathly screech from inside the incident room drowns out everything. Terror stifles his senses for a moment, the delay almost costing him dear. Directly in front of him, the creature he saw feeding has risen from the floor and is poised to burst forward to attack.

Cal manages to gather himself to bring his weapon to bear on the terrifying creature. The beast's face is smeared in deep-red blood that paints its skin from its nose and all the way down its neck. Cal stares at the fearsome creature, ready to defend himself, his finger brushing the trigger of his sidearm, but something familiar causes him to delay.

Mike? Cal screams in his head. *Please, no, don't let it be.* Cal's trusted partner, mentor and friend has fixed his eyes upon Cal with only one thought: to feed. He rushes forward, leaving the body below him behind. Mike's hideously distorted face twists even further as he moves to attack at astounding speed. His arms reach forward, fingers like claws ready to sink into Cal's skin.

His emotions in turmoil, Cal's head spins. He knows what must be done but he delays, hoping another option may present itself. It is a forlorn hope; he understands that. For Mike, all hope is lost and Arnold is not in a position to take responsibility for killing Mike as she is still behind Cal. The responsibility falls to Cal. He must put his friend out of his misery. Perhaps that is only right. Mike is his friend and he needs Cal's help, now more than ever.

Mike is almost on top of Cal when Cal depresses his sidearm's trigger. Cal's eyes meet his partner's evil pools of blackness. There is no recognition from his partner, not even at the very end. Cal tells himself that it isn't Mike any longer as his bullet pierces Mike's forehead. Mike died at the hands of another. It isn't Mike's brains that erupt into the air as the bullet smashes out of the back of the beast's head. It is not Cal's friend that collapses, hitting the ground dead.

"Defend yourself!" Arnold's voice bellows from beside Cal.

Bullets blast from Arnold's gun, the sound echoing in Cal's eardrums. He forces Mike out of his head and, in an instant, his wits return. Arnold fires again, her face urgent, determined. Cal follows her lead, turning toward the ghoulish figures moving across the office.

Multiple creatures come at Cal. Some tear across the office floor whilst others leap across desks. Apparitions of familiar faces that Cal once conversed with are now distorted by fearsome features that want nothing but bloody slaughter. Cal fires at the closest beast, any misgivings about shooting his former colleagues forgotten. Killing Mike put pay to that. He understands that it is now, kill or be killed and, right now, the latter option is odds-on. There are too many creatures attacking for him and Arnold to deal with, especially with their limited ammunition.

Cal's first shot misses its target hopelessly. That is a bullet that he could ill afford to waste. Nevertheless, he fires again at the beast, which is low down on his left. This time his aim is true: the bullet smashes into the female creature's right temple. Blood and brain matter spray into the air, the target killed instantly. Cal doesn't afford himself a slap on the back; there is no time for such indulgences. At least another five zombies are coming at them, all of them closing in rapidly to overwhelm them.

"They're too fast!" Arnold shouts, above the crack of gunfire.

Registering his agreement in his head, Cal has no time to answer his superior. There is only time to fire again in desperation at the next-closest threat. Not enough bullets are hitting their targets though. *How many bullets do I have left? Two, three?* Cal panics. The battle is lost. At any moment both he and Arnold will be cut down where they stand and ripped to shreds.

"I'm out. Run!" Arnold shouts in terror.

Visions of his beautiful wife and unborn child flash into Cal's head as his weapon clicks empty. *It is too late to run!* Cal screams in his head at Arnold, his fear preventing the words from coming out of his mouth. Death is upon them, only inches away.

Arnold doesn't run. She also realises it's futile. She cowers, ducking in reflex as the assault comes. Cal cowers

153

too, but he raises his hands over his head in the vain hope that his arms will offer some protection against the impending onslaught.

Forgive give me, Kim. I wish I could have been there to help you raise our child, Cal laments in desperation. His thoughts are suddenly stunned into oblivion, his mind goes blank and it takes a couple of seconds for his consciousness to return. Time seems to stop. The realisation slowly dawns that no attack has hit him and that he is still standing. The overpowering crashing noise that stunned his fragile mind is gunfire. A barrage of gunfire.

"Get them outta here!" a bellowing voice demands.

Something touches Cal's arm. He flinches from it. Is it a human touch or the touch of the undead? The touch tightens around his arm. Cal is defenceless and he succumbs to the irresistible pull of the force grabbing him, putting his faith in it.

"Are you okay, Cal? Are you injured?" Arnold's voice questions urgently above the sound of gunfire.

Cal has lost his bearings and is not even sure if he is still breathing. Something heavy and solid is in his hand. He grips it tightly, hoping the gesture will stop the room spinning around him and help bring him back to reality. He is still breathing. Cal is sure of that now. Arnold's voice assures him at least of that much. *Kim, I'm still here for you!* he cries in his head, hoping an unseen connection will take his words to his wife.

"Cal!" Arnold demands.

"I'm here," Cal replies cryptically, still thinking of Kim. "I'm okay, I mean," he quickly adds.

"Jesus, that was close. A second longer and we'd have been mincemeat," Arnold pants, as the gunfire dies down.

"What happened?" Cal asks embarrassingly, realising he is standing back in the corridor.

"Jackson must have sent a firearms team after us," Arnold surmises. "Thank heavens he did."

"Did you see Mike in there? What they'd done to him?" Cal demands, a shiver running through his body.

"I saw," Arnold replies. "So many of our colleagues. What a waste."

"Are there any survivors?" Cal asks.

"I don't know. Not yet," Arnold answers, sorrowfully.

"The investigation will be in tatters," Cal says.

"That was the target. I do not doubt that," Arnold states.

"How could this man possibly infiltrate police headquarters so easily?" Cal asks.

"He must have had help," Arnold replies.

"Inside help?" Cal presses.

"More than likely," Arnold concedes.

"We have to find him. There could be other targets. Who knows where else they intend to infiltrate next?" Cal insists.

"I intend to. Starting with the lobby, if you're feeling up to it?" Arnold questions.

"He'll be long gone by now," Cal tells Arnold.

"Not necessarily. You alerted us as soon as you saw the facial reconstruction and Commissioner Jackson will have certainly put the building in lockdown just as soon as he'd sent the firearms team. Our man could be trapped in the building," Arnold says, hopefully.

"Let's go," Cal replies, urgently.

Cal and Arnold rush toward the lifts, re-holstering their sidearms as they move. Both of them would dearly love to keep them in their hands for their pursuit. But neither weapon has ammunition, however, rendering them useless for the time being.

The lobby is in chaos when they step out into it. Arnold was right: the building has been put into lockdown. Nobody in or out until Commissioner Jackson says so. Police officers stand idly by, watching the commotion or jabbering into their phones. It is the general public that is up in arms, the majority of them congregating around the security station. The security guards behind the cordon demand that everybody move back, but with little success. People have things to do, places to be.

"Can you see him?" Arnold asks, urgently.

"Not yet," Cal replies, as he scans the faces of the people gathered there.

Arnold barges her way past irate members of the public until she reaches the security cordon. Cal follows in her wake, studying every face in the crowd.

"He isn't here," Cal tells Arnold.

"No. No, he's not," Arnold agrees.

"He's either somewhere else in the building or he got out before Jackson gave the order to lockdown," Cal insists.

"We need to check the street," Arnold says, looking at the security guard blocking the exit. "Move aside, Officer, we need to get through," she tells the large, unimpressed security guard.

"Nobody is permitted to leave," the burly man informs Arnold flatly.

"I am Chief Arnold, Officer. We are in pursuit of a suspect and I'm ordering you to move aside, or I'll arrest you for obstruction. Now move!" Arnold orders.

After a moment's contemplation, during which the guard probably considers the prospect of losing his job if he is arrested, he reluctantly moves aside.

"Don't allow anyone else to leave!" Arnold orders the man, as she passes him, with Cal right behind her.

"Have you seen this man?" Cal stops to ask the guard, holding up his phone with the picture of the suspect displayed. Arnold hovers next to Cal while the guard studies the image.

"I don't think so, but I can't say for sure," the guard says.

An uproar sounds as Arnold and Cal pass the cordon and the security guard moves back into position. They pay no heed to the protests. Cal shows the same picture to the other security guards manning the security cordon, but he gets the same response from all of them. Only then do they rush toward the main entrance.

Outside the sun is shining and the street is busy with both pedestrians and traffic. Without having to say a word, Arnold begins to scan the right-hand side of the street, while Cal takes the left, both working their way out from the centre.

"Anything?" Arnold asks, impatiently.

"Don't worry, Chief, I'll let you know if I see him," Cal replies.

In the distance, further down the street, a taxi stops at the kerbside. Cal squints to see who gets into the vehicle, but it's difficult to see with other cars passing and pedestrians criss-crossing. He thinks he glimpses a flash of a person ducking down to get inside the taxi. He also thinks that the person is wearing a baseball cap but, before he can decide for sure, the taxi silently pulls away. Cal has no view of the taxi's registration number and, within moments, it disappears altogether when it turns right. *Shit*, he thinks, *was that him?*

"I've got nothing," Arnold announces.

"I've just had a possible sighting," Cal replies. "The suspect possibly just got into a taxi."

"Possibly?" Arnold questions, frustratedly.

"It was further down the road," Cal points. "Difficult to see from here."

"Did you get a reg number or anything?" Arnold asks.

"I didn't get a good enough view," Cal replies. "But it was a city taxi, not a private one."

"Shit," Arnold bursts out.

"Sorry, Ma'am," Cal says.

"Sorry, Detective, that wasn't directed at you. Just frustration, you understand," Arnold tells Cal.

"I do, Ma'am. Believe me, I do," Cal assures.

"It might not have been him. But we'll get onto the taxi company. He could still be inside the building," Arnold says, unconvincingly.

"It's possible, Ma'am," Cal agrees.

"Something tells me we've missed him, but we'll sweep the building just in case," Arnold says, turning back to the entrance.

"And assess our losses," Cal says, causing Arnold to pause.

"Yes, unfortunately, Detective," Arnold replies. "I'm sorry about Detective Turner. I know you were close to him, and not just in an official capacity."

"He was a good friend. I'm going to miss him," Cal replies, sombrely.

"As will we all, Cal. It was a shocking turn of events and I'm sorry you had to deal with him," Arnold says, sincerely.

"Thanks, Chief. In some ways, I'm glad it was me. I think that's the way Mike would have preferred it," Cal replies.

"That's very magnanimous of you, Detective. If you need to talk, my door is always open," Arnold offers.

"Thank you, Ma'am."

Back inside, things haven't calmed down. Instead, they have deteriorated. The lobby is becoming packed as more people descend in an attempt to leave. Cal and Arnold revert to scanning faces once more as they approach the throng trying to leave. New people have assembled in the lobby, all of whom need to be checked, just in case. However, there is no sign of the man they are looking for.

The oversized security guard who'd try to stop them leaving sees Cal and Arnold approaching to re-enter. This time he doesn't stand in their way but moves briefly to the side to allow them through before retaking his position. Cal nods his thanks to the guard as he passes, deciding it's best to keep the man onside.

"Still no sign of him here," Cal observes, as they rejoin the melee.

"That doesn't mean he's not still inside the building," Arnold counters.

"No, it doesn't, Ma'am," Cal agrees.

"We're going to need a new base of operations," Arnold states.

"Chief Arnold!" a voice calls before Cal can agree.

Cal turns to see Tilly, Arnold's assistant, approaching them. She has just exited a lift. She has a stern expression on her face and looks like she means business.

"What is it?" Arnold asks, as Tilly approaches.

"I've been trying to phone you. I was terribly worried when
I heard what has happened," Tilly says, as she reaches Arnold, putting a concerned hand on her superior's shoulder.

"I'm sorry. Events took over and I didn't hear my phone," Arnold replies with a hint of embarrassment at Tilly's display, her face blushing.

"It's probably on vibrate," Tilly suggests.

"Possibly," Arnold concedes.

Cal wonders if Arnold and Tilly are in some kind of relationship. They suddenly seem very familiar, whilst Arnold also appears to be feeling awkward. He quickly puts the thought out of his head. It's none of his business and there are more pressing matters to attend to than office gossip.

"Anyway," Tilly continues, taking her hand off Arnold's shoulder, "I think we have another breakthrough. The facial recognition team have put a possible name to the face they constructed."

"Really!" Arnold gasps. "What is it?"

"Merle Abital," Tilly announces.

"How certain are they?" Cal interjects.

"It's not 100 per cent. But that's the name the computer came up with and he just happens to live in the city. He lives in Billingham," Tilly answers, confidently. "We have his address."

"What are the odds? It must be him!" Arnold states, feverishly.

"It can't be a coincidence, Ma'am," Cal says, just as eagerly.

"We need a team of specialist firearms officers and full backup," Arnold announces, even as she moves for the lifts.

"I took the liberty of speaking to Commissioner Jackson when I couldn't get hold of you, Ma'am," Tilly announces. "He's assembling a team for you now. They will be ready to move out in thirty minutes. I understand that he will also be accompanying you."

"Excellent," Arnold says, urgently, stopping to press the call button. "We need to go via the armoury for ammunition, and lots of it!"

Chapter 13

The taxi ride home goes by in a flash. Merle had only made it out of police headquarters by the skin of his teeth. He had anxiously seen the security guards suddenly bar the way through their security station just as he had managed to reach the main entrance. He had then rushed away from the building before anyone could change their mind. Thankfully, he'd hailed a taxi easily, which took no time to leave the area completely.

Adrenaline must have been flooding his bloodstream. It took a good ten minutes or so before Merle had managed to get his breath back, and even more time until he could gather his thoughts. Once he had calmed down, he still struggled to come to terms with what he had managed to accomplish. He doesn't mind admitting that he is proud of himself and feels that Janus will be just as proud, and extremely impressed to boot.

In no time, the taxi is entering Billingham. It doesn't take a genius to work out that they have entered the wrong side of town. The abandoned cars, protruding weeds and unsavoury-looking locals make it obvious. Especially after just returning from the big city, where everything is shiny and manicured and the public don't act as if they'd mug you as soon as look at you.

Merle makes sure the taxi drops him off a fair distance from his apartment block. A short walk will do him good anyway and allow him to clear his head before he reports to Janus. Nobody will trouble him on these streets. People around here instinctively know when they see someone with as little as they have and it's not worth the bother of robbing them.

The fresh air is welcome as Merle begins his walk after the taxi has dropped him off a block or two from his apartment. He breathes in the air greedily, the oxygen restoring balance to his head after his adrenaline overdose. He discards the evidence of his disguise at the first opportunity, throwing it into a large refuse container proudly parked at the corner of an apartment block. The city has its monuments and so does Billingham.

Have you got any change? he's asked, as he walks past an impoverished person with a sleeping bag around their shoulders. The poor soul clings onto the scraggy warmth for dear life. Their hand outstretched, bony fingers ready to catch some change. They still smile as Merle walks by, ignoring them.

Merle isn't heartless, far from it. He feels desperately sorry for every one of the unfortunate citizens of Billingham, of which there are many and he is one of them. He is not on the lowest rung of the ladder but close enough to see the desperation. Only one, or perhaps two, broken rungs away from falling to join his most unfortunate neighbours. A lost job here, an unexpected bill there or a ruinous robbery might tip the balance for most people and, God forbid, the families in this neighbourhood.

He keeps the hard-earned wad of cash Janus entrusted to him buried out of sight. The appearance of such riches on these streets would attract unwanted attention, like moths to a flame. Some of his neighbours have a sixth sense for these things. They can smell newly minted notes on the breeze, like a shark sensing blood in the water miles away.

Nobody gives Merle a second glance as he approaches his apartment block. The staff in the chicken shop look through him as if he wasn't there when he orders his greasy meal. None of his neighbours say 'Good evening' when he passes them in the corridors on the way up to his apartment. And his next-door neighbour, Mrs Wallace, doesn't emerge holding a newly delivered package and moan about being disturbed again.

Shutting his front door, Merle pauses for a moment to gather himself. Another day of excitement and trauma has left him drained of energy. He wonders how many people have met their demise through his actions recently. Dozens certainly, more even. He has barely had the chance to properly study the news after last night's events in Trinity Square and now there is also today's horror to contend with. Has the news of the carnage at the heart of the police force broken yet, or is it still hush-hush?

The aroma of fried chicken rising from the plastic bag at his side takes Merle's mind off such things, at least for now. He finds that he is famished. He suddenly regrets not adding the extra piece of chicken to his order that the young man had offered him at a bargain price.

Janus will understand Merle delaying reporting back while he refuels his batteries. Surely that is not too much to ask for after such a successful day? Merle doesn't want to have to rush his report because of a growling stomach.

In any event, Merle does have a growling stomach when he presses the power button on his computer. Growling of a different nature, however. The chicken isn't sitting well inside him. Actually, his stomach is vehemently protesting at the assault caused by the greasy fast food. It won't be long before his meal makes a fast exit, but he can't delay contacting Janus any longer.

Janus18 is online, Merle sees that as soon as he logs on to their chatroom. He wonders how long his friend has been waiting for him to log on. Before Merle has a chance to write his first message, Janus's voice sounds through his computer's speaker.

"Hello, Merle. I was waiting for you. I have been worried about you, but it seems that congratulations are in order from the news I have been watching," Janus says.

"The operation went as well as can be expected, Janus. I haven't had the chance to see the news yet, but everything went just as you planned," Merle responds.

"So I see, Merle. Well done. I knew you would succeed. I am very proud of you," Janus tells Merle, as if he were congratulating one of his children for winning the science competition at school.

"Thank you, Janus. I can't deny it was the scariest thing I've ever done. On multiple occasions, I was sure they would challenge me and stop me. And I only just made it out before they locked down the whole building," Merle tells Janus.

"People, even the police, generally don't see what's right in front of their noses, Merle. I had every confidence in you. Tell me about when you entered the incident room and planted the release system," Janus pleads.

"Well, after I passed through security, which was nerve-racking, it was quite straightforward. The security pass got me into the incident room and nobody gave me a second look when I was inside. They were all too busy with the investigation, which appeared to be progressing at pace. From what I saw, you were wise to decide to take this action. It looked like the police would have been onto us rapidly if we hadn't," Merle observes.

"You're quite right about that, Merle. We couldn't risk that happening, could we?" Janus says.

"Absolutely not," Merle agrees.

"What happened next?" Janus asks.

"Once inside, I walked right into the centre of the office, took the release system out and placed it on the floor, next to a desk and close to the senior officer overseeing the investigation."

"Yes, Merle. And then?" Janus asks, excitedly.

"As I was walking out, that senior officer challenged me, but it was too late by then. He was standing right above the release system when I activated it. He was blasted with the toxin and was the first to turn," Merle continues.

"How quickly did it happen?" Janus asks.

"He turned in less than a minute, Janus. I thought that was because of the large dose of toxin he was showered with," Merle answers.

"That may have played a part, but that new formula is designed to act quickly," Janus informs Merle.

"It acted astonishingly quickly. The cloud of vapour spread into the room, infecting others. A young female police officer tried to stop me from leaving the incident room. I had to deal with her," Merle says, sadly.

"Really. What happened?" Janus asks, eager for detail.

"She showed such courage, Janus. She was just the sort of young woman the new world is going to need. She was brave, young and pretty. I was forced to strike the girl to get her out of my way, which I did reluctantly," Merle answers.

"She does sound remarkable, and it's a pity she had to be dealt with, but these things are going to happen, Merle, I'm afraid. Many good people will be lost in the cleansing, it is unavoidable, so don't dwell on her loss and don't beat yourself up about it," Janus insists.

"I won't. It was just a shame that such a fine specimen was lost," Merle replies.

"I understand that. More than most, Merle. What happened after?" Janus presses.

"I watched the beginning of the chaos in the incident room. The slaughter unfolded quickly and brutally, as expected, and then I had to make my escape," Merle answers.

"And your escape was touch and go?" Janus asks.

"It was, but I made it out of the building just in time," Merle replies.

"Excellent, Merle. The operation was a complete success. Bravo, my friend," Janus congratulates.

"I hope so," Merle blushes.

"Don't doubt it, Merle. You've done a superb job. Credit where credit is due. Accept the plaudits," Janus insists.

"Thank you, Janus. I'm pleased I can be of service. What's next?" Merle enquires.

"Next, my friend, you receive your rewards," Janus answers. "Outside your front door, a man is waiting for you to let him in. He has something for you."

"A man is waiting outside here?" Merle asks in confusion.

"Yes, Merle. He has been waiting for you to return home to give you your reward," Janus confirms. "Exciting, isn't it? Can you let him in, please?"

"Okay," Merle agrees, still in a state of confusion. "I'll be back in a moment," he tells Janus.

Someone is at my front door. What could they possibly have to give me? Merle thinks, apprehensively. He doesn't see another choice but to go and let whoever it is in. *Perhaps the man has more money to give me*, Merle thinks, *or a new piece of equipment needed to continue the struggle.*

Nervously, Merle opens the door and sheepishly peers out into the corridor.

"Mr Abital?" a gaunt-looking man asks. The trilby-style hat and long raincoat he is wearing seem to suit his late middle-aged years.

"Yes," Merle answers, eyeing the worn bag hanging over the man's shoulder.

"My name is Mr Easter. Janus has asked me to come and see you. May I come in?" the man asks.

"Yes," Merle agrees, wondering if the name Easter is significant. *Easter might suggest rebirth. Is that the man's real name, or an assigned covert pseudonym?* Merle continues to wonder. "What is this about?" he asks, as he stands aside to allow the man to enter.

"Janus would like to explain that to you himself. Shall we go and talk to him?" Mr Easter suggests.

"Yes, okay. This way," Merle agrees, and leads Mr Easter over to his computer.

"Thank you," Mr Easter replies.

"Mr Easter is here," Merle says toward the computer's microphone.

"Please sit down, Mr Abital. You'll be more comfortable," Mr Easter offers before Janus replies.

"Thank you for coming to see Merle, Mr Easter," Janus's voice sounds. "I trust you found his apartment okay?"

"Yes, Janus. There were no issues," Mr Easter replies. "I believe you wanted to explain to Mr Abital why you sent me to visit with him."

"Yes, thank you, Mr Easter, I would certainly like to tell him," Janus replies, as Merle stares at his computer as if Janus was there with him. "We have all been extremely impressed with your commitment to the cause, Merle," Janus continues. "You have done excellent and vitally important work, enabling our work to progress at pace. I am pleased to be able to inform you that Foundation Day is now in the offing."

"Really?" Merle replies anxiously, wondering what part he will play in the event.

"Yes, Merle, really," Janus confirms. "We are all very excited, as I'm sure you are, to hear this news. The project will proceed tonight in the city. The virus has been reverted to its natural state so that it is transmittable again. The enhancements to the virus that your work has helped prove are so effective that we feel that now is the time to move forward. The release will happen in the city at 8 pm tonight. Once we have evaluated the results, the release will proceed across the country and then the world."

"This is very exciting news," Merle says, nervously.

"It is very exciting, Merle. Finally, we will give the planet the breathing room it so desperately needs," Janus tells him. "Overpopulation, climate change and extinction will become things of the past. Humanity will survive, we have ensured that, but in greatly reduced numbers. Only the fittest and strongest will survive the forthcoming cleansing. That is why this type of virus has been engineered.

169

"Once the cull has run its course, we will have the opportunity to control future population growth. Humanity will thrive once again, without poverty, hunger and starvation blighting it. There will be a plentiful bounty for those who survive and their offspring will be a wonder to behold. Balance will return to the planet, bringing with it Eden, here on earth."

"This is what we have been working for," Merle says, now guessing why Mr Easter has come to see him. *Mr Easter has come to bring me my dose of antidote*, Merle decides. *Is he also here to take me to the secure colony to wait out the cull, as Janus promised? Or is he here to help me play my part in the release tonight?* Merle wonders. "What do you need me to do? Merle volunteers.

"Thank you, Merle. Your commitment to the cause is admirable and beyond doubt," Janus replies. "Which is why I know you will understand when I tell you that your work is complete. But I do need to ask you to make one more sacrifice."

"I will do anything to help, Janus," Merle insists, staring confusedly at the flickering computer screen. "And I want to continue to help."

"I know, Merle, and I wish that were possible," Janus replies. "Unfortunately, our comrade with the authorities has given us some bad news."

"What news?" Merle questions nervously, glancing at Mr Easter, who is standing over him, a few paces behind.

"A witness has come forward and has given the police information that has led to them identifying you as the person responsible for the attacks. As we speak, they are en route to arrest you, Merle. As I am sure you can understand, we cannot afford to let that happen. You hold information that might allow the authorities to interfere with our work in the future. It pains me to have to tell you this, Merle," Janus says, sincerely.

"I would never say anything," Merle insists. Fear erupts within him as he suddenly realises the real reason why Mr Easter has come to visit him. Reluctantly, Merle turns toward Mr Easter. He hasn't moved from his position behind Merle, but now there is a gun in his hand. His outstretched arm aims the gun directly at Merle's head.

"I know you wouldn't, my friend, but we simply cannot take any risks. I know that you will understand that this decision is in the best interests of our work," Janus replies.

"If the police are coming, then take me to the colony now. They won't find me there," Merle pleads, desperately, his fear stifling.

"That was considered, Merle. But unfortunately, you don't fit the profile of the citizens allocated to populate the colony and your application was turned down," Janus informs Merle, sadly. "I'm sorry, my friend, there is no other way. Rest easy knowing what you have done for our cause, and that you won't be forgotten, Merle. Goodbye."

Merle is totally gripped with terror. How can Janus do this to him? After all the promises he made him. After all that he has done for Janus and his friends. Sweat pours out of Merle as his heart races, his mind scrambling to think of something to save himself. He cannot move but just continues to stare, the light of the computer screen blurring under his faltering vision.

"Mr Abital," a voice sounds from behind Merle.

Merle ignores the voice. He's too afraid to look. He pretends he cannot hear, pretends that nobody is there. *Don't pretend*, Merle tells himself. *Act. I must act if I'm going to live. Turn now and fight. Jump up from the chair and fight!*

"Mr Abital," the voice sounds again.

Slowly, Merle swivels his chair toward the dreaded voice, struggling to find strength in his legs. He must though. As soon as he turns, he must spring out of his chair and attack his assassin. Mr Easter is older and smaller than he is. Surely he will be easily overpowered?

Merle finds himself facing Mr Easter. His legs have failed him and his body is paralysed with fear. There is no attack and Mr Easter stares down at Merle for a moment from behind the gun he is holding in his outstretched arm. Merle's vision miraculously clears now, at the end, allowing him to see the stern, unforgiving face.

"Are you ready, Mr Abital?"

Merle doesn't answer. He cannot. Fear has completely consumed him.

Mr Easter's eyes squint slightly in the instant before he pulls the trigger. He feels no emotion and certainly no guilt for his actions. He suspects that Mr Abital felt exactly the same when he was running around the city playing God. No mercy was offered then. Why should it be offered now?

The bullet pops out of the silenced pistol he is pointing. Mr Easter is well practised in such work. There is no need to worry about alerting neighbours in the apartment block to the fact that an assassination is taking place. There is no crack of gunfire or terrified scream. Everything is planned for, controlled and as it should be.

Mr Easter sees the overpowering fear in his target. Terror is written all over Mr Abital's blood-drained face. The eyes are what Mr Easter studies, however. They are the window into the soul, are they not? He pays no heed to the bullet discreetly piercing the centre of his target's forehead. The eruption of blood, bone fragments and brain matter out of the back of his head is hard to ignore. They spray across the desk behind Mr Abital, splattering onto the computer screen to be illuminated by its multicoloured light.

Mr Easter doesn't see anything in Merle Abital's eyes as he slumps down dead in his chair. There is no divine moment during which he crosses over to the other side. He has never seen any enlightenment in the countless people he has ended over the years. He wonders if this is because there is nothing to see but terror and desperation at the end. Or perhaps it is because his victims are all soulless heathens. Most if not all of whom have brought their demise upon themselves, through their own nefarious decisions. Mr Easter doesn't know the reason, but he will keep looking.

Time is of the essence. The police are on their way to make their own visit to Merle Abital and Mr Easter doesn't delay to consider the meaning of life any further. Instead, he aims his pistol again and fires six more shots at the computer behind his victim. The computer's screen flickers as the first bullet smashes through the plastic-fronted façade. The noise of the bullet hitting the computer is loud, but not loud enough to draw attention. The screen blanks out with the second bullet and the rest of the bullets rip the computer to pieces.

There is just one more thing for Mr Easter to do before he can leave. He leans over the corpse of Merle. Reluctantly, he sticks his hand into the front pocket of Merle's jeans. Thankfully, he pulls out the phone on the first attempt. He drops it onto the floor, next to the growing pool of blood, and spits a bullet directly at the phone's screen. Pieces of glass, plastic and metal erupt from the obliterated phone. A second bullet isn't required.

Satisfied that his work is done, Mr Easter slips out of the apartment, closing the door securely behind him. He has no concerns about running into the police as he makes his way out of the building. The information he received informed him that it will be at least another fifteen to twenty minutes until they arrive at Mr Abital's apartment block, and he will be long gone by then.

Chapter 14

Cal finds himself riding shotgun to Commissioner Jackson's driver as they race toward Billingham. Chief Arnold sits in the back of Jackson's official car, next to the commissioner. In front of them, two police motorcycle outriders and two police cars clear their path. All the vehicles are flashing their blue lights and blaring their sirens as they speed along. Behind them is the special operations tactical truck, filled to the brim with special operations firearms officers. Behind that is a column of police support vehicles transporting as many officers as they can hold, many of whom are carrying firearms.

Cal has never been to war but he can be forgiven for thinking that is exactly where he is heading now. He feels like he is part of an armoured column about to cross the border into an enemy country but he reminds himself that they are only travelling to Billingham. Although Billingham can be quite rough around the edges, it certainly isn't a war zone. The residents are residents of the city, just as he is.

Cal himself is loaded up with more ammo than he has ever carried before. The Glock nestling under his jacket has a fresh magazine loaded into it and he has a further two magazines stuffed into his pockets. Initially, the armoury back at headquarters was reluctant to issue such a large amount of ammo to them. However, they quickly relented when Arnold angrily gave them a dressing down. In their defence, they were unaware of the horror that had taken place in the incident room, at that time.

Behind Cal, Jackson and Arnold mutter small talk about the case and other subjects. Cal, however, is lost in his thoughts, not registering what his two superiors are discussing. His thoughts are dark and threaten to consume him. He thinks about the team in the incident room, all of whom are now dead. The image of Mike keeps flashing through his mind. The sight of his friend turned into a horrific zombified creature scrambling across the floor to attack him. How can he tell Janet and Mike's family that? How can he tell them that it was he who shot and killed Mike? How can he face them?

"Cal, you're very quiet. Are you okay?" Arnold's voice interrupts Cal's thoughts.

"Yes, Ma'am. I'm okay," Cal lies.

"If you're thinking of Mike, you need to put that to one side for the time being," Arnold says softly, leaning forward in the back seat. "I know it's hard, but I need you in the here and now. We will deal with the loss when we have this man in custody, I promise you that. Can you do that?"

"Yes, Ma'am. I just got lost in my thoughts for a moment. I will be ready when we arrive," Cal assures.

"Thank you, Cal. It's tough. So, let's apprehend this man and put a stop to it," Arnold insists.

"I'm with you, Ma'am. Let's get this asshole," Cal replies, his mind clearing.

After entering the Billingham neighbourhood, the police convoy kill their sirens a few blocks out from the destination building. The last thing they need is for their target to hear the sirens and run. There is no guarantee that the target will be at his residence but the less warning he receives the better.

"That's our building," Cal says, pointing through the windscreen, his phone pinpointing the apartment building.

The rundown block of apartments is about seven stories high. It is a concrete monolith of social housing that should have been knocked down decades ago. Cal finds it difficult to understand how a neighbourhood of the city has been allowed to become so deprived. He thinks the same each time he comes to Billingham, which he does often in his line of work.

Tyres screech as a prelude to the action. The two police cars at the front stop urgently just past the main entrance to the building. Commissioner Jackson's driver skids to a halt next to them, making sure there is plenty of room for the cavalry at the building's main entrance. The two motorcycle outriders swing around to block the road ahead as Cal jumps out of the car.

Black-clad special ops officers swarm out of the tactical truck the instant it grinds to a stop. They fan out to cover the front of the building like a well-oiled machine behind their combat-style M4 automatic rifles. Other police vehicles brake to stop whilst others thunder past to circle round and cover the rear of the building. If the target is inside, there will be no escape. Not this time.

Commissioner Jackson stands overseeing proceedings, his hands on his hips and his chest billowing outwards, like a proud father watching his children. Jackson doesn't interfere; he knows when to let his children play.

The special ops commander waits, his men poised, waiting for his signal like a tightly wound spring. He is patient though; he won't move until every exit from the building has been secured. No risk will be taken that might let his quarry slip away.

Without warning, the commander's hand whips up to the earpiece in his left ear. This is it, Cal thinks, his anticipation rising the moment the commander's signal arrives.

Disappearing like fading shadows, the special ops officers begin to file through the building's main entrance. Once the team is through, others close in on the entrance to take up covering positions, but not before Cal and Arnold have followed the assault team inside. Their sidearms are in their hands, at the ready.

Both plain-clothes officers know they need to keep their distance from the assault team. It is the team's job to secure the area. That is what they are trained for. The target's apartment is on floor three of the building. Four firearms officers take the lift up, securing it as the means of escape at the same time. The bulk of the team takes the stairs, however, their rifles pointing up, leading the way.

Cal and Arnold also take the stairs, making sure they stay back from the men ahead of them. On each floor of the ascent, the team run into residents innocently going about their daily business. They are politely but firmly asked to return to their apartments. None of them argues when faced with the fearsome masked and armed police officers, and two officers remain behind at each level for crowd control.

On floor three, the squad of special ops clog the corridor as they move along to the target's front door. Cal and Arnold don't need to be told to wait at the exit to the stairwell, where they take cover, watching proceedings from a distance.

Dark figures aiming their weapons gather around a doorway halfway along the corridor. Cal sees a battering ram in the hands of one of the men. He knows there will be no customary knock on the door or ringing of the doorbell. Tension rises as the men prepare to breach the apartment.

One ferocious swing of the battering ram smashes into the apartment's door, throwing light from beyond across the scene. 'ARMED POLICE! ARMED POLICE!' is bellowed over and over again as the special ops team pile into the apartment the moment the door gives way, while Cal and Arnold watch on anxiously, waiting for what happens next.

No gunfire erupts from Merle Abital's apartment after the team has entered it. The corridor goes mysteriously quiet while Cal and Arnold are left watching the two officers who have taken up positions outside the apartment, their rifles at the ready.

"What do you think?" Cal whispers.

"I don't know. Perhaps he isn't home," Arnold replies.

"Shit. That's probably it," Cal responds.

"Let's wait and see. He might have surrendered without a fight," Arnold offers.

"Fingers bloody crossed," Cal hopes.

"Chief Arnold, the apartment is clear," a voice shouts down the corridor.

"Here we go," Arnold says to Cal, as she rushes out of the stairwell.

Cal follows Arnold out eagerly, slipping his sidearm back into its holster, praying that Merle Abital will be in cuffs when they get inside the apartment. "Ma'am," the two officers stationed outside say, as they make their way to allow their two colleagues through and into the suspect's lair.

"Someone got here before us," the team's commander says, as Arnold and Cal enter the otherwise silent apartment. His entire team stand looking, rifles across their bodies, at a morose scene of murder framed by the large window behind it.

The body of an overweight man is slumped in a chair positioned in front of a desk. Blood is splattered across the desk, staining the clothes of the victim, and is pooling on the floor beneath the chair he is slumped in.

"Nobody touches anything," Arnold orders, as she lowers herself to her haunches to get a good look at the man's face. "It's our suspect," she confirms, as she peers at the victim.

"Are you positive?" Cal asks, redundantly.

"Yes, I'm positive. Fucking hell!" Arnold barks as she rises, her face filled with anger.

"Is the apartment all clear?" Cal asks the team's commander. He knows that it will be. The special ops team are as good as they come.

"Yes, it's clear," the commander confirms.

"Thank you, commander," Arnold replies. "Please have your team clear the apartment. Keep two officers stationed on the door and have forensics sent up."

"Yes, Ma'am," the commander replies, turning to his men, who have already started vacating the apartment.

"One step forward and two steps back," Arnold says despondently to Cal.

"Not necessarily, Ma'am. This place could be a treasure trove of evidence."

"Have you seen the computer?" Arnold asks, sarcastically. "Something tells me there will be very little to find in here. This goes a lot deeper than we imagined. This man was probably a pawn in someone else's horrific plan. We have only found a dead stooge."

"Nevertheless, there must be something here to connect the two," Cal offers, more in hope than expectation.

"I hope you're right, Detective," Arnold says, trying to sound upbeat. "Look: his phone. Shot to pieces just the same as the computer. Someone didn't want us to look at either of them."

Cal bends down, taking a pen out of his pocket. "We may yet be able to access information from both. It's amazing what can be extracted from even the most damaged tech nowadays," Cal says, poking the phone on the floor with his pen to try to see how damaged it is. "There might also be prints."

"Doubtful. These aren't amateurs we are dealing with," Arnold counters.

"Mistakes happen," Cal replies.

"Forensics will tell us," Arnold points out.

"Although we might not be able to access his devices, his internet usage will tell us what sites he's been looking at and using, and what searches he's made. We will find something," Cal insists, as he leaves the phone and gets up.

"I'm already getting that information compiled back at base," Arnold informs Cal.

"I'd expect nothing less," Cal smiles, taking a closer look at the desk.

"We couldn't have been far behind whoever did this. The blood has barely congealed. It's still dripping from beneath the chair," Arnold observes.

"I bet we just missed them," Cal agrees, as he studies the contents on top of the desk.

He sees fragments of bone in amongst the blood and other white material, which he recognises as brain matter. A half-full mug of coffee sits in the centre of the desk, in front of the blank computer screen. Next to the screen, a well-watered small plant sits in a dull pot, save for its red speckles of blood. Next to that is a notepad. Cal would dearly love to have a look inside the pad immediately, but that is a job for the forensics team. He can't risk contaminating it and spoiling evidence.

His eyes wander to the computer tower, which is shot to pieces. Bending down, he peers into its destroyed innards to see if he can see the machine's hard drive. He can, but it looks seriously damaged and he doesn't hold out much hope that it can be salvaged to any degree. As he rises, something catches his eye: a bright piece of yellow paper is stuck to the side of the mangled computer. He can't touch the paper; it may have evidence on it. Instead, he moves around the side of the desk to see if there is anything of interest written on it.

"Ma'am," Cal says, when he sees writing on the paper.

"What is it?" Arnold asks, taking up a position next to Cal.

"It could be a username and password for a website," Cal suggests.

"Possibly, or one of them could be a password for his computer," Arnold replies.

"MA.5689.AM definitely looks like a password," Cal observes, as he takes a photo of the paper with his phone.

"Yes, and Janus18 could be a username," Arnold adds.

"Some research is going to be needed to find out what it's for but there's a good chance it's significant," Cal says.

"It's another lead," Arnold replies.

"Yes, and forensics will certainly unearth more leads in here. We need to get a look at that notepad for starters," Cal says.

"Soon, Detective, soon," Arnold encourages. "This investigation is turning out to be a can of worms."

"I have full confidence that you will unravel it, Chief Arnold!" Commissioner Jackson insists, as he appears next to them.

"Thank you, sir. We will do our best," Arnold replies.

"It's a tough break we have here, though," Jackson adds, surveying the gruesome murder scene.

"Yes, Sir. We are, however, uncovering evidence already," Cal volunteers.

"Very good, Detective. I will expect a full report once it has been investigated," Jackson replies, without asking for details of what Cal is referring to. "In the meantime, I have some unfortunate news," Jackson continues.

"Sir," Arnold says.

"Disease control have quarantined headquarters. The entire building is under their control and it is off-limits to us. Our investigation there is effectively shut down until they are satisfied there's no further risk of contamination," Jackson announces.

"Sir, we cannot afford to delay this investigation. Something sinister is going on that we're currently unaware of. What we've witnessed so far is just the start, I'm positive of it. We need to be putting all our resources into this, not shutting down our biggest asset!" Arnold insists. "I have already just lost almost my entire team."

"I am well aware of that, Chief Arnold. This is out of my control, but rest assured I am applying as much pressure as I can to get headquarters reopened," Jackson replies.

"Sir," Arnold says.

"Your investigation will continue from Mercury House," Jackson informs them, somewhat timidly.

"But, Sir!" Arnold begins to protest.

"Chief Arnold," Jackson cuts her off abruptly, "it cannot come as a surprise to you that these attacks are of concern to the government. The mayor has been having discussions at the highest level since last night and you know what they say: shit rolls downhill.

"He's ordered me to hand this investigation over to Secret Intelligence, but I argued against it. In the end, we came to a compromise: this investigation will work out of Mercury House. You will have the backing of their full national and international resources. An extensive team of investigators will be allocated to you. You can also take your own people over with you although, following today's dreadful attack, I can't think that there will be many to take, other than Detective Chambers. Wouldn't you agree?" Jackson asks Arnold.

"I see your point, Commissioner," Arnold concedes, readily.

"Look, Sarah," Jackson says to Arnold, softening his stance. "We need all the help we can get on this. None of us has dealt with an investigation like this before, never mind that we are also under attack. Use their resources. Find these people."

"We will, Sir. You can count on us," Arnold agrees, confidently.

"I know you will. Keep me informed," Jackson orders, before turning to leave.

"He's right," Cal says, once Jackson has left. "Our team is decimated. Have you had many dealings with Mercury House?"

"Enough to be extremely wary of them," Arnold replies. "Nothing is as it seems with the intelligence services. But, as the commissioner said, they have the resources we need. Just watch your back when we're there and be careful what you say, and who you say it to."

"Understood, Ma'am," Cal confirms.

"Come on, Detective, let forensics get on with their work," Arnold says, as the first suited-up members of the forensics team step into the apartment.

As they leave, they see that two firearms officers are stationed outside the apartment, as Arnold had ordered. Nobody will be gaining access to Merle Abital's apartment for the foreseeable future without express permission.

"Let's see what his neighbours have to say," Arnold says, as they leave.

Cal nods his agreement as Arnold turns right to knock on doors, while Cal turns to the left. Firstly, Cal knocks on the door overlooking their suspect's apartment, just to the side on the opposite side of the corridor. His forceful loud knocks go unanswered, however, so he turns. Next, he crosses the corridor to knock on the door of the adjoining apartment, hoping for better luck. The moment he reaches the door, even before he has raised his hand to knock, he hears a bolt being unlocked, followed by the removal of a security chain.

"Hello," Cal says, as a crack appears in the door. "I'm Detective Chambers. Can I talk to you about your neighbour, Merle Abital?"

"He was up to no good," the simple reply comes from the elderly woman who slowly opens the door.

"Really, Mrs...?" Cal replies.

"I'm Mrs Wallace," Cal is informed abruptly.

"Hello, Mrs Wallace. Can you tell me why you think he was up to no good?" Cal questions.

"I hardly knew him. He only moved in seven or eight months ago," Mrs Wallace replies.

"But you think he was up to no good?" Cal asks again, holding onto his patience.

"Of course, he was up to no good. He was shifty. Coming and going at all hours. Strange packages arriving for him. The delivery man kept getting me out of my chair to take in parcels for him, even when my shows were on television. Most annoying," Mrs Wallace explains.

"What type of parcels, Mrs Wallace, and how many? Can you remember?"

"Of course, I can remember, young man. I'm not senile," the old lady insists.

"I'm sorry, I didn't mean to imply that. It's just that it's very important," Cal assures his frail witness, forcing a smile.

"What's all this about anyway? There's been a lot of commotion and I've seen all the police out of my window," Mrs Wallace asks.

"If you could tell me about the parcels, Mrs Wallace," Cal presses.

"They were boxes of all shapes and sizes," Cal is told. "All marked with 'Fragile' tape. I took in four of them, but there were more."

"How many more?" Cal asks.

"I don't know exactly, but I saw the delivery company's van pull up several times and then knock on his door."

"Was it always the same delivery van, and do you know which company it was?" Cal asks, excitedly.

"It was always the same. I don't know the name of the company though. It's the one with the brown vans and uniforms," Mrs Wallace confirms. Cal immediately knows which company she is referring to.

"Did you ever see inside any of the parcels?" Cal asks.

"How could I see inside? Do you take me for a busybody who opens other people's parcels? I was just glad to get rid of them when he came home. Besides, they were all very neatly secured," Cal is told, suggesting that she might have sneaked a peek inside, if she could have.

"Is there anything else you can tell me about Mr Abital, Mrs Wallace?" Cal wonders.

"No, Detective. As I said, I didn't know him, apart from his parcels and the strange hours he kept. Do I need to be worried about my safety with him?" Mrs Wallace enquires, reasonably.

"You don't have to be worried, Mrs Wallace. Unfortunately, we found Mr Abital deceased in his apartment just now," Cal confirms.

"Oh, my," the old lady gasps, her hand moving over her mouth. "What happened?"

"I'm afraid I cannot divulge that information. All I can say is that he is a suspect in an ongoing police investigation," Cal offers.

"I'm not surprised. I knew he was shifty. Didn't I tell you so?" Mrs Wallace says, triumphantly.

Arnold arrives behind Cal just as he is finishing up with Mrs Wallace. She has not managed to find out any relevant information from the neighbours who answered their doors to her. All of them told her that they'd seen the suspect in and around the building but had never spoken to him. Arnold is impressed by the information Cal has garnered from Mrs Wallace, however, especially concerning the delivery company. That information should prove exceptionally useful to their enquiries and arrangements will be made for an officer to visit Mrs Wallace to take a formal written statement.

They use the stairs again to descend the building, dodging more forensics officers coming up as they go.

Outside, dusk is falling over Billingham, the dimming light making it appear more sinister. Cal takes little notice; he is used to trawling the city's streets after nightfall, including the neighbourhood of Billingham. Crowds of local onlookers that are being held back by uniformed officers and cordons vie to see what is going on. All of them will be used to seeing police units on the local streets but nothing on the scale of this operation.

Inevitably, at the forefront of the crowd are the press, who become quite excited when they see Chief Arnold emerge from the building. Spotlights are hastily switched on, bathing Cal and her in harsh white light. Red LED lights blink into life on the news cameras, suggesting that they are recording, and questions are bellowed across by the overzealous reporters.

Arnold ignores the jumble of shouted questions, preferring instead to make a beeline for the anonymity of the major incident vehicle, which has arrived on the scene. Cal follows her, unable to stop himself from wondering who might be watching him on their televisions.

Mike's wife Janet could be watching, confused as to why Mike isn't with him. She will be worried, or has she already been informed of her husband's tragic death? Is she watching Cal in anger, because he didn't go to see her, to break the awful news and tell her what happened himself? He turns away from the cameras, embarrassed and ashamed to be seen.

His wife Kim could also be watching, angry and upset at having received no call from him to tell her he is safe and well after the events at police headquarters. His guilt weighs heavily as he follows Arnold inside the major incident vehicle. He should have phoned Kim and he should have gone to see Janet. There are so many things he should have done.

Chapter 15

"Are you alright?" Arnold asks, after they enter the major incident vehicle.

"Yes, Ma'am. Why?" Cal replies, pulling himself together.

"No reason. You just looked a bit overawed," Arnold says.

"I'm fine. It's just that Mike and the others occasionally play on my mind," Cal tells Arnold.

"It's to be expected. I feel it too," Arnold confesses.

"We've got to get to the bottom of this," Cal insists.

"We will, Detective. Rest assured," Arnold replies.

"Do you mind if I go and make a quick phone call, Ma'am?" Cal asks. "I need to phone my wife to let her know I'm okay after the attack at HQ".

"Certainly, Cal. It's long overdue," Arnold observes.

"Thank you, Ma'am. I won't be long," Cal says, turning to leave the vehicle.

"Chief Arnold, Detective Chambers?" a female voice asks from the rear of the vehicle, stopping Cal in his tracks.

Cal and Arnold turn to see a brunette with shoulder-length hair rising out of a chair. There is an immediate air of sophistication about the attractive woman as she stands, dressed in an immaculate dark-grey trouser suit and stub-heeled patent-leather shoes. Alarm bells ring immediately with Arnold when she sees the woman, whilst Cal stands looking, unsure what to make of her.

"Can I help you?" Arnold replies.

"I hope that it's me that can help you, Chief Arnold," the woman replies. "I'm Agent Sutton and I've been assigned as your liaison with Secret Intelligence. I'm here to see that you have everything you need to succeed."

"Oh?" Arnold replies, dubiously.

"I see that you may have your reservations about S.I., and I can't say that I blame you," Sutton concedes. "I think that we all need to put our reservations aside in the face of this threat, however. I assure you that, in this instance, we all want the same thing. I am just as determined as anyone to put a stop to these attacks, as is every agent at S.I."

"I'm sure you all are. I just don't like all the games you play. The cloak-and-dagger mentality," Arnold admits.

"I am here to ensure that it won't interfere with this investigation, Chief. I am here to help. I promise you," Sutton insists.

"I hope you are," Arnold replies. "In any event, it looks like we're stuck with each other."

"I'm afraid we are. So, shall we make the best of it?" Sutton suggests, smiling widely.

Her smile manages to disarm Arnold to a certain degree. So much so that Arnold agrees to bring Agent Sutton up to speed with the latest on the investigation and the evidence discovered in the suspect's apartment. While Arnold is doing that, she tells Cal to go and make his phone call. Cal leaves the two women to it, reluctant to be left out of the briefing but knowing he must make his phone call to Kim.

Cal steps out of the major incident vehicle, hoping he slips out unnoticed by the gathered press. He doesn't give them a chance to act as he quickly steps around to the back of the vehicle, moving out of sight before they can switch their spotlights back on.

Cal looks at his phone, thinking and hoping that Kim might have messaged him. There is no message from his wife. *Perhaps she doesn't care if I'm alive or dead*, he thinks, tapping on her number.

"Hello, Cal. I just saw you on the news. I was wondering when you would let me know if you are okay. I don't know why I bother," Kim answers.

"Why you bother!" Cal growls, seeing red. He can't help himself. "Have you phoned me to see if I'm alive or dead? Have you even messaged me to check if I'm okay? You have no idea what I've been through today. I'm sorry I haven't been able to phone you. I've been chasing down the person who attacked us. This is the first chance I've had.

"Our whole team is dead, all of them. It was only luck that I wasn't in the office when it happened. Mike is dead and, guess what, it was me who killed him. I shot him in the head before he attacked me. He'd turned into some kind of undead zombified creature, Kim. And I shot him in the head," Cal rants, becoming upset.

"Please, Cal," is all that Kim replies, her voice cracking.

Cal knows he has said too much. He should be protecting his wife from those sorts of horrors, not laying them out on a plate for her to worry over. That is the reason why she left in the first place and he's just put his cause back by God knows how much.

"I'm sorry, Kim," Cal quickly says, holding back his tears to try and salvage the situation. "I shouldn't have told you all that. It's been a very stressful and upsetting day."

The other end of the phone goes stony silent.

"Listen, Kim, I'm okay. We're just trying to stop these horrific attacks. I know you don't approve but it has fallen to me and my colleagues to try and I'm sorry for my outburst. I'll message you later to see if you're okay and want to talk. I love you," Cal says into the silent phone.

He waits a moment to see if Kim responds but still receives nothing back. Dejected by his wife's silence and lack of concern for him, Cal ends the call. Now, a tear does escape from his eyes. Sadness rises within him, threatening to become uncontrollable.

A young, uniformed policeman stands guard near the perimeter of the apartment building, doing his duty. The officer looks at him strangely, possibly in sympathy. Cal hadn't noticed him standing there; he was too caught up with phoning Kim. *How much of that did he hear?* Cal wonders, embarrassed, knowing it was the whole exchange.

Still too upset to head back into the major incident vehicle, Cal rummages in his pocket for his pack of cigarettes and quickly lights one up. He draws deeply on the first drag before billowing smoke into the night sky, the lung-killing procedure cathartic. By the time he has dragged half of the cigarette away, he finds himself feeling calmer. With a flick of his fingers, he discards the rest of the cigarette in the street. Bright-orange embers spark brightly against the night as the cigarette hits the road and Cal turns to rejoin the investigation.

"What's happening?" Cal asks, as he moves next to Arnold. She is standing behind Agent Sutton, who is sitting in front of a computer screen, feverishly tapping away at its keyboard.

"Agent Sutton is digging into the suspect's internet history," Arnold replies, with a hint of excitement.

"She can do that so easily?" Cal replies in amazement. "How have we got a search warrant and contacted his internet provider so quickly?"

"Ask no questions and I'll tell you no lies," Sutton answers with a wry smile, and without breaking her keystroke.

Now it is Cal's turn to feel the excitement. Maybe Agent Sutton is going to be of more use than Cal thought initially. Normal police procedure for gaining access to a person's internet history is laborious and time-consuming and often ends in a frustrating refusal. First, a warrant would need to be applied for and, if that is granted, and that's a big if, the internet company would have to be tackled. Cal suddenly wonders how easy it is for the intelligence services to gain that kind of access. Do they just log onto their system and hack into the internet company's servers to gain access to the records? Can they do that for anyone's records? Cal fidgets uncomfortably for a moment, hoping that it's not that easy. Of late, since Kim left, his history might raise an eyebrow or two. He feels himself blush when he considers the possibility that the sophisticated Agent Sutton had checked his history when she learned that they would be working together.

"Oh dear," Sutton says, downbeat.

"What is it?" Arnold asks, immediately.

"I'm afraid I've hit a brick wall," Sutton responds.

"That can't be," Arnold protests.

"There is nothing out of the ordinary in the suspect's records, just the usual porn sites and general websites. Some of it's hardcore, but nothing to raise a red flag," Sutton informs them.

"Shit," Arnold seethes.

"Wait a minute. I see," Sutton says, cryptically.

"What, what do you see?" Arnold questions.

"We're not out of the game yet. The suspect had searched for tools to use the dark web," Sutton reveals, her fingers tapping rapidly. "Hold on."

"Well," Arnold asks impatiently after a minute.

"We need to continue the search at Mercury House. I can't do it from here," Sutton tells them.

"What do you mean?" Arnold demands.

"I'm certain that Mr Abital made use of the dark web. He must have used it to communicate with his cohorts. I can't access the dark web, certainly not from here. It will need expertise and the computer power at Mercury House. Algorithms are held on our computers that may give us access, along with my colleague's help," Sutton replies, rising from her position in front of the screen after she has logged off from whatever she was on. "Shall we? My car's parked close by."

Agent Sutton doesn't wait for an answer. Instead, she almost glides toward the exit door to leave. Arnold and Cal follow her like puppy dogs, eager for a treat. Arnold doesn't even get a chance to hand over the crime scene to another officer as they follow Sutton. Instead, she has to make a frantic phone call as they walk.

Orange lights flash on a normal, unimpressive black car when Sutton presses the button on the fob she has plucked from her luxurious handbag. Cal was half expecting her to have arrived in an Aston Martin, James Bond-style and he laughs at himself for such a ridiculous notion as he climbs into the back seat of the car.

He can tell, however, that the car doesn't pack a standard engine when it growls into life. *A sleeper*, Cal decides. An understated run-of-the-mill car, with an engine that will go from nought to 60 in fewer seconds than the number of fingers he has on his right hand. He is certain the car will have the suspension and brakes to match.

Agent Sutton doesn't waste the horsepower the car offers her either. She speeds away from the apartment block and out of Billingham rapidly, paying no heed to the speed limit.

"What do you think is going on, Detective Chambers?" Sutton asks, above the roar of the engine.

For a moment, Cal doesn't register that Agent Sutton is addressing him. His brain assumes she is talking to Arnold in the front seat next to her.

"Sorry, Agent Sutton, I thought you were talking to Chief Arnold," Cal quickly blurts, as he registers that Sutton is talking to him.

"My first name is Cassie, not Agent," she replies, smiling into the rear-view mirror, catching Cal in her gaze.

"I think it's best if we keep things formal, Agent Sutton," Arnold interjects from beside her.

"As you wish, Chief," Cassie agrees. "So, Detective. You were saying."

"I think I'm probably thinking the same as all of us," Cal replies, feeling Cassie's gaze on him again.

"Which is?" she presses.

"That Merle Abital was a patsy, suckered in by the real person, or persons, behind the attacks. He was drawn in and used by them to carry out the attacks on their behalf. Who they are has yet to be determined and we can only hope they are deranged psychopathic chancers and nothing more sinister," Cal answers.

"What do you mean 'more sinister'?" Cassie tests.

"I mean an organised group or cult that have designs on something bigger. So far, the attacks, though dreadful, have been concentrated and contained. Supposing the attacks become more widespread or, God forbid, the toxin becomes transmittable. That is my fear," Cal admits.

"You're right then," Cassie responds.

"Sorry?" Cal says, confused.

"We are all thinking the same," Cassie smiles into the mirror. "Have you any theories about what group could be behind it? If indeed it is a group."

"A few, but I thought that you might tell us that," Cal replies, trying to turn the tables.

"Please, Detective, don't keep me in suspense," Cassie fences.

"Okay, so long as you don't take offence," Cal replies.

"This sounds interesting and I do love a good conspiracy theory. Please go ahead," Cassie requests.

"Fine. It wouldn't surprise me if it was someone in authority behind it. Possibly part of the government, or perhaps the intelligence community. Much like I think that there's more to the recent COVID pandemic than meets the eye. Who's to say this isn't a continuation of that. The next phase," Cal admits. "Or maybe it's just some crackpot lunatic."

"Bravo, Detective. I think you've made an interesting argument," Cassie congratulates.

"Do you know something you're not telling us, Agent Sutton?" Arnold questions, as Cal sits back in his seat.

"Not at all, Chief. If I had any evidence, I would share it with you. I only have theories, much like Detective Chambers," Cassie insists. "However, I intend to find out. With your help," she adds.

Cal pulls his phone out of his pocket whilst his two female colleagues continue to debate in front of him. He has mixed emotions when he sees that Kim has messaged him, as he hoped she would. *Is this the message he has been dreading, the one where she finishes their relationship completely?* Cal thinks, as he taps the notification. That's more than likely after his earlier outburst.

I'm sorry that I haven't been more supportive and that I didn't try to contact you after the attack today. It's not that I don't care about you, because I do, deeply. I just find it extremely difficult to deal with. I couldn't bear it if I'd phoned and you hadn't answered because the worst had happened. How could I deal with that loss? I can't imagine what you're going through with the loss of Mike and your other colleagues under such terrible circumstances. I'm thinking of you and wish there was something I could do, but there isn't. I think we need to sit down and talk properly once this is all over. Do you? Please be careful, Cal. Our baby is going to need you, and so will I. Xx

Cal sighs, trying to digest the things that Kim has said and what she means by them. Pressure builds in his head with everything that is going on. He understands how difficult it must be for her when he is in danger. When he is working, full stop. She says she cares for him deeply and will need him but, to him, she has a funny way of showing it. All he can agree to do is talk as she has suggested and hope that they can resolve their issues. Cal quickly taps out a message to that effect and presses 'Send'.

Up front, things have quietened down. Cal isn't sure if any conclusions were drawn by the two women. His concentration was taken up by Kim's message. They are approaching the city, he sees, looking out of the window.

Bright lights burn in skyscrapers against the night sky, tempting them closer.

Chapter 16

As Cassie takes them into the city, Cal notices there is a high police presence. He knows that all leave has been cancelled and understands that the purse strings have been loosened for overtime. Thankfully, the mayor didn't decide to scale back once the suspect was found dead. He couldn't afford to take that risk, especially considering the circumstances of the death. Cal suspects the mayor has been tapping up central government for extra resources and funding.

"I'm going to make a quick pit stop before we get to Mercury House," Cassie announces.

"What for? We haven't got the time," Arnold protests.

"It won't take a minute. I know a fabulous sandwich shop nearby. We can't perform to the best of our ability without fuel to burn. Wouldn't you agree, Chief? We'll get them to go," Cassie replies, marvellously.

"When you put it like that," Arnold concedes, her stomach immediately grumbling.

"I could eat," Cal agrees, realising he is starving.

"You won't regret it," Cassie assures. "They do fantastic coffee too."

Cal has taken to Cassie Sutton. She has a lovely way about her. *Under different circumstances...* he begins to think, but immediately stops himself. He hears Arnold's words of warning about the intelligence services ringing in his ears. Is Cassie trying to lure him into dropping his guard by using her feminine charms? A smile here, a show of interest there and her appealing appearance could all be part of a finely tuned act designed to sucker him in. *She nearly caught me in her net*, Cal thinks, deciding that he won't be caught on the hook so easily.

"My treat," Cassie says, as she pulls up outside a traditional, but clearly upmarket, sandwich shop. "What do you fancy?"

"There's no need for that," Arnold insists. "We'll get our own."

"In a way, you will be," Cassie replies, smiling. "It's a company credit card. So what'll it be?"

"Our tax dollar being put to good use for once," Cal jokes, before giving Cassie his order.

Arnold says that she will go with Cassie to choose, pushing her door open before Cassie can argue. Cal watches the two women walk inside the sandwich shop with interest. They couldn't be more like chalk and cheese if they tried.

Chief Arnold: a stern, plain-looking woman dressed in a thigh-length drab blueish coat, her hair scraped back into a ponytail. A highly intelligent, matter-of-fact, no-nonsense professional who will get the job done at all costs.

Cassie, by contrast, is definitely cut from a different cloth. She is high maintenance, there is no doubt about that, and takes pride in her appearance. It costs time and money to achieve her sophisticated, attractive look. Whilst Cal has only just met Cassie, he thinks that both women share the same drive and determination. Both must be driven to have arrived where they are in their chosen professions.

Cal continues to watch the two women through the glass-fronted shop. Cassie takes the lead, conversing animatedly with her server, laughing and joking, while Arnold stands to the side watching proceedings, and only talking when necessary. Cal realises that these are unfamiliar surroundings for Arnold, but he is sure that the dynamics would be the same if the women were ordering lukewarm coffee from the cafeteria at police HQ.

His phone buzzes in his hand, bringing his amateur anthropological deliberations to an end. Kim has sent a simple 'Speak soon and be careful' message in reply to his, and Cal sends a couple of kisses in return. By the time he looks up again, Arnold and Cassie are leaving the sandwich shop, weighed down with goodies.

Arnold suddenly pauses halfway to the car to pull her phone from her front pocket and Cassie stops to wait for her. Arnold doesn't move as she answers the call and begins talking. At that moment, as Cal watches her, he decides that she would brush up nicely if she were so inclined. The thought is fleeting and Arnold's face reverts to business in an instant. Cal lip-reads her saying "We're on our way" into the phone, her expression stern.

There goes dinner, Cal decides in dismay. Arnold then turns and unceremoniously dumps the coffees she is carrying into a nearby waste bin before saying something to Cassie. Cassie rushes around to the driver's side of the car, thankfully bringing the impressive-looking paper carry bag with her that contains the sandwiches. Arnold slams the car door behind her, whilst Cassie virtually throws the bag of sandwiches into the back of the car at Cal.

"What is it?" Cal demands, as Cassie shoves her key into the car's ignition.

"That was Commissioner Jackson. A suspect device has been discovered at City Arena," Arnold replies, as Cassie wheelspins the car away from the roadside.

"Shit. Is there an event on there tonight?" Cal asks, guessing there must be.

"Yes, a sold-out music concert. More than 16,000 people will be there, and that's just inside the main arena," Arnold confirms.

"Are they evacuating the arena?" Cal asks.

"I don't know," Arnold snaps back. "Jackson didn't have any more details, he just told us to get over there. The bomb squad and disease control are already inbound."

"So it could be a false alarm," Cassie offers, tugging at the car's steering wheel.

"Let's hope so," Cal says, unconvinced, "or this could be the start of another phase."

"We'll soon find out," Arnold replies.

Cal is swung from pillar to post as Cassie swerves in and out of traffic. He holds on for dear life as she careers around corners. Cassie takes no prisoners as she speeds through the city's streets in the direction of City Arena.

Situated slap-bang in the centre of the city, the Arena District is a focal point for the entire city. Shopping malls, cinemas and untold numbers of bars and restaurants feed off the complex. In addition to housing the main concert venue, the arena also has a convention centre and several conference halls to draw business in from across the city, the country and the world. Not to mention the arena's associated art gallery and central library. The Arena District is constantly busy but, when the main arena is sold out, it is chock-a-block with people.

A chill shivers down Cal's spine when he considers an attack at the complex. There have been scares in the past, resulting in security reviews and extra measures being put in place. Security there will be tight, especially when the main music venue is in use. It won't be as tight as the security precautions in place at police headquarters though, and they have just failed disastrously.

His fears are not only due to the concentration of people an attack would affect at the arena, there is another reason. Cal has been visiting this side of the city centre more than he'd like to of late. Kim's sister's apartment is situated in the Arena District, not far from the complex. The apartment is in an excellent position. The building overlooks the complex, and has easy access to the amenities it offers. Only last week, on his day off, he'd met Kim at a bar. They'd sat in the sun on the bar's terrace, talking and watching the world go by. The terrace has amazing views of the water basin, which sits on the periphery of the complex. Cal had a lovely afternoon, as did Kim, he thinks, but nothing came of it. He'd left after a couple of hours when Kim said she needed to run a few errands and said she'd make her own way back to her sister's.

"I've got a bad feeling about this," Cal says from the back seat, anxiously.

"Let's not jump to conclusions," Arnold insists. "We've had false alarms before."

"Not under these circumstances," is Cal's reply, to which Arnold stays silent.

Traffic becomes heavy as they cross the city and approach the Arena District. Cassie is forced to slow down, something that tests her patience... and her language. Cal assumes that her car is fitted with hidden blue flashing lights and sirens, but he doesn't mention that. He knows as well as Cassie does that bringing them into play can often do more harm than good. At least they are currently moving along steadily. Switching on blue lights and sirens can cause drivers to panic and take unwise evasive action. That often results in accidents, snarling up the traffic completely.

Ahead, the bulbous roof of the large main arena comes into view and Cassie turns off the main trunk road to reach it. She throws another expletive into the air when a car in front decides to make the same turn, but at the last second, cutting across them. The foul language doesn't sound right coming out of her mouth, Cal decides. It's the sort of colourful language he is prone to use. *Perhaps Cassie isn't quite as refined as she first appears*, he thinks.

"Go left here," Arnold suggests, at the same instant that Cassie indicates left.

"Great minds think alike," Cassie replies, as she makes the left turn.

The traffic thins, allowing Cassie to lurch the car forward, picking up speed. They begin to pass multistorey car parks offering parking spaces, but they are ignored. Cassie heads straight for the outer perimeter of the complex and to a service road they are all familiar with.

As expected, the road is cut off from general traffic by a barrier reaching across it. Cassie flicks a switch on her dashboard as she approaches the barrier and blue flashing lights suddenly burst into action as a warning to the person in control of the barrier. She is forced to slow as the barrier begins to rise but she doesn't come to a stop as she glides underneath it.

Cassie leaves the blue lights flashing when they enter the arena complex. The service road may restrict motorised traffic but not pedestrians. There is no sign of an evacuation; the road is busy with people walking in all directions.

Thankfully, most take heed of the blue lights and get out of Cassie's way. The road gets busier and busier the closer they move toward the bright lights and razzmatazz of the complex's main entrances. So much so that Cassie is forced to slow the car to a snail's pace.

"Would we be better off on foot?" Cal wonders.

"There's a small parking area up ahead for official vehicles. Let's make our way there," Cassie replies.

Cal doesn't disagree; Cassie seems to know the road better than he does. The blue lights bounce off the faces of the people in the road. Most seem unconcerned by the warning lights. They simply move out of the car's way, some quicker than others. Cal hopes their relaxed demeanour will not be disturbed tonight and that the alert Arnold received from Jackson is nothing more than a false alarm.

Sure enough, there is a small parking area close to the complex. Cassie carefully turns into it when there is a break in the flow of people, stopping the car in one of its spaces.

Arnold is first out of the car as soon as Cassie applies the brakes and Cal follows her out, pulling his suit jacket straight as he stands. Both wait for Cassie, who takes a minute to emerge.

"Sorry, I was just reporting in," she tells them above the chatter in the air around them from the crowd.

She presses a button on her key fob as she moves round and the back of her car pops open. She lifts the lid and pulls out an overcoat, which she asks Cal to hold for her. Cal is confused as to why she needs a coat; the night isn't cold. He doesn't have to wait long to get his answer.

A moment later, Cassie produces a shoulder holster from the rear of her car, which she expertly swings over her back and through her arms. Cal and Arnold stand watching in surprise as Cassie retrieves an automatic handgun which she pushes into the holster. Their surprise turns to awe when Cassie then produces a compact sub-machine gun from out of the back of her car and proceeds to clip it to the left side of the holster, so that it hangs down the side of her body.

Thanking Cal, Cassie takes the overcoat off him and slips it on, the garment hiding her weapons perfectly. 'Almost there,' she tells them, as she delves once more into the back of the car. Only after she has transferred four magazines of bullets, according to Cal's reckoning, into her coat does she close the lid and turn, ready to go.

"Do you think you've got enough weapons?" Cal jokes.

"I've seen the footage taken at Trinity Square and at police headquarters, Detective," Cassie replies. "If this is what we think it might be, I think we all might need more."

"Fair point," Cal concedes, glad he's loaded up with as much ammo as he could get.

"When we're all ready," Arnold says impatiently, itching to get moving.

"Let's go," Cassie says, calmly.

Arnold filters into the crowd of people buzzing around the complex. The main entrances are close by where white lights burn, illuminating the area. There is no sign of a police presence around the complex. Private security and stewards in high-vis uniforms take responsibility for crowd control.

"When are the bomb squad due to arrive?" Cassie asks.

"All I know is that they're on their way," Arnold replies.

"Who called in the threat? Because security don't seem to have got the message. They're still allowing people inside the complex," Cal points out, concerned that no action is being taken. "Surely the complex should be evacuating?"

Arnold agrees with Cal's assessment entirely, and decides to act. She approaches a security guard who is standing nearby, watching over the crowd near one of the entrances.

"Where is the security control room?" she urgently asks the guard, showing him her credentials.

"What's this all about?" the man asks, looking at Arnold's police badge.

"I need to speak to the person in charge of security," she replies, ignoring the question.

"It's up the escalator, at the back," the guard tells Arnold.

"Take me there," Arnold orders.

"I can't leave my post," the man protests.

"Now!" Arnold demands.

"Follow me," the security guard says, after a moment's hesitation.

Turning, the security guard leads Arnold inside the entrance, with Cal and Cassie following. Disturbingly, there are throngs of people inside the extensive main foyer. Many are rushing to get to their destination before show time, while others stand unconcernedly at bars and food outlets, taking sustenance on-board. Arnold is led straight to one of the many escalators that crawl up to the next level.

"Have you received any security alerts tonight?" Arnold asks the security guard as they travel up.

"Nothing out of the ordinary," the guard replies, looking back down at them. "Why? What's going on?"

"Let's get to the control room," Arnold replies, avoiding his question.

The escalator deposits them at the next level, which is just as busy. As he walks them toward the rear, the guard skirts groups of people. Cal sees a sign reading 'SECURITY' mounted over a door in the direction in which they are being led.

"Thank you," Arnold says to the guard when they reach the door. "You may return to your post now."

"Okay," the guard replies, uncertainly.

"Keep your wits about you," Cal warns, as the guard leaves them.

Arnold tries the handle on the door but finds it locked.

"Police. Open up," she shouts, banging on the door with the side of her fist.

Almost immediately, the door opens and a worried-looking, older man dressed in a security uniform appears.

"Please come in," the man invites them, without asking to see their ID. "I'm Richard, head of security."

"Thank you, Richard. We've had a report that a suspect device has been found. What can you tell me?" Arnold asks, as she heads into the control room.

"We're not sure what it is. One of my men came across it about 20 minutes ago. He found it in the ventilation room for the main arena," Arnold is told. "At first he thought it was part of the room's equipment, didn't you, Kevin?" Richard says, looking at a younger man sitting in the corner of the room.

"What made you suspicious of it, Kevin?" Arnold asks, looking across the room.

"It isn't normally there," he replies.

"Are you familiar with the ventilation room then?" Arnold questions.

"Apparently he's been sneaking in there to smoke, regularly," Richard interjects, angrily.

"Nevertheless, could it be a new piece of equipment that's been installed?" Cal wonders.

"I don't think so. It looks completely out of place and a pipe has been drilled into the main system. It's fixed into place with gaffer tape. Do you want to see a picture?" Kevin rises from his chair to show his phone to them.

"We need to evacuate the entire complex," Cassie insists the moment she sees the picture.

"We do?" Richard asks, nervously.

"The device appears almost identical to the one used at police HQ," Cassie says, looking at Arnold and Cal fearfully.

Neither Arnold nor Cal has had the chance to review the evidence found after the attack earlier in the day. They haven't seen the device used in the attack, but neither questions Cassie's assessment that the two devices are the same.

"Richard, instigate the complex's evacuation protocol immediately," Arnold demands, urgently. "We don't want to cause panic that leads to a stampede but get the people out. Starting with the main arena."

"You've practised it, Richard. You can do it," Cal encourages, when he sees Richard hesitate.

"Sir," a woman sitting behind a large bank of CCTV screens suddenly says. "There's a fight happening in the arena."

Arnold, Cal and Cassie turn in unison toward the woman. As does Richard, the man she was talking to, and they all rush over to the screen the woman is looking at with dread in their stomachs.

"We're too late," Cal says, absently, as he looks in horror at one of the screens showing the main arena.

Nobody responds to Cal's words; they are all too shocked to speak. It appears that scuffles and fights are breaking out in the crowd across the floor of the arena. People are beginning to panic and chaos is breaking out.

"Can you zoom in?" Cal asks the woman sitting in front of them.

Cal has no doubt about what they will see as the image increases in size on the screen. He doesn't want to look at it but must, if only to confirm what they are dealing with. Just as suspected, at the centre of the carnage, zombified creatures wreak havoc. The fearsome beasts viciously attack anyone in their vicinity. Crowds on the packed floor are penning the victims in and blocking their escape.

"Sound the fire alarm," Arnold declares in shock. "Get everyone out now. Is there one in here?" she asks desperately, looking around the control room.

"There's a trigger over there," the head of security replies, moving toward the red box containing the button.

"WAIT!" Cassie shouts. "Can we lock down the arena?"

"Lock them inside?" Arnold gasps in disbelief. "Are you crazy?"

"I think we must consider it. Can we risk them getting out and entering the city?" Cassie counters.

"It would be a bloodbath in there!" Arnold protests.

"And what would it be like if they get out? We don't know if this attack is different. God forbid, but suppose the virus has become transmittable and spreads? The whole city could be at risk," Cassie insists.

"We can't stop people leaving the arena, even if we wanted to. There are too many exits," Richard announces.

"That settles it," Arnold says.

Without further discussion, Arnold walks over to the trigger for the fire alarm mounted on the wall. She takes one last look at Cal and Cassie before pulling down on the switch.

Inside the control room, a red warning light begins to flash the moment the trigger is activated, and a loud siren sounds outside the room. The volume is too loud for the door of the security room to muffle. Thankfully, the alarm doesn't sound directly inside the room they're in. After approximately 30 seconds of the alarm sounding, it suddenly stops to allow a pre-recorded public address announcement to play.

"This is an emergency," the voice announces over the public address system. "Please make your way calmly to the nearest exit and evacuate the building," the voice says. The second the message finishes, the alarm resumes for another 30 seconds or so before the announcement plays again.

Arnold is on her phone as soon as she has activated the fire alarm. Cal hears her bellowing into her phone in near hysteria. She has called Commissioner Jackson and urgently informs him of the dire situation. She orders him to get every available unit to the arena complex immediately, with all the firepower they can lay their hands on.

"Call the government. Get the army here. Get everyone here. We need backup and we need it now," she shouts into her phone, before hanging up.

Chapter 17

Arnold lowers the phone, a look of desperation fixed on her face. The alarm continues to sound, and the announcement continues to play in the background. Cal expects her to act, to issue orders, but she doesn't. She stands looking, peering at one face and then another of the people in front of her and, for the longest time, nobody speaks. Nobody knows what to say or what the hell to do.

"We'd better evacuate." Richard, the head of security finally breaks the silence.

"You have no idea what we are dealing with here. This is the same type of attack that happened in Trinity Square last night and at police headquarters today," Cal tells him. "Vicious monsters that will slaughter you are just about to pile out of that arena," he adds, not knowing how else to put it.

"I'd rather be out there than stuck in here, if that's true," Kevin insists, from beside Richard.

"Me too," the woman at the CCTV screen agrees.

"We need to get out and kill as many of these things as we can before they move into the city," Cassie says, pulling her machine-gun from under her coat and unclipping it from her holster.

The three security guards stand back in amazement when Cassie produces the weapon, as if by magic. Their faces would be comical if the situation wasn't so serious.

"Cassie is right," Arnold announces. "We take as many of them out as we can. The backup will be here shortly and we do what we can until they arrive."

Following Cassie's lead, Cal pulls the Glock from the holster hidden under his jacket. Arnold quickly has her sidearm in her hand as she turns for the door.

"Are there any spare guns?" Kevin asks, as they prepare to move. His question goes unanswered.

"Stay behind us," Arnold orders the three security guards, as she slowly opens the outer door.

The volume of the fire alarm moves up a notch when the door is opened but, thankfully, it isn't overpowering. The alarm is designed to create urgency, not out-and-out panic.

Arnold leads them out into the main complex. Crowds of people are moving in the direction of the escalators, which will carry them down to the exits beyond. Nobody seems to be panicking; most people have worried expressions on their faces while they walk briskly along in an orderly fashion. In fact, some revellers are laughing and joking with each other as they go, many of whom appear to have made the most of the 'refreshments' on offer before they were rudely interrupted.

All three officers carrying weapons change their stance to hold their firearms discreetly, hiding them under their overcoats. None of them wants the sight of guns, especially Cassie's machine-gun, to cause panic in the crowd.

To the credit of Richard and his security colleagues from the control room, they detach themselves from Cal, Arnold and Cassie and begin to help direct the public toward the escalators, whilst making their own way to the exits. Soon, they are lost in the crowd.

Cal's heart thumps. He knows that this is the quiet before the storm. Despite the impending chaos, he feels an inner calm, however. Whether that is because he has already experienced the terror these attacks create or whether it's because he's exhausted and cannot afford to waste the energy, he is unsure. He doesn't know why he feels so calm but savours the feeling while he can.

As they reach the top of the escalator, Cal sees that the lower level spread out before them is packed. Everyone is moving in the same direction, toward the exits. For a fleeting, deluded moment Cal imagines that it might be possible for the evacuation to be successful. That casualties will be kept to a minimum and the horror will be short-lived.

His misplaced optimism is horribly crushed just as the escalator begins to carry them down toward the ground level. A bone-chilling scream rises from the floor below, echoing across the cavernous space, and a stunned hush falls. People pause, turning in all directions, searching for what has caused such a horrendous sound.

Cal also searches, uncertain which direction the scream came from. Tension rises as the crowd slowly begins to shuffle forward again, telling themselves the scream was just drunken antics.

"It's happening," Cassie's voice sounds in Cal's head. She's right, Cal doesn't doubt it now, and his increasing anxiety is warning in the same way.

Below them, as they pass the midpoint of their descent, the attack becomes visible for the first time. A surge in the crowd occurs like a wave on the ocean travelling toward the coast and the surge spreads out from the right of the escalators, its origins out of sight. People turn to protest at being pushed, but the growing sounds of terror carrying on the air from deeper within the complex give them more pressing priorities. Instead of protesting at being shoved from behind, they look forward, applying pressure in that direction to try and reach the exits.

Without warning, the escalator judders to a stop and Arnold topples forward slightly into the people packed into the confined space in front of her. Cal manages to grab the handrail to steady himself. Gasps of confusion and frustration sound as Cal searches for a way to traverse the last third of the descent. They need to get to the exits urgently and attempt to stop the infected from moving out into the city. There are only three of them, but they must try.

"Police! Make a hole," Arnold bellows at the people in front of her. She is ahead of Cal, but there's nowhere for the people to go.

"Let's go!" Cassie shouts.

Cal sees a pair of bare feet with pink-painted toenails travel past on his left. He looks up to see Cassie above him, her shoes in one hand and the machine-gun in the other. She steps down the centre panel between their escalator and the next one. Her feet grip the stainless-steel in a way that her heeled shoes could never have done.

Luckily, Cal and Arnold are wearing rubber-soled shoes, much more sensible for police work. They both climb up to follow Cassie down. Other people decide to try and follow suit, but Cassie fiercely orders them back down and out of her way. 'Police,' Arnold shouts behind her, to ward the people off their runway.

Another scream shrills out from below, followed instantly by another. Cal risks looking over to see what is going on as he steps down. He nearly stumbles and falls when multiple zombified creatures burst into view, cutting their way into the surging crowd on his right.

Screams of terror sound out continually from the people below. The chilling screams intertwine with horrific screeches from the massing undead creatures appearing from the rear and hysteria builds on the floor below. Nobody here has failed to see the news of the last day or two. Their thoughts that it could never happen to them are obliterated in an instant. Hysteria turns to panic which spreads to the people on the escalators who are looking down at the slaughter unfolding in front of their eyes. This was not the show they expected to see tonight.

There is no stopping the deadly clamour to escape the complex and no stopping people from following Cassie's lead and climbing up onto the central panel to fight their way down the escalators. People fall, taking others with them, until groups of bodies tumble. Some even try to descend on the edge of the outer escalator, trying to shimmy down the handrail. Most, if not all, fall, dropping straight down into the carnage below and the waiting beasts.

Luckily, Cassie has already jumped off at the bottom by the time that real panic sets in. Arnold and Cal jump down behind her into the crowd, fighting to reach the exits and the possibility of safety outside.

Cassie, still clinging onto her shoes, is in front of them as they push to reach the exits, but their efforts are futile. All they can do is to go with the flow of people as everyone pushes forward. Cal has been to plenty of concerts, especially in his younger years. He feels like he is at one now, in a mosh pit at a hardcore gig, fighting to stay upright.

Something flies over Cal's head and he ducks in reflex. He doesn't see what it is, but screams cry out from the direction in which it landed. Unconsciously, he pushes forward; he can't help adding to the crush. The exit doors are closed, but things are deteriorating around them. Arnold stumbles in front of him, threatening to fall under the feet of the desperate crowd, which stomp forward like those of a herd of cattle.

Cal manages to grab her arm, pulling her back from the abyss, his legs straining to keep the two of them on their feet. Perhaps all the time spent moshing in his misspent youth wasn't completely wasted. Arnold's head glances back, to see who had helped her. Any gratitude she feels is masked by her fight to escape the claustrophobic crush.

Howling screams of terror blast into the frenzied atmosphere from every direction, but mostly from behind Cal. A waft of fresh air blows across his face, the breeze welcomed by his gasping mouth, his overheating body and his mind. The cool air confirms that they must be close to an exit, and his hopes are suddenly revived.

"Keep going. We're nearly there!" Cal shouts to Arnold and Cassie in front of him.

Neither woman answers or acknowledges Cal's encouragement. They are too busy dealing with the crush. Every face around him begs to be released from the turmoil.

Cal passes beneath a green 'Exit' sign and then suddenly they burst out into the freedom of the night. The relief is tremendous. Fresh air billows into their lungs, even as they are carried further outwards on the human tide. Eventually, the tide dissipates somewhat in the expansive square outside in which they find themselves. The crowds flow into the surrounding roads beyond the square, further easing the crush.

Cassie takes the opportunity to quickly put her shoes back on and Cal wonders how she managed to keep hold of them as she bends down. Her feet must have taken a battering. Arnold stands beside her, gulping down air, her eyes looking up to the heavens in thanks.

Cal turns back toward the arena complex to survey the situation. He notices blue lights flashing off the complex's façade, raising his hopes again that they may be able to contain the situation. He recoils as a shadow races past him, streaking by on his left. Gripped with terror, he follows the creature, which moves at astonishing speed.

Cal raises his arm, the Glock in his hand, his mind racing. The beast crashes into Arnold, her mouth still gaping open, taking in air. *Nooo!* Cal's mind screams as Arnold is smashed off her feet, her gaping mouth unable to even scream. The two figures fly through the air before slamming into the ground with terrific force. Arnold's gun clatters against the paving and skids to a halt against Cassie's shoe. The intelligence officer turns to see what is happening.

Before Cal can bring the Glock to bear, he sees the beast's head dart against the side of Arnold's neck. He fires, shooting too soon and hitting the creature between its shoulder blades, with little effect. Cal aims again, trying to get a shot at the creature's head but it is low down, nestling into Arnold, near her head.

Gunfire blasts from Cal's left, a short burst of machine-gun fire, the weapon secured against Cassie's shoulder. The bullets hit their target. Blood erupts from the beast's head, splattering across the ground.

"Cover me!" Cal shouts at Cassie desperately, as the creature's dead body slumps on top of Arnold.

Diving forward, Cal grabs hold of the body and pulls it off Arnold. Blood gushes from the side of her neck when the beast is removed. In a panic, Cal shoves his Glock back into its holster and rips off his jacket as he falls onto his knees beside Arnold. He presses his jacket into the side of her neck to try to stem the flow of blood. Her eyes are wide, pleading with Cal to save her, and he increases the pressure on the side of her neck.

"Hold on, Chief, help is coming," Cal says, earnestly. "Can you see a medic?" he demands, looking at Cassie.

Cassie doesn't answer. She has other problems. The machine-gun in her hands lights up again, her feet fighting to keep their balance in her heeled designer shoes.

"Medic!" Cal shouts to anyone who will listen, looking around urgently for help.

Arnold coughs horribly below Cal and blood ejects from her mouth, splattering warmly over Cal's hands, which are already wet with blood. Arnold's face is so pale, in contrast to the blood. She is slipping away. Her eyes shift to look straight into Cal's, searching for a saviour. He is helpless though. All he can do is maintain pressure on the wound and call for help but nobody comes to help. Arnold's death is inevitable.

"Cal, you need to fight! There are too many!" Cassie shouts through the sound of her own gunfire.

Arnold's eyes are beginning to roll into the top of her skull and blood pours out from the side of her mouth. Her breathing is unrecognisable—she is all but dead—but Cal still doesn't want to leave her to die alone.

"Now, Cal, or we both die!" Cassie screams in panic.

Cal turns on his knees, his hand reluctantly releasing the pressure on Arnold's neck. Whether she was dead before or after he left her, he doesn't know.

He takes hold of his Glock, the metal slick in his blood-soaked hand. People run in every direction, away from the complex, their shadows hiding something more sinister amongst them. Figures are everywhere. *How is Cassie differentiating between the good and the bad?* Cal asks himself.

Cassie fires again, even as Cal searches for a target. He follows her direction of fire but all he sees is people scattering. All of them have faces of terror, he sees, as they run through the intermittent artificial light. Just as he's telling himself to get his eyes tested, he sees a creature coming straight at them. The threat is heading directly at Cal. The creature races across the ground, its deadly eyes fixed.

Taking aim with his weapon, Cal hesitates to fire. If he misses his target, there's no doubt his bullet will hit something behind the beast and there are innocent people in the background.

He waits, waits until his target comes closer, and is larger in his sights. Cal prepares to fire. With the ferocious creature almost upon him, something touches his ankle, just as he hones in to take his shot. *Arnold,* the back of his mind cries. *She is still alive!*

His euphoric surprise must be ignored, pushed out of his mind. The deadly creature is about to attack. Cal fires without another thought and his aim is true. Brains spill out of the creature's head, its body going limp, ready to crash into the ground.

Cal doesn't wait to see the result of his kill. He turns to check on Arnold. She was dead, he was sure of it. Thank God he was wrong. "Chief," he blurts out, as he turns toward Arnold, praying that she is still breathing.

A hand closes around his ankle and he sees that Arnold's arm has moved to his leg. Following the arm up to Arnold's neck to check on her injury, Cal's eyes are drawn away by the face staring at him.

Fear and panic instantly bolt through Cal. Arnold has turned into one of them. Her face has become evil and contorted, turned into horror personified. Her stare is black and malignant. She sees nothing but prey. Teeth drawn out of her perished gums close in on Cal's leg, which she holds in her grasp, wanting to bite into his flesh.

"Nooo!" he shouts in shock, falling away from Arnold, ready to scramble away from the monster. His leg is caught though, stuck in Arnold's hand, held in her vice-like grip. Machine-gun fire sounds above him, but the bullets don't come to save him as Arnold's teeth close in on his helpless leg.

Without thinking, Cal raises the Glock, the gun's muzzle only inches away from Arnold's head. A pang of regret in his stomach doesn't stop him from pulling the gun's trigger. The force of the bullet knocks Arnold's head back, her brains exploding into the air. Suddenly his leg is released, allowing him to scramble to his feet. Shock makes his head spin. Not enough oxygen is reaching his brain and, for a moment, he thinks he is going to pass out.

"Fall back!" Cassie's voice bellows into his head, as more rapid-fire rings out.

Cal's eyes blur. He has lost all sense of direction. All he sees is Arnold's horrific features. Another hand grabs him, this time around the arm, alarming him again. At first, he pulls against it, wanting no part of what the owner has to offer.

"Fucking move, Cal!" Cassie shouts, coinciding with another tug on his arm.

Cal relents. He must trust the owner of the hand. Cassie drags him back, away from the complex. His legs move with her, helping to circulate his blood. Oxygen begins to nourish his brain once more in sufficient quantities to revive him. Air flows into his lungs readily, assisting in his revival.

"Keep going," Cassie insists, dragging him along.

Steadily, Cal's vision clears, his mind returns to reality and he again sees the chaos around him. People are running for their lives in total panic. A wretched scream howls out, dangerously close behind them. Cassie pulls his arm to get him away, but can they escape the oncoming slaughter? The speed of the zombified creatures is too great to outrun them. The creatures are closing in on them and Cal senses the danger at his back.

"We need to turn and fight!" Cal shouts at Cassie.

Close by, bodies tumble to the floor as people are taken down from behind. Their screams shudder through Cal. He expects to be hit at any moment. Is this the end for them both? Are they fated to die on the paved ground amid this chaos and to go the same way as Arnold?

Cassie hears Cal's call, sees the bodies falling and turns to fight. Immediately, rapid fire bursts from her weapon. Targets are everywhere. Cal spins, raising his Glock. His first bullet blasts into a beast's head. The creature, only feet away, was ready to attack. They've turned to fight not a moment too soon.

Another target presents itself as the first beast hits the ground. Cal fires again but misses the head shot, hitting the creature in the shoulder. The creature's upper body whips away sideways under the force of the bullet. No more than an inconvenience, the bullet has little effect, the creature's evil eyes not wavering from its target prey.

Multiple bullets rip into the beast from Cassie's machine-gun. They slam into the creature's chest and neck and finally Cassie finds the kill shot. Cal mentally thanks Cassie, his newly found fighting partner, as he retargets his Glock.

Shadows are everywhere, all of which seem to be swarming toward their position. Members of the public run hysterically for their lives. Loved ones are abandoned to their fate in the panic for survival. The speed at which the virus is spreading is astounding, frightening. Ferocious creatures appear from in amongst the shadows in growing numbers, all desperate to feed. Cal realises they will be overwhelmed by the onslaught. It's just a matter of time. The extra ammo he loaded up with is no match for the battle he finds himself in.

"We can't keep this up," Cassie shouts in desperation. "I'm low on ammo!"

Cal doesn't answer her. His concentration is totally consumed with repelling the attack. He fires again, hitting a careering beast that is almost upon him. His bullet disappears into the creature's face. *Should we have kept running?* he asks himself, firing again. *We are stranded, with overwhelming force bearing down on us. It is hopeless*, he tells himself. *This is the end.* He knows it.

"I'm out," Cassie shouts, throwing the machine gun to the ground.

Cassie has her sidearm in her hand and is firing within a couple of seconds. The pistol is no match for the machine gun's ferocity, however, paling by comparison. With the main defence gone, the creatures begin to close in. The single-action guns kill some beasts, but not enough. *Our fight is over*, Cal concedes, thinking of Kim. Shooting one or two more creatures isn't going to stop the inevitable.

Just as he accepts his fate, gunfire erupts from behind them. Cal turns to see black-clad operatives closing in on their position. A full team of armed officers has arrived on the scene. Their fire is controlled but overpowering. Arnold was right: backup did arrive but why couldn't it have arrived in time to save her?

"Fall back!" one of the officers orders, and neither Cal nor Cassie delay.

Cassie leads Cal behind their lines, where they see more officers protecting the rear. As soon as Cal is through to a relatively safe position, the rescue squad begins to retreat. Cal notices relief written all over Cassie's face, a feeling that is mirrored by his own. They move back with the squad, whilst keeping their own guards up. Their guns are still pointing outwards, ready to fire.

"Fuck me! I thought that was it," Cal gasps.

"You and me both," Cassie replies.

"Talk about, just in the nick of time," Cal adds.

"We're not out of the woods yet. Stay alert," Cassie growls, her eyes focused, searching for targets.

Cal shuts up, does as he's told and watches through the lines of the men firing in front of him as they all retreat. As he shuffles back with their guardians, he wonders where they are being taken. *Where is safe now?* he asks himself. *If the virus can spread this quickly, who knows where it will end?*

Steadily, they move further away from the arena complex. They are being directed in a different direction from the one in which they left the car. That must surely now be classed as abandoned. Cal looks behind, sure that this direction leads to the car-parking areas for the complex. Is that where the reinforcements are? There are blue flashing lights behind, but he can't make out any detail. He hopes that it isn't just police officers waiting to receive them. They need the firepower of the army to deal with this carnage.

"Climb up the slope," somebody shouts, as the movement backwards suddenly stops.

Cal struggles to get his bearings. He doesn't recall a slope near the car parks. Nevertheless, he does as he's told, quickly going through the line of men at the rear, where he meets a grass verge. Cassie grabs onto his hand as they begin climbing up the verge. *Her shoes will be the death of her,* Cal thinks, as he pulls her along.

The verge is steep but manageable and they quickly approach the top. Muzzle flashes and gunfire erupt over their heads but, thankfully, whoever is firing sees them coming.

"This way," someone shouts through a gap in the barrage of gunfire.

A hand reaches down to pull Cassie up the final section of the verge. Cal grabs onto the railing perched on top to pull himself up and over it. Have they made it to safety, or just reached a waypoint in the chaos? Either way, relief washes over Cal having survived the horrendous carnage below.

Chapter 18

"Where's Chief Arnold?" a voice asks, as Cal and Cassie gasp for breath.

Cal doesn't register the question immediately. His mind is a jumble of horrific thoughts. He watches absently as the team that came to their rescue battle to retreat up the verge, trying to regather himself. Aided by the covering fire, it isn't long until officers begin to reach the peak and climb over the low railing. Cal wants to thank each one separately and to shake their hands but, in the event, he just watches them.

"Sir, where's Chief Arnold?" the voice asks again, over the sound of gunfire.

Cal turns toward the voice and finally registers that it is Matt talking to him. The time he spent with the young officer last night in Trinity Square was shocking enough. How things have deteriorated in only 24 hours.

"She didn't make it," Cal replies, solemnly.

"What happened?" Matt asks, to Cal's dismay.

"Not now, young man," Cassie tells him, to Cal's relief.

Matt doesn't press the subject, he just looks at Cassie, trying to decide who the hell she is. His compulsion to question her is quenched by her air of authority and he lets the 'young man' slight go this time. This is not the time to poke the bear. She looks like she would eat him for breakfast. Whoever she is, she has just survived a terrible ordeal and looks ready to snap.

"Where is Chief Arnold, Detective?" a commanding voice asks from behind Cal.

Turning toward the voice, and before he has seen who is asking him, Cal reluctantly realises that this time a simple answer won't suffice.

Even before he pulls down the black material covering the lower part of his face, Cal recognises the special ops sergeant, who is standing waiting for an answer. He is the same sergeant who called them to the massacre in Vision bar last night at Trinity Square.

"She was attacked just before you arrived with your team, Sergeant. She didn't make it, I'm afraid," Cal replies, with a heavy heart.

"We wouldn't have survived, either, if you and your team hadn't arrived when you did, Sergeant," Cassie interjects, seeing that Cal is struggling. "We owe you our gratitude. Thank your team for us please, Sergeant," she adds, sincerely.

"And who are you?" the sergeant questions, not beating around the bush.

"Agent Sutton, S.I. I'm aiding in this investigation. I'm pleased to meet you, Sergeant," Cassie replies.

"We haven't got time for pleasantries," Cal growls, looking around. "What's the situation here as you see it, Sergeant?"

While he waits for the sergeant's assessment, Cal sees that the police have arrived in numbers. At least a dozen police cars are parked in the area he finds himself in, which seems to be a small car park overlooking the arena complex. The special operations tactical truck and two other police vans are also in attendance.

"I don't need to tell you that the situation is catastrophic, Detective," the sergeant replies, as a helicopter flies overhead. "The complex is overrun and the danger is spreading. We haven't the numbers or the firepower to stop it and we can't hold this position. We must evacuate, immediately."

"Evacuate!" Cal shouts over the gunfire to make his point. "What about the survivors? Are you suggesting we abandon them? If we don't stop the spread now it will be out of control!"

"It is already out of control, Detective," the sergeant insists. "This isn't like the other attacks. The virus, or whatever it is, is spreading easily."

"I am well aware of that, Sergeant. But we can't just leave," Cal replies.

"We are going to be overwhelmed if we stay here. Our orders were to find you and Chief Arnold, not to go to war with an undead army that we have no hope of defeating. I have 25 firearms officers here and there are hundreds, if not thousands, of undead already. We have to retreat and regroup," the sergeant explains. We are already getting reports of attacks in the surrounding area."

"The army are on their way," Cassie interrupts, looking at her phone. "They will be here imminently. I was aware that they were on standby after the other recent attacks."

"I'm glad that you knew that!" Cal replies, angrily.

"The sergeant is right. We need to evacuate, regroup and let the army deal with it. We still have an investigation to carry out, Detective," Cassie insists, ignoring Cal's anger.

Another helicopter swoops overhead. This one flies in low and, even in the darkness, Cal sees that it is of military origin. He watches it fly over the plaza square near the complex's entrances, where it reduces its speed.

"Holy shit!" Matt shouts, as ferocious gunfire, intertwined with red flashing tracer fire, erupts from the side of the aircraft. His words of shock and awe are all but drowned out by the thundering sound of the bombardment. Bullets rain down onto the ground, indiscriminately shredding anything in their path. No quarter is given to any survivors who might miraculously still be alive and yet in the line of fire. They are consigned to become collateral damage on the arena's battlefield.

"Sergeant, they are moving along our right flank," a masked officer pants, as he arrives at the sergeant's side.

"We're moving out. End of discussion," the sergeant announces to all.

"We need a ride," Cassie states, like they are leaving a bar after a few drinks.

"I can take you," Matt offers.

Another helicopter arrives on the scene as Matt leads them to his car. It too has begun bombarding the area with gunfire by the time they reach Matt's police car. *The situation is out of control*, Cal worries, his thoughts turning to Kim.

"Give me a minute," Cal tells Cassie and Matt, his phone already in his hand.

He sees that he has two missed phone calls. Both are from Kim and he urgently redials her number.

"Cal!" Kim answers immediately. "What's going on? There is gunfire nearby," she panics.

"There's been an attack at the arena. Are you at your sister's?" Cal asks.

"Yes. What should we do?" Kim asks.

"Stay where you are. You should be safe there," Cal replies.

"Are you serious, Cal? It's like a war zone here!" Kim shouts down the phone.

"Is it? How close would you say it is?" Cal asks. *Surely the undead haven't spread as far as her sister's apartment building?*

"Wait a second," Kim demands.

Cal waits, his worry growing. He feels Cassie's eyes on him.

"I just looked out of the window. It's close and getting closer, Cal. Lauren says we should leave. Should we?" Kim asks.

Cal doesn't know what to say for a moment, or what advice he should give. He doesn't want Kim out on the streets. Not with all hell literally breaking loose. But if they stay where they are they will probably become stranded in the middle of the outbreak. Who knows what will happen then?

"Stay where you are. I'm coming," Cal tells Kim.

"How long will you be?" she asks.

"I'm close. I won't be long. Get ready to leave when I get there," Cal insists.

"Okay. Please be as quick as you can, Cal. I'm frightened," Kim replies.

"Sit tight. I'm coming," Cal assures.

Cal puts his phone away and looks at Cassie, who gives him a knowing look. She might try to convince Cal to stay on task. Tell him that the quickest way to bring this nightmare to an end is to find out who's behind it and that his wife will be safe where she is. But she has read his file, and she knows his wife is pregnant. Even a cursory read of his file would tell her that he's not the type of man to leave his pregnant wife behind, and in danger.

"I know, Cal," she concedes, without him having to say a word. "I'm coming with you."

"That's not necessary," Cal objects.

"I know it's not, but I'm coming. Tell yourself it's because I can't let my star investigator out of my sights if you like," Cassie replies. "We need to get some better weapons before we go though."

Cassie is already jogging toward the special ops truck before Cal can protest again. Secretly, he is relieved that Cassie will be with him as he follows her. He suspects he will need all the help he can get.

"Sergeant," Cassie says.

"Yes," he replies, just as he was about to board the special ops truck.

"We need weapons. Two rifles and fresh magazines for our sidearms," Cassie demands.

"Well, you aren't getting them off us, Agent Sutton," the sergeant replies, nonchalantly. "All our equipment must be accounted for."

"Are you serious? We're in the middle of a fight for our lives and you're telling me it's more than your job's worth!" Cassie responds, angrily.

"I don't make the rules," he replies.

"You can allocate the equipment to me. I can assure you it won't be an issue," Cassie assures.

"I'm sorry, Agent Sutton. I can't give you weapons," the sergeant insists.

Cal sees Cassie is about to blow her top when he steps in.

"Sergeant, I will take full responsibility. We need to move on a vital lead, but I'm sure you can appreciate we don't want to go unarmed. Therefore, I'm ordering you to issue us the weapons we need," Cal blags.

"This is very irregular, Detective," the sergeant replies.

"As are the times, Sergeant. We can't afford to stand on ceremony, not now," Cal reasons.

"When you put it like that, Sir," the sergeant replies.

A few moments later, Cal and Cassie are walking back to Matt's car carrying automatic rifles, spare magazines and extra ammo for their sidearms.

"Nicely done," Cassie says, as they walk away.

"You just have to know how to deal with them," Cal replies.

Back at the car, Matt is standing waiting, only now he too is holding a rifle.

"No, Matt, I'm afraid not," Cal says to him.

"Sir, you need a driver and I'm a trained firearms officer," Matt reasons.

"Where did you get that?" Cassie asks, referring to Matt's rifle.

"From my car's weapons locker," Matt replies, simply.

"I think he will be an asset," Cassie tells Cal.

"I don't want to be responsible," Cal replies.

"Responsible for who? With all due respect, I can look after myself, Detective. Jay, my partner and friend, was slaughtered in that incident room. I'm in this fight, whether you like it or not," Matt argues.

"We haven't time to argue," Cal relents. "You're driving, that's all. Now let's go."

Other vehicles have already started to leave the car park. The special ops truck is waiting for all the vehicles to evacuate before the last of its officers gets on-board. The team continue to guard the grass verge, firing almost constantly, waiting for their signal to move.

"Where are we going?" Matt asks Cal, as he gets in the front seat next to him.

"It's the Waterside apartment block. We're going to have to go the long way round though. Hopefully, that will cut out any trouble," Cal answers.

"Is that one of the new blocks on the waterside near the complex?" Matt asks.

"Yes, it's one of those. Now, let's get moving," Cal orders. "I'll direct you."

"I know the way," Matt tells Cal, as he drops the car into gear and speeds out of the car park.

Matt brakes hard when he reaches the exit, waiting for a slower car to move through the opening. The moment he's through, Matt switches on the car's blue lights and floors the accelerator. He swerves, crossing over to the other side of the road to overtake the slower-moving police cars leaving the area.

Cal realises that Matt is trained not only in firearms but also in tactical driving. He handles the car like a professional racing driver. *Hopefully, Kim won't be waiting long at all*, Cal thinks, as he is forced back in his seat.

"Control, this is Agent Sutton, 452879," Cassie says into her phone from the backseat. "Put me through to Director Khan."

Cal's ears prick when he hears Khan's name. Director Khan is head of the city's Secret Intelligence branch. His reputation is formidable in law enforcement circles throughout the city. He is known for his aloofness, sharp mind and unforgiving attitude. Cassie must be well connected to be on professional speaking terms with the director and Cal is interested in what she has to say to him.

"Good evening, Director," Cassie says, with Cal listening intently. But just as she begins to speak, Cal's phone lights up, with Commissioner Jackson's name displayed.

Shit! Cal says to himself, as he answers his phone.

"Commissioner," Cal answers.

"I can't get hold of Chief Arnold. Is she with you, Detective Chambers?" the commissioner asks.

"I'm sorry to have to tell you that Chief Arnold is dead, Sir," Cal says, wondering how many more times he will have to break the sad news. "She was attacked outside City Arena by one of the zombie creatures, Sir."

"Jesus Christ, where will this end?" Jackson replies.

"I don't know, Sir," Cal responds. "The City Arena complex is overrun and the virus is now transmittable. I expect you know how dire the situation is, Sir."

"I'm afraid I do, Detective. Are you still at the complex? Have the army arrived?" Jackson asks.

"We have just left the complex, Sir. Two helicopters were there when we left and I believe the army were right behind them, Sir," Cal answers.

"Given the awful news about Chief Arnold, I'm appointing you lead investigator for this investigation, Detective Chambers. Are you up to the task?" Jackson questions.

"Yes, Sir, I am," Cal replies, wondering if he should mention to the commissioner what he is currently doing.

"Very good. I am relying on you, Detective. Anything you need, just let me know. Is the S.I. agent still with you?" Jackson asks.

"Yes, Sir. She is," Cal replies.

"Is she proving useful?" Jackson enquires.

"Very, Sir, although it's early days," Cal tells him.

"Just be wary, Detective. You report to me, no one else. Understood?" Jackson insists.

"I understand, Sir," Cal confirms. "Do the army expect to be able to defeat this attack, Sir?"

"That remains to be seen, Detective. The generals are confident, but they always are. We will have to see how the operation progresses," Jackson replies, sounding less than convinced.

"If it does fail, Sir?" Cal cautions.

"The government are on this, Detective. They have contingencies. We must trust in them. Your job is to discover who's behind these attacks and I'm sure I don't need to tell you that's the best way to stop them," Jackson insists.

"No, Sir. You don't," Cal replies.

"We're counting on you, Cal. Keep me informed," Jackson orders.

"I will, Sir," Cal replies.

Surprised that Jackson used his first name, Cal lowers his phone. He has completely missed Cassie's call with her superior. In the event, it was she who was able to listen to most of his call.

Jackson has just put him in charge, replacing Chief Arnold. Jackson wouldn't be impressed if he knew that, instead of getting on with the investigation, he was on a rescue mission.

"What did the commissioner say?" Cassie asks.

"What did Director Khan say?" Cal says, abruptly.

"Nothing," Cassie replies. "I was just updating him, as I've been ordered to do. Why? What's wrong?"

"Sorry, I didn't mean to snap," Cal replies. "I'm just a bit stressed. Commissioner Jackson put me in charge of the investigation. He told me to concentrate on that and to let the government deal with the latest outbreak."

"That's more or less what Khan said to me, and they're right," Cassie confirms.

"I know they are, but that's not what I'm doing. I should have been honest with Jackson and told him to find somebody else," Cal stresses.

"I don't agree. We're merely taking a detour. Once your wife is safe you will be able to concentrate on the investigation. You are integral to it, Detective. You know more about it than anyone, and that is invaluable," Cassie insists. "This is a necessary detour. How can you concentrate until you know your wife is safe?"

"My pregnant wife," Cal adds.

"Exactly, Cal. Let's get this done and then we can dive back into the investigation," Cassie suggests.

Just as Cassie finishes her sentence a shocked hush descends on the occupants of the car. On the other side of the road, a column of military vehicles begins to thunder past, grabbing everyone's attention. Loud diesel engines work overtime speeding the column in the opposite direction, toward the arena complex. Troop carriers, military SUVs and trucks form a column as far as the road is long. Wide, low-slung multi-wheeled beds loaded with tanks are hauled past, shaking the road as they go. Troops in open-sided trucks gripping rifles pay no attention to the police car as they pass. Their eyes are fixed on their brothers in arms as they psych themselves up for the battle ahead.

"I guess the authorities are taking this seriously," Matt says, from the driver's seat.

"How can they not?" Cal replies.

"They're going to need every man they can get," Cassie adds.

Matt indicates and tugs at the steering wheel as he peels off the road, away from the column, which shows no sign of ending. The slip road circles round, forcing Cal and Cassie to grab hold of handrails to stop them from toppling over. Matt accelerates again as the road straightens. They begin to travel back toward the Arena District and toward Kim's sister's apartment block.

A constant stream of cars drives in the opposite direction on the other side of the road's central barrier. The public are already taking it upon themselves to evacuate the part of the city near the arena, and who can blame them? Matt moves into the outside lane of the two-lane highway to overtake another column of military vehicles, this one shorter than the other but extensive, nevertheless.

Matt guns it past the column just in time to cut across its front to take the next exit. Another slip road takes them back down into the Arena District and its narrow streets. Cars driven by nervous drivers, all looking over their shoulders, queue to join the trunk road they have just exited, their frightened families peering out of side windows with eyes like saucers.

"Which way?" Matt asks, urgently.

Cal directs Matt deeper into the district, toward the water basin that the apartment block towers over. The night sky flashes with white and red as helicopters continue the bombardment around the arena complex, as they draw closer. Cal hopes that the stretch of water around the complex will deter the attack from moving into the residential area, at least until they have rescued Kim and her sister.

"That's the building." Cal points through the windscreen at a shiny new apartment tower.

"Tell them we're almost there," Cassie says from behind.

Cal quickly taps out a message to that effect and receives one back immediately.

"They're waiting," Cal announces.

"Tell them to come down," Cassie suggests.

"I'd rather not in case there's danger around the building. I'll go and get them. It won't take a minute," Cal replies.

Cassie huffs but doesn't protest.

Nearly there, Cal thinks, looking down at his phone to check if there are any new messages. He doesn't see the dark figure wander into the road, straight in front of the car.

Matt sees the figure move out of the darkness immediately, but even his specialist tactical driver training cannot prevent the inevitable. His eyes try to adjust in a split second to decide if the figure is human. The speed that the car is travelling at doesn't give him enough time to decide and so he is forced to take evasive action.

Cassie gasps as Matt swerves sharply to avoid hitting the figure head-on. Cal's head shoots up from his phone in a confused panic, his stomach dropping horribly, alerting him to the car's sudden change of direction.

In the road, the figure continues to shuffle forward, unconcerned by the speeding car bearing down on it. No attention is paid to the sound of screeching tyres as Matt works the car's steering wheel desperately, trying to keep control.

The back of the car fishtails as the tyres lose traction. Matt has lost control. He knows it even before the front wheels crash into the roadside kerb and gravity seems to disappear. The car is launched into the air, its rear section coming round as the four wheels spin in the air.

Before the car hits the ground again it has spun three-quarters of the way round on itself. Still moving forward, the front of the car smashes through the plate-glass window of the building adjacent to the road. The front of the car crashes through another window as it continues to tumble sideways over and over again, bouncing across the unforgiving ground. Glass shatters into the air. The momentum of the car is unrelenting. Steel panels crush under the force as airbags explode throughout the car's interior.

Finally, with one last resounding crash, the car skids to a halt, ending up on its side. The rear of the car finishes up in the road whilst the front section billows steam into the front of the building and up to the nearby street lamps. And then nothing moves.

Chapter 19

Inside the car, dust swirls through the air and pieces of glass and debris fall as the car settles. Cassie coughs first, a cough of distress that is followed by a bruised groan. She moves, trying to determine whether she is seriously injured. She realises that the car is on its side and that she is hanging in the air, only kept from falling by her seatbelt.

Cal pulls his face out of the remnants of the airbag, which has deflated and fallen across his face. He is on his side against the door of the car and glass crunches beneath him as he tries to move. He joins Cassie in coughing out dust and debris. His joints ache but he doesn't think anything is broken.

Something moves above Cal through the haze of dust. Matt dangles in his seatbelt, which pins him into his seat, but his arms and head dangle down toward him. Cal thinks he sees Matt's arm move.

"Matt, are you okay?" Cal splutters. "Cassie?"

A long moan sounds from above Cal and now Matt does slowly move. More glass and debris fall off the young officer, showering Cal's face and forcing him to cough again and to cover his face with his hand.

"I'm okay," Cassie coughs from the back of the car.

"Me too. I think," Matt says, finally.

"How are we going to get out of here?" Cal asks.

"I should be able to climb out. Hold on," Cassie replies.

Cassie grabs onto her seatbelt with one hand and presses its release button with the other. Her legs and body fall away from her, her grip on the seatbelt stopping her from completely falling to the bottom. She finds a standing position through the shattered window below her and looks up. The window in the door above her has completely vanished. That is her exit point. She just needs to climb up to it. She finds her rifle in amongst the glass at her feet, throws it over her back and begins to climb.

Cal sees Cassie pressing forward and decides it's time for him to get moving. He unbuckles his belt and tries to move into a position that will allow him to get out of the car. Pain cuts into the side of his upper arm as it scrapes against the shards of glass covering the ground below him. Ignoring the pain, he at least manages to get into position to look at Matt.

"Are you okay?" Cal asks Matt, who is still hanging in the air.

"I think so, Sir. I just want to get out of here," Matt replies. "I'm sorry about this," he adds guiltily.

"Don't be ridiculous. This isn't your fault. That thing came out of nowhere," Cal assures.

"I should have expected it," Matt replies.

"Rubbish, Matt. It couldn't have been avoided," Cal insists. "Now let's get you out of here."

While Cal begins to help Matt escape the overturned car, Cassie has begun to pull herself out. Using the back seat for leverage, her foot pushes her higher. She is careful where she places her hands as she pulls herself through the broken window. Glass still clings on around the frame and she can't afford any more injuries.

The moment her head appears outside the car a chilling screech sounds in their proximity. Fear courses through her body, the hideous noise causing her to rush to defend herself. Her arms strain to pull herself through but her foot slips off the material of the back seat. She nearly falls back into the void, her fingers grip in reflex and thankfully her scrambling feet manage to find something solid to push against.

Cassie takes a breath and goes again. This time she makes sure of her footing. Her arms go through the window and she finds herself in a position to push herself free. Her backside lands on the solid rear quarter of the car, her head turning to find the source of the threatening noise.

Shadows move across the road beneath the orange–white man-made light of the street lamps. Urgently, Cassie pulls her legs out of the car and swivels to defend herself. Precariously, she manages to rise into a position where she has one knee on top of the car and her front foot finds a position on the wheel next to her, helping her to balance.

Creatures close in to attack even as Cassie reaches for the rifle slung over her back. She pulls on the weapon's strap to swing it round into her hands just as the first creature reaches striking distance. The beast launches itself into the air at Cassie. She has no idea if it is the same creature that their driver swerved to miss as she pulls the trigger on the rifle.

Cassie has the high ground as the creature flies through the air. The rifle recoils into her shoulder when the first bullet blasts out in a downward trajectory. A loud crack of gunfire bounces off the surrounding buildings, reverberating back to assault her ears. But Cassie's aim is perfect: the bullet smashes through the beast's skull, killing it instantly. She wobbles, along with the car, when the body hits the underside of the vehicle with a crunch.

Another heinous screech wails out in protest from the creatures at the killing of their kin and more of them rush in to seek their revenge. Cassie swivels on her perch to meet the onslaught and fires again. This time, one bullet follows another. They must, if they are to have any hope of repelling the oncoming attack. Numerous undead creatures appear out of the shadows. The building behind Cassie offers some protection to the rear, but that is her only advantage. Her rifle continuously jerks back into her shoulder. Bullets erupt out of the rifle's muzzle, slamming into the fearsome twisted beasts, which close in on her position.

"Cal!" Cassie shouts desperately, knowing she needs help. There are too many creatures for her to deal with alone. Even with the help of Cal and Matt, it might not be enough to repel the oncoming offensive.

Gunfire cracks down into the stricken car, pounding into Cal's head. Matt is free from his seatbelt and Cal helps push him upwards through the glassless window above. Cal is already passing Matt's rifle up to him as he disappears through the window.

After the second front of rifle fire opens up from above, Cal looks for his best option to escape the steel cage he is trapped inside. He decides against climbing out the way Matt went; he doesn't want to interfere and climb into the middle of the ongoing gunfight. Instead, he looks toward the car's windscreen.

Potholed and cracked, the windscreen still manages to cling onto its frame, haunting Cal. He braces his back and slams the bottom of his foot into the edge of the windscreen with a crunch. The first blow dislodges a section of the windscreen. He kicks again at another area. This time the glass peels away from its glued fixings, falling away to land on the concrete, where it completely shatters with a loud crash.

The smell of cordite wafts into the interior on the breeze through the open front of the car. Cal's shock is instant when he looks through it, into the street beyond. Dark figures dart between contorted fallen bodies in the street and they are aiming at the new opening. They are coming for Cal.

He curses himself for not picking up his rifle before he started kicking at the windscreen. A schoolboy error, one that could cost him dearly. Cassie again calls out his name as he scrambles to pick up the weapon from where it has landed amongst shattered glass. *Give me a break, Cassie!* his mind demands, as he brings the rifle up. Shoving the rifle out front, he opens fire without a thought about aiming the weapon.

Hoping the burst of fire has hit something, Cal moves to get into a more suitable position. Creatures close in, he sees, as he crouches down to get a better view. He must fire again even before he is settled, releasing another burst of bullets. This burst is more targeted and at least some of the bullets hit the attacking creatures. None of them are head shots, though. The bullets buy him a small amount of time at best.

Finally getting himself into a firing position of sorts, Cal urgently aims at the nearest threat. Now he joins the fight properly. He fires three bullets at the closest hateful creature, a young female beast. The third bullet blasts the side of its head off and it tumbles to the ground. He has no time to lament the poor youngster who, only a short while ago, must have been excited at attending the concert at the arena.

Cal shoots again, the rifle's crack stinging his ears in the enclosed space he squats in. After two more creatures fall under his fire in quick succession, he lowers the rifle slightly. No more targets present themselves as he peers out and, above him, the constant sound of gunfire has reduced to occasional small bursts. *It's time to move*, he urges himself, hesitantly.

Cal thought he would be relieved to leave the mangled wreckage of the car when it is time to step and squeeze his way through the gap where the windshield once was. But he finds himself reluctant to leave. Leaving the relative safety of the enclosure fills him with dread. At least there are steel walls hiding and protecting him on most sides inside. He will be exposed when he is out in the open. Fair game for the hungry enemy.

Windshield glass scrapes and crunches under his feet as he climbs out. His eyes are wide, his head turning, searching for the next attack. Cal fits through the gap relatively easily and positions himself near the front end of the car, using it to cover his back as he acclimatises to being back out in the open. His eyes flick from side to side, checking, his heart jumping at every shadow.

Cal's heart nearly stops when Matt suddenly lands on the ground next to him, giving Cal no warning that he was leaving his perch on the driver's door.

"There will be more coming," he tells Cal, who nearly gives Matt a round of 'Fucks' for scaring him to death.

"No shit," Cal settles for.

"We need to find shelter, or find a way out of here," Matt gasps.

Cal ignores his suggestion for now and moves round behind his rifle to find Cassie.

"Help me down," she orders Cal. "I don't want to turn my ankle in these shoes," she adds, as Cal offers her his hand.

As soon as Cassie's feet hit the ground her rifle is back up in a defensive position. Blood runs down the side of her face and her cheek is bruised. Neither of the injuries look serious and she pays them no attention. Cal wonders if his face looks as beaten up. It sure feels like it, as does his body.

"What's the plan?" she asks, as she ejects the magazine from her rifle and checks it before pushing it back home.

"I'm going for my wife. Their block is just around the corner," Cal replies. "You and Matt should evacuate the area."

"What? You'd leave me to it, would you, if it was me? Bullshit, you would," Cassie challenges. "Let's get it done. Lead the way, Detective."

"We're carrying on," Cal tells Matt. "You find a way out."

"No chance. I'm with you," Matt insists, moving to Cal's side, his lip split and bleeding.

There's no time to argue the toss. They need to get off the street, not stand around having a debate.

"Okay, thanks," Cal says, as he leads them off, his rifle up, out in front.

A speeding car makes them all stop and turn, its headlights catching them crossing the road. The car doesn't slow down. Instead, it races past them in the direction of the trunk road out of the area. Two petrified occupants pay them no more than a glance as they motor past, hoping that they aren't shot at as they go. The car is a reminder that the public are still in the area. Some have already left, some will

246

be cowering in their homes, whilst others will be in the process of leaving. As if to prove the point, another car emerges from an underground car park, its engine over-revving. The driver continues labouring the engine as the car heads in the same direction as the other one.

"Keep moving," Cassie encourages.

Cal doesn't need telling twice. Distant gunfire is a constant reminder that they aren't on a sightseeing tour.

On the other side of the road, they stay close to the buildings, using them for cover. They need to move down further before they turn right to reach the apartment block they are heading for and every step they take brings them closer to the sound of gunfire, and danger.

"Contact, ten o'clock!" Matt shouts, like a professional soldier.

Cal's eyes dart, looking for the threat, and it takes him a second to see the movement in the shadows ahead, on his left. The figures sway unpredictably as they move forward, the movement inhuman. There is no confusing the figures with ordinary members of the public.

Matt's call may have sounded professional, but it does them no favours. His voice carries on the breeze, all the way over to the creatures. The words unnecessarily give away their position.

There is no hesitation. As soon as Matt's call carries across to them, the beasts act. By now familiar, but dreaded, high-pitched screeches sound out in reply to Matt, who glances at Cal and Cassie in regret and fear.

"We need to find cover!" Cassie barks. "Somewhere we can defend!"

Cal is already searching for any cover on offer. The glass buildings lining the streets offer none and he can't even see a doorway or side street that might lead to shelter. All he sees is walls of glass and steel.

"Run!" Cassie shouts in the instant before her rifle blazes into life to lay down some covering fire.

Cal follows Cassie's lead and fires a burst of bullets at the oncoming creatures. He sees at least six beasts as he pulls in his rifle and sets off, running. Matt is in front of Cal and Cassie is just in front of him. They need to turn right at the next junction.

"Go right!" Cal shouts at Matt.

Cal shoots a look at the pack of beasts that are trailing them. The pack is closing fast, coming at them from their left flank. A car's engine sounds moments before headlights turn onto the road in front of them. It is another evacuating car, which guns its engine as it straightens up onto the road.

Don't stop or turn, Cal begs, hoping that the car will divert their hunters, giving them a chance to escape. The car carries on toward them, picking up speed as it travels. Matt reaches the turning point as the car blares its horn. Cal doesn't know whether the driver sounds the horn to distract the pack of zombified creatures, or to genuinely alert the figures in the road that they are coming so they can get out of the way. He realises that whoever is driving will probably have no inkling that the figures are ferocious monsters. How would they know? All they see are people in the road.

Whatever the driver thinks, they don't slow down. Swerving onto the other side of the road, the car steams past, driving around the pack of creatures, which take no notice of the vehicle. The car gradually disappears in the distance as quickly as it had appeared, and any hopes Cal had of a diversion fade just as fast.

Cal approaches the corner, his legs burning, his heart racing. He is running out of time; he can feel it. Any second now his race will be run and he will be taken down, swamped by bloodthirsty creatures and ripped to shreds.

Gunfire blasts out from in front of Cal and bullets cut through the air, whizzing past his head. Matt, taking cover behind the corner of the building, his rifle poking out, fires again. Thuds intersect the sound of gunfire as bullets hit the creatures behind Cal. Cassie disappears around the corner in front of him as bullets continue to fly past.

Trusting in Matt's accuracy, Cal reaches the corner and speeds round it. Cassie is already turning to open fire with Matt, and Cal immediately slams on the brakes to also bring his weapon to bear. He sees crumpled bodies already on the ground and only three creatures still on their feet, closing in. He opens fire the second he has a beast in his sights and, one by one, they fall until the gunfire ceases.

"Where now?" Cassie asks, exasperatedly.

"We're nearly there. The entrance to the building is along this road," Cal answers, feeling guilt for putting Cassie and Matt in danger.

"Thank God," Cassie replies, panting.

"Thanks, Matt, nice shooting," Cal says, looking at the young officer, who looks pleased with himself.

"Yes, nice shooting, kid," Cassie agrees, her sentence sounding as if has been stolen from a Western movie.

Cal sees Matt's face light up even more as a result of Cassie's praise. The young officer even blushes. However, Cal doesn't see the shadow bearing down on them until it's too late.

He sees the movement out of the corner of his eye while he is still looking at Matt. Panic rushes through Cal as his head turns toward the shadow, his fear rising when he registers the evil features of the beast, which has appeared from out of nowhere. In reflex, his arms react and his rifle swings up and around, his body twisting to catch up. Matt and Cassie don't see the danger, only the terror on Cal's face.

Both see that something is terribly wrong and their heads turn in slow motion in the direction Cal is trying to aim his rifle. If Cal was holding his sidearm in his hand it would be up and firing in a flash. The rifle is bulky to use, though. It requires two hands, and that delays Cal's reactions.

Racing across the road from the opposite direction to that of the pack of creatures they have just eliminated, this beast is a large male, wearing jeans and a bloodstained white T-shirt. Its grey leathery skin is slashed and battered with festering wounds. Blood-matted, shoulder-length hair streaks back from its head in the wind as it careers across the ground. The creature's speed is terrifying, and it appears unstoppable.

Cal's panic hinders his urgency and he fumbles to bring the rifle into a shooting position. Just as he is getting close to achieving something like an aim, the beast launches itself into the air, on a collision course with Matt.

His defences breached, Cal can only watch as the creature slams into Matt with terrific force. The colossal energy of the hit lifts Matt off his feet, stunning him instantly. He has no idea what is happening. Directly behind the two airborne bodies stands a building with a glass-and-steel façade.

Cal flinches uncontrollably when Matt's back crunches into a tall wall of glass at almighty speed. The pane of glass instantly disintegrates, shattering into a million pieces. Matt and the creature disappear into the building as the glass comes crashing down behind them.

Sickness fills Cal's stomach. He is stunned, in total shock. In front of him, Cassie gawps wide-eyed, in utter disbelief. Neither of them moves for an inordinate amount of time, their shock paralysing them.

Shards of glass flow over their feet until, finally, they snap out of their shock. Cal slips on the glass but then pushes himself forward into action. He stumbles but saves himself from falling to rush into the building after Matt, with Cassie hastily following him inside, her head in turmoil.

Matt is spreadeagled on the marbled floor of the building, his head angled to the right. The young officer's face stares up into oblivion, his mouth gaping open, lifeless. Only the beast clinging to him moves. Pinning Matt to the ground, the creature's head bobs around Matt's neck area in a chomping motion.

"No!" Cal screams uncontrollably, knowing Matt's life has expired.

Gunfire blasts from next to Cal. Bullets thud into the back of the creature, trailing up until they slam into the back of its head. Cassie doesn't stop firing. Bullets rip into the creature's skull, sending blood spraying over the white marble floor. The beast's skull disintegrates in a mush of brain, blood and bone. Only when her weapon clicks empty does the onslaught end. Even then, Cassie's finger remains in position, pulling on the rifle's trigger. She doesn't move, just stands like a statue, staring down.

Silence envelops Cal and Cassie. Neither of them can bring themselves to speak, never mind move. They just keep staring at the horrifically gruesome sight laid out before them.

Time stops for both as their minds reel in shocked sadness. Cal's guilt is all-encompassing. He should never have allowed Matt to come here, nor Cassie for that matter. Will she be the next to die a hideous death because of his decisions and responsibilities? Kim is his wife, his responsibility. She was nothing to Matt and she is nothing to

Cassie. Matt is dead because Cal agreed to let him come along on his rescue mission. This is nothing to do with the investigation, despite what Cassie said. This is personal for him and he has put others in danger for his own selfish reasons.

Admit it, Cal shouts at himself. *You were happy they came with you. You wanted their help. You didn't want to face this alone and now look what's happened! You selfish bastard!*

Blood spurts out of Matt's mouth and splatters onto the floor. Another cough sends more red liquid into the air. *Is he still alive?* Cal questions, through his despair. *Will he be let off the hook? Is my guilt to be pardoned?*

Cassie ejects the empty magazine from her rifle, bringing Cal back to reality. There is no salvation in exchange for his guilt. A chilling groan follows the blood out of Matt's mouth to confirm Cal's continued suffering. He is not alive. He is infected and turning into one of the undead. A fate worse than death.

Cal knows what he must do. He steps in front of Cassie. His selfishness caused Matt's suffering. He cannot allow Cassie the trauma of putting an end to the suffering. She is not to blame for this situation, he is, and it must be he who suffers this trauma. He will carry this extra guilt.

Reluctantly, Cal raises his rifle. He aims carefully, ensuring that Matt's end will be instant. There will be no more turmoil for this brave young police officer. Cal is numb as his rifle releases its bullet. The shot enters Matt's head straight through his forehead and Cal turns away immediately, not wanting to see more of Matt's blood spilled than he must. He allows himself that small solace.

Chapter 20

Cassie watches Cal as he turns his back on the dreadful scene and sees that he is on the edge of despair. He looks broken, his guilt threatening to consume him.

"This isn't your fault," Cassie tells him.

"Whose is it then? Matt was here for me, and so are you," Cal responds, drearily.

"Matt made his own decision, and so did I," Cassie insists. "You're not responsible for these monsters. We're just doing our best to deal with them."

"We're not here to deal with them. We're here because of me. She's my wife. I don't think Matt even knew her name, and now he's dead," Cal replies.

"He's dead because someone decided to release a deadly virus. He's dead because he wanted to make a difference, just as we do. You can't blame yourself, Cal," Cassie insists again.

Cal doesn't reply to Cassie. He just stands dejected, even as evil sounds rise in the streets outside.

"We must carry on or his death will be for nothing," Cassie continues. "Let's get your wife and get out of here.

253

Then we can concentrate on finding the bastards behind this barbarity," Cassie seethes.

Cal looks at Cassie, her expletive hammering home her determination.

"Are you ready?" she asks. "We've got to move. They're out there and all this noise will be like a magnet to them."

As if on cue, an ominous screech cries out from beyond the hole in the side of the building they are standing in. Glass scrapes under their feet when they turn to look, street lights flicker and shadows move. Something is approaching and neither Cal nor Cassie wants to wait around to greet it.

Cal looks urgently around the building they find themselves inside. He hadn't realised the size of the interior; it could almost be described as cavernous. A large company logo mounted on a large marble wall across from them gives no indication as to what type of business the company occupying the building is involved with. Cal doesn't care, he only looks to see if they can move through the building to get closer to their goal.

"This way," Cal tells Cassie as he sets off, deciding to stay off the streets, at least for now.

"Is this your wife's building?" Cassie asks, confused, as she jogs to follow Cal.

"No," he replies. "It's the building opposite. I think it's best if we keep off the street for as long as possible."

Cassie doesn't argue with Cal's logic, despite her reservations. The undead will surely follow the sound of smashing glass and enter the building. How are they going to exit the building when the time comes? Might they become trapped inside with bloodthirsty creatures? On the other hand, the streets outside are far from safe.

Cal leads them further along the building and follows the wall of glass on their left-hand side. Their footsteps echo as they run, no matter how light on their feet they try to be. Cassie's steps echo loudest, every click of her heels making them wince.

Cal sees the entrance to Kim's building approach through the glass, on the other side of the road. As he suspected, the entrance to that building is opposite the entrance to this one, which they are rapidly nearing.

He plans to phone Kim when they are in position and tell her to get ready to buzz them into her building. When she's ready, they will shoot out another piece of glass to exit this building and run across the street. He hasn't worked out how they will leave the area yet, though. Neither Kim nor her sister has a car.

Just as Cal settles on the first part of his plan, the atrocious sound of death reverberates above them.

"They're inside," Cassie says, fearfully, "and they've seen us!"

Cal stops adjacent to the building's locked entrance. He knows the doors will be locked without having to try them. Over the road is the entrance to Kim's building. Its doors, as expected, are shut. He needs to phone Kim.

"Cal, they're coming. What's the plan?" Cassie asks, urgently.

Cal puts his phone to his ear as he looks in trepidation back to where they entered the building. *Answer the fucking phone, Kim*, Cal demands in his head when he sees numerous figures chasing toward them.

"Cal!" Cassie exclaims.

"Hello," Kim answers.

"Get ready to buzz us in." Cal cuts her off. "We're being chased. Get ready now!"

He doesn't wait for an answer from Kim but shoves his phone away as another deathly scream rings out and raises his rifle. *At least the street appears clear*, Cal thinks, as he pulls the rifle's trigger.

Bullets slam into the large glass entrance door. Cal prepares to run as soon as the glass shatters to the ground. Cassie is primed to move next to him, but her rifle and focus are pointing toward the oncoming horde of the undead. Cal sees the glass shatter into a web of small shards, but it doesn't fall. He fires again. Bullets smash into the shattered glass, breaking through to leave small holes in it, but still it remains in place.

Cassie opens fire next to him at the same moment that his rifle clicks empty. *Shit*, he thinks, *what now?* The horrendous memory of Matt and the large beast crashing through the pane of glass flashes through his mind. Before he can think again, he runs straight at the shattered glass in front of him.

Cal feels his rifle smash into the glass. He feels his fists break through. Pain cuts across his hands as he bursts out into the street, glass raining down on top of him, and onto the surrounding area.

Shards of glass trickle inside his clothes and down the back of his neck. He is stunned for a moment. He feels the glass in his hair and on his face. Cal is afraid to open his eyes, despite the urgency of their predicament.

"Fucking move," Cassie's voice sounds in his ear, as a hand grabs his arm.

Cal prises his eyes open as his legs are forced into action by Cassie's pull. There is a crashing sound behind as Cal decides that his eyes are clear and they sprint across the road. He assumes that a creature or creatures have slid over across the shards of glass. That may just give them the valuable seconds they need, Cal hopes.

Cal is only brought to a halt by hitting the apartment building opposite, directly in front of the panel of call buttons. Cassie spins while she waits for Cal to gain them entry into the building. She opens fire immediately, aiming at the creatures emerging through the building's shattered entrance.

"Cal!" she shouts again, as more beasts appear on the street. She won't be able to keep them at bay for long.

A second later, which feels like an eternity, Cassie hears a loud buzzing noise. She doesn't stop firing until Cal taps her on the shoulder. Turning to see Cal holding the entry door open, she bolts for its refuge.

Inside, Cal helps pull the spring-loaded door shut. He watches the grotesque creatures, freed from the onslaught of bullets, race across toward the glass door.

"Take cover," Cal shouts the moment the lock clicks into action.

Cassie is already using the thin alcove in front of the lift door for cover and she presses the call button as soon as she arrives at the stainless-steel door. Cassie has no more idea than Cal whether the glass front of the building will repel the bombardment of the undead or whether it will shatter, leaving them completely exposed.

Cassie watches the attack approach down the sights of her rifle. Cal races past her to take up a position while they wait for the stainless-steel door to open and for the lift to whisk them away. Her finger twitches over the rifle's trigger, ready to squeeze their defences into action.

The first beast arrives at the glass but doesn't slam into it in a rage. Instead, it slows its approach, as do the other members of the pack behind. They almost become like confused pedestrians on the street. One after the other they look around in frustrated bewilderment, searching for their prey, which seems to have disappeared into thin air.

Cassie breathes a sigh of relief, whilst not letting her guard down. She keeps her rifle aimed at the closest creature through the glass right up until the door next to her slides open with a ping. Only then does she roll herself from her covering position and into the refuge of the steel box.

"Never a dull moment with you is there, Detective?" Cassie says, trying to lighten the mood as they are transported upwards.

"It does seem that way, I must admit," Cal replies.

"Something tells me this is going to get worse, Cal. Please don't try to carry everything on your shoulders. All we can do is our best. We are not responsible for this horror show," Cassie reasons.

"I know. It doesn't make it any easier though," Cal replies.

"This is far from easy," Cassie sighs.

"Thanks, Cassie, for your help," Cal says, looking at his new partner. "You have been so impressive today."

"Oh stop it, Detective. You'll make me blush," Cassie smiles. "Besides, you're no slouch yourself," she adds.

A ping accompanies their arrival on Kim's floor. Cal lets Cassie off first and he hears Kim's voice before he exits.

"Cal?" Kim asks, uncontrollably, the moment Cassie appears.

Cal isn't surprised by how happy he is to hear Kim's voice, especially after all that has happened since he last saw his wife. He rushes after Cassie and, as soon as he appears, he sees Kim running down the corridor from her sister's apartment.

Cassie clears out of the way to allow Kim to race past her and into Cal's arms. Cal is somewhat taken aback by surprise by Kim's show of affection. It has been some time since she allowed him anywhere near her. However, he doesn't allow himself to get overexcited. *This is more about the dire situation than anything else*, he tells himself.

Cal only allows himself to savour Kim's hug of relief for a few seconds before he pulls away to look at his wife for a moment. Her eyes are wet and when she has a proper look at him, the look on her face changes to one of concern.

"You're bleeding, Cal, and your face is bruised. What's been going on?" Kim asks, her hand taking hold of his.

"It's a long story," Cal tells her. "I'm okay, don't worry."

"Is that a machine gun?" Kim asks, looking at Cal's other hand.

"Come on. Let's get inside. We need a drink," Cal says, ignoring Kim's question.

"Who's your friend?" Kim asks, turning to Cassie.

"Oh, sorry. This is Agent Cassie Sutton. We have been working together today," Cal answers. "Cassie, this is my wife, Kim."

Cassie forces a weary smile at Kim, who nods a greeting in return. Cassie is unsurprisingly looking quite dishevelled, a far cry from the immaculate appearance she sported when Cal met her only a short time ago. He can only imagine how rough he looks right now, with cuts and bruises and glass in his hair and down his back.

"Come on, let's get you two cleaned up," Kim says, turning to lead them down the corridor.

Cal sees Lauren, Kim's older sister, waiting for them just outside her apartment. He always used to have a good relationship with Kim's sister but recently things have become quite frosty between them.

"Hello, Lauren," Cal says, as he follows Kim into the apartment.

"Hi, Cal," she replies, surprisingly putting her hand on his back as he passes her.

She is pleased to see me, Cal thinks. The two sisters must have been going out of their minds holed up in the apartment with all hell breaking loose around them.

Cal is familiar with Lauren's home. He and Kim often visited when they were together. They helped Lauren move in when she bought the apartment and they often stayed over after a night out in the city.

Cal isn't familiar with the middle-aged, handsome man who is waiting inside the apartment, though, and he looks at the man with suspicion for a second.

"You must be Cal," the man says, approaching. "I'm Alex. I live in the apartment opposite. Kim has told me all about you."

"Has she indeed?" Cal replies, suspiciously, wondering if this man has been offering his shoulder for his pregnant wife to cry on.

"We haven't time for pleasantries," Cassie announces. "We need to arrange transport out of the area!"

"Didn't you come in a car?" Kim questions.

"We had an accident. The car is out of use," Cal replies, simply.

"I'm going to leave you to it," Alex interjects. "Donald will be waiting for me. He's quite worried."

"Donald?" Cal questions.

"My partner," Alex replies.

"I see," Cal says with some relief as he realises that the man is probably not a threat regarding Kim.

"Have you any advice for us?" Alex asks Cal.

"Do you have a car?" Cal asks.

"Yes. Both Donald and I do. They're in the underground lot. Why?" Alex answers.

"Then, if I were you, I'd use them to leave this area as soon as you can. Things are going to get worse around here, but be careful on the roads," Cal advises.

"I see," Alex says, with a worried expression. "I'd better go and speak to Donald."

With that, Alex turns to leave. Although it may be selfish, Cal is pleased to see him go. He is one less person to worry about.

"Do you want to freshen up?" Kim asks Cassie.

"Later," she replies, abruptly, not looking up from her phone.

Kim turns back to Cal like a scolded cat. Cal gives her a reassuring smile, knowing how temperamental Kim can be, especially in her current condition.

"She's rather rude," Lauren says, quietly, facing Cal and Kim.

"No, she's not, Lauren," Cal replies, angrily. "You have no idea what we've just been through and I expect she is trying to arrange transport out of here for us, unless you'd prefer to stay put."

"Alright, Cal. I'm sorry," Lauren says, wounded. "I didn't know."

Cal sighs, before apologising to Lauren himself for his reaction. She smiles at Cal and offers to get him a drink.

"What do you want to drink, Cassie?" Cal asks.

"Coffee, please. Milk and a shot of whisky if you have some. If not, one sugar," Cassie states.

"Same for me please, Lauren," Cal says.

"Two Irish coffees coming right up," Lauren replies with raised eyebrows, as she heads off to the kitchen.

"Are you trying to arrange transport?" Cal asks Cassie.

"I'm trying. But there's a backlog," Cassie replies, frustratedly.

Cal decides to leave her to it and wanders over to the window to see what's happening outside. Gunfire vibrates off the windowpane and, in the distance, helicopters are still throwing down tracer fire onto the ground below. Behind the aircraft, Cal sees the silhouette of the arena complex, which has become a battlefield. He still finds it hard to get his head around what is happening and, if he thinks about it too much, he believes his head might explode.

The apartment is on the eighth floor. Cal diverts his eyes downwards to the surrounding streets to see the latest situation as best he can from the height he is at.

"What can you see?" Kim asks, from beside Cal.

"Figures are moving through the streets down there. More than when we arrived, from what I can see," Cal replies.

"Figures?" Kim questions.

"Do you really want to know, Kim?" Cal replies.

"I think I have to know," Kim answers. "I need to know what we're up against."

"They're ferocious monsters, Kim. Zombies that are only after one thing," Cal tells her.

"Blood?" Kim asks.

"I'm afraid so, and they'll stop at nothing," Cal replies, as Kim takes hold of his hand.

Cal struggles to remember when he last held hands with his wife and a warm fuzzy feeling rises inside him. He wonders if it feels the same for Kim or whether she is just frightened and needs reassurance.

"How has this happened?" Kim asks.

"That's what we're trying to find out, but they seem to be one step ahead of us and, whoever they are, they are ruthless," Cal answers.

"I'm sorry about Mike, Cal. I really am. I know how much he meant to you. He was a lovely man. I'm going to miss him too." Kim squeezes Cal's hand.

"I can't think about that right now," Cal replies, his warm fuzzy feeling extinguished.

Cal releases Kim's hand and turns to Cassie, just as Lauren arrives with steaming mugs.

"Any luck, Cassie?" he asks.

"In a word, no," Cassie replies in frustration. "I can't get hold of Director Khan, or anyone else in authority. My other contacts aren't helping much either. Everyone's going out of their minds."

"So, what do we do?" Cal asks. "We can't just sit here and wait for things to deteriorate."

"I'm open to suggestions," Cassie replies, looking up from her phone.

"Is it safe to drive out?" Lauren asks.

"I wouldn't call it safe, but we don't have a car in any case," Cal replies.

"Alex and Donald have two cars. I'm sure they will lend us one," Lauren suggests.

Cal and Cassie look at each other, considering the suggestion.

"It's an option," Cassie says, shrugging her shoulders.

"Our only option by the look of it," Cal replies.

Neither Cassie nor Cal is overjoyed by the thought of another dangerous and traumatic car journey, but Cassie isn't getting anywhere with arranging another option and so Lauren takes Cal to see Alex. A short time later they arrive back in Lauren's apartment, with Cal holding a set of car keys.

"They've decided to stay here and ride it out," Lauren tells Kim and Cassie, slightly distressed.

"Really?" Kim says. "Are they sure?"

"Cal tried to convince them to leave. He said they could follow us out, but they weren't interested," Lauren replies. "Donald was insistent."

"It's their decision," Cassie states, as a matter of fact. "Are you two ready to leave?"

"As ready as we'll ever be," Kim replies.

"Where are we going?" Lauren asks.

"Cal and I have work to do," Cassie responds.

"We can go to Dad's," Kim suggests.

"I'll phone him to warn him we're coming," Lauren replies.

Cal is happy that Kim will be at her father's. He lives in the suburbs of the city and away from the trouble, at least for now. Lauren makes her call and then she and Kim gather the belongings they are taking with them. Needless to say, they haven't packed light but this is one time when Cal won't be able to help with hauling the luggage. He will need both hands for his rifle.

Chapter 21

In the event, Cal finds himself helping Kim with her luggage, at least as far as the lift. They are cramped on the ride down and Cassie looks less than impressed at being squashed up against the door. Her position hinders her from checking her rifle again, but she manages it, and so does Cal. They have no idea what will be waiting for them in the underground parking lot.

Cal looks at Cassie, her beaten and bruised face a study of total concentration, and he wonders what she actually thinks about tagging along with him on this rescue mission. She has been through the wringer for him, and that's something that Cal won't forget easily.

They glide to a stop at the parking level. The door slides open on Cassie's side and she brings her rifle down as soon as bright fluorescent light floods into the lift. As Cal passes the door, he does the same. He is conscious of Kim watching him wield his weapon. She is used to seeing his sidearm, but she has never seen him aim it in anger, never mind an automatic rifle. He wonders if she is impressed by his performance. He can't help it; he's only a man after all.

"Stay here and hold the door," Cal orders Kim and Lauren. "We'll bring the car to you."

"Be careful," Kim whispers, as Cal steps out.

Cassie is already out and her rifle moves through the air, following her eyes, which are on stalks looking for danger. Cal pauses at her side to help her to search. The array of parked cars in front of them could be hiding anything.

"Let's move," Cassie finally says, satisfied that nothing is moving.

"This way," Cal tells her.

Alex gave him clear instructions about where his car is parked. Painted yellow sequential numbers in front of each parking space confirm the direction they are heading in. Cal clocks the exit ramp as they deliberately step deeper into the car park. The exit ramp is open to the elements, with no more than a single, long, thin, horizontal barrier to protect the car park from unwanted visitors. Cal is surprised that the area isn't secured more tightly. The barrier wouldn't stop a car thief and certainly wouldn't deter the undead if they decided to wander down the ramp, if they haven't already.

Cal's anxiety heightens upon seeing the exposed exit and he urgently searches for the red paint of the classic BMW they are looking for.

"There," Cassie says, as she changes direction to move down in between cars.

Releasing one of his hands from his rifle, Cal fishes the keys out of his pocket and quickly presses the old-style alarm button attached to the key ring. Flashing orange lights and a beeping sound confirm that it is the right car. Cassie rushes to the passenger side and Cal turns for the driver's door. The central locking releases the doors and they both pull in their rifles so that they can get inside.

"I thought you said it was a classic BMW?" Cassie says, as Cal inserts the key into the ignition.

"That's how Alex described it," Cal replies, as he turns the key.

"Delusions of grandeur," Cassie scoffs, as the engine turns over.

"Beggars can't be choosers," Cal retorts, as the engine fails to start.

"Try it again, for fuck's sake," Cassie snarls.

"What do you think I'm doing?" Cal insists, turning the key.

Again, the starter motor whirls loudly and, this time, the engine coughs once before dying.

"We've got movement at the ramp," Cassie says, urgently.

"Come on, you fucker," Cal encourages, and turns the key.

The engine chugs reluctantly before finally firing into life. Cal puts the car straight into 'Drive' and hits the accelerator. He turns right, staying away from the exit ramp in the hope that the creatures up there may pass it by. Ignoring a left turn, Cal instead powers down to the end and swings around to point the car in the direction of Kim and Lauren.

Cal sees Kim's head poking out of the lift just as he applies the brakes to stop directly outside it and Cassie is out of the car the instant it stops. She takes up a covering position at the front of the car. Cal jumps out and runs around the rear of the car to help put the luggage in the back.

"Quickly!" Cal tells an apprehensive Kim and Lauren, neither woman keen to leave the relative safety of the steel box that could whip them up and away to safety at the touch of a button.

Cal hauls two travel cases over to the back of the car and throws them in. He turns to see Kim leading Lauren out of the lift, both carrying oversized hand luggage and both displaying fearful expressions.

Without warning, gunfire erupts from Cassie's rifle. The sound of rapid fire blasts into the car park, and has nowhere to escape. Kim ducks in reflex at the sudden assault of noise, which ricochets off the low ceiling and closed-in walls. Lauren screams in terror and falls to the ground completely, her arms dropping her luggage as they move to protect her head.

Ducking as well, Cal glances to see shadowy figures moving straight ahead of them at the bottom of the exit ramp. Seeing his pregnant wife in such close proximity to the horrific creatures that have slaughtered so many, including Mike, Arnold and now Matt, fills Cal with raw terror.

"Get in the car, Kim!" Cal shouts in a panic, grabbing her arm to direct her onto the back seat. Kim drops whatever she is carrying and jumps inside the car. As he turns, Cal grabs Kim's stuff and throws it into the back of the car behind her. He then takes hold of Lauren, who is still cowering on the ground.

"Cal, we need to get out of here!" Cassie shouts in between blasts of gunfire.

More gunfire blasts out as soon as Cassie has shouted. Cal dives down to grab Lauren, her head buried in her arms. He grabs the closest arm whilst bellowing at her to get up, but she has frozen, and Cal cannot move her.

"Lauren, get in the car with me," Kim shouts from the back seat. "Quickly. Then we can leave."

Finally, Cal feels Lauren's weight shift and her arms begin to move. He pulls her to her feet and bundles her in next to Kim. He throws her luggage into the rear of the car and slams the door shut.

Cassie keeps firing as Cal runs back and jumps in behind the wheel. The engine is still running, but he revs it just to make sure.

"Let's go, Cassie!" Cal shouts urgently, as he sees ominous figures massing in front of them.

Cassie releases one last volley of bullets before swivelling toward the passenger door. Cal is accelerating forward even before the door slams shut. Cassie, breathing hard, aims her rifle at the windscreen. She is taking no chances, the weapon held out in front of her, ready to explode into action.

There are so many figures down by the exit ramp. Some bodies are on the ground, thanks to Cassie's covering fire, but more are on their feet, heading directly toward them. Ploughing into so many creatures head-on would be carnage, and probably not just for the enemy. Snarling beasts would fly over the front of the car and crash through the windscreen, still baying for blood.

"Turn left!" Cassie orders.

Cal is already preparing to turn. Distressed noises emanate from the two women behind him as Cal yanks the steering wheel hard left. He'd rather take a joyride around the car park for a minute or two if it means that the exit will clear. Hopefully, the creatures will follow the sound of the car's engine and spread out, away from the exit ramp. Hopefully.

Rubber squeals against concrete. Cal isn't afraid to over-rev the car's engine. Right now, noise is his ally, calling the undead deeper into the car park so as to clear their exit.

"What do you think?" Cal asks Cassie, stopping when they reach the far side of the car park. "Shall we go for it?"

Cassie sits up in her seat, looking through the car's windows to search the brightly lit cavern.

"I can't see any of them, but we can't drive around here all night. Let's give it a go," Cassie agrees.

"Sound the horn!" Kim insists from behind.

Cal does exactly that for a few seconds, impressed by Kim's idea. Perhaps she is already beginning to understand the threat.

"Ready?" Cal asks, taking his hand off the horn.

Cassie nods nervously, her knuckles whitening on the grip of the rifle. The car rolls forward, Cal gently bringing it up to a reasonable speed. He doesn't gun it; stealth is their friend now. He keeps a steady speed and doesn't drive too fast. An accident now would be a disaster.

An attack could come from anywhere at any time. Cal's eyes search desperately for the first signs of one, knowing an attack is inevitable.

"Keep your eyes peeled. They're coming," Cassie says, reading Cal's mind.

Just as Cassie speaks, Cal sees movement from the right. He feels panic, but he doesn't answer, forcing the panic down. Cassie's rifle is on the threat immediately.

The creature stumbles out from behind parked cars a few metres ahead of them. The male beast seems confused. It shuffles around aimlessly, not sure which way to turn. Cassie lines up her rifle on the beast. Cal is sure she is going to shoot at the creature right through the windshield.

"Don't fire," Cal says urgently, and presses the car's accelerator.

He closes in on the creature fast, the beast still in a world of its own. Cal doesn't mean to hit the creature, he means to slide by it, but the gap between it and the parked cars is too small. The front quarter of the BMW clips the beast hard, sending it flying back toward the cars it

271

appeared from. A deathly screech vibrates into the car as the creature crashes into the closest parked car in a spin. Cal doesn't check the damage in his rear-view mirror. His concentration is fixed forward, knowing there will soon be more obstacles to overcome.

"Nice shooting," Cassie congratulates, sarcastically, from beside Cal.

"Thanks, I think," Cal replies, as he straightens the car up.

An exit sign mounted overhead ensures Cal doesn't become lost in the maze of cars. He takes the next right to follow the sign, the tension inside the car building as they draw nearer to the exit ramp, which is still out of sight.

Almost as soon as the turn is made something thuds into the back of the car, hitting the door where Lauren is sitting. She takes a sharp intake of breath in fright, but the thud is short-lived as the car moves forward. Cal flicks his eyes to the mirror and sees a fallen figure in the middle of the lane behind.

In that split second, Cal misses a creature that launches itself at them from out of nowhere, this time at the front of the car. The beast lands on the front of the car, right next to the windscreen, directly in front of Cassie. The female creature's body becomes lodged over the windscreen wipers, its legs hanging down over the side. Cassie's face is inches away from the beast's, separated only by glass. Fearsome eyes lock onto Cassie and the creature's lips prise apart to bare its gruesome teeth. It is of no concern to the tormented female creature that it is being carried along by the car, or that its legs hang precariously down the side of the bodywork. Only one thing is of concern to this wretch, and that is to feed.

Cassie appears stunned for a moment. She doesn't react to the bloodthirsty passenger right in front of her.

Groans of horror sound from the back seat as the two women sitting there come face to face with malevolent evil for the first time, their disgust taking any words of terror away from their lips.

Cal recoils as far away from the beast as he can, despite the protection of the windscreen. Even through his fear he sees an opportunity approaching and carefully eases the car over to the right, increasing his speed marginally.

Suddenly, the beast's terrifying face races away from the windscreen as the lower half of its body smashes into the concrete pillar Cal is aiming for. The creature pivots from the force of the blow, its eyes not leaving Cassie's for a second, not even when the side of the car crushes its body between it and the immovable concrete pillar.

In an instant, the creature is pulverised. Dark-red blood bursts out of its body like water from a balloon to spray across the windscreen and down the side of the car. The beast's eyes still search for Cassie in the second before its head becomes trapped between the car and the blood-soaked pillar. The head bangs against the side of the car before a sickening crunch sounds as it pops like a crushed melon.

Cal sees the creature's face mash as its brains erupt out of the top of its burst-open skull. Sickened by the horrific display, he belatedly diverts his traumatised eyes. Bile bubbles in the back of Cal's throat as he wonders how much of the hideous display Kim has seen. She has gone very quiet behind him.

Soap and water hit the windscreen to try and clear the red-stained carnage, together with the windscreen wipers. Cal keeps his hand on the washer lever as blood continues to hinder his view. The worn rubber of the washer blades struggle to remove the pieces of flesh and lumps of body innards.

"I can't see anything," Cassie's strained voice reports.

Cal doesn't answer her. He is too busy concentrating on looking out through the streaks of blood and guts. Another exit sign directs him left and then the lane leads around to the right, bringing the car directly in line with the exit ramp.

With the windscreen finally beginning to become clear of the gruesome mess, Cal's vision becomes clearer. His hands tighten on the steering wheel and Cassie sits bolt upright as the remaining challenge to reach the exit presents itself.

Ominous figures become alert in front of them as they see the car appear. At least five creatures block the car's path to the exit ramp. Their diversion around the car park has thinned the pack of undead at the exit but not dispersed it entirely. They were fooling themselves if they thought it would.

"Put your foot down and go for it!" Cassie demands.

A hand touches Cal's shoulder from behind at the moment when he decides that Cassie is right. Kim's grip tightens when Cal's foot pushes down and the car picks up speed. Her touch is electrifying and fills Cal with confidence and determination, determination to get his wife away from this horror and to reach safety.

As the car picks up speed the undead launch a counteroffensive. The creatures spring into action, rushing forward to meet the car head-on. Their resolve in the face of a speeding car dents Cal's confidence, but not his determination.

Within a second, the car hits the first beast. The car's speed is too fast to allow the creature time to react. Squeals of protest ring out as the front of the car smashes into the creature's legs and it flies up over the front of the car. Its body slides across to fall out of sight over the side.

As the car's back wheels ride over the beast and it bumps up into the air, the next creature launches itself into the air at them. Cal fights the steering wheel over the body, whilst swerving as far as possible to the side to avoid the airborne monster.

With a thud that threatens to smash the side window, the creature bounces off the side of the car but Cal clips one of the parked cars on Cassie's side. The blow knocks the car over to the right and straight into the path of another flying creature. This one hits the top of the windscreen, cracking the glass immediately. Kim's hold of Cal's shoulder wavers as the beast's body tumbles over the top of the car, thudding against its roof before falling away over the back.

Cal has no chance of reacting to the next collision and instead hits the next terrifying figure head-on with a crunch. The legs of the creature are dragged under the car until the midsection of its body is caught on the nose of the car, where it jams and remains. Trapped, the beast goes berserk, its arms flailing to try and release itself, its twisted face turning in the air in anger.

The exit ramp approaches at speed with the creature still stuck to the front of the car. Another creature is waiting at the bottom of the ramp, appearing indecisive about its next move. Behind that creature is the entry barrier, which Cal has no idea how to raise to let them out.

With no other options, Cal ploughs into the last remaining creature blocking their escape. The car crashes into the confused beast on Cassie's side and it is flung up into the air. At the periphery of his vision, Cal sees the body hit the exit ramp's wall, but he pays no attention to the creature's troubles. He has his own.

Cal keeps his foot pressed on the accelerator, aiming for the barrier. With a crash against the already cracked part of the windscreen, the barrier snaps off from its anchor, finally releasing them.

All four wheels of the BMW leave the ground as Cal powers over the crest of the ramp. He looks at the beast still stuck to the bumper of the car in the instant before the front of the car slams back down, hitting the ground hard. The beast is suddenly dislodged and disappears down, out of view. As the front wheels regain traction and the back ones return to the road, Cal turns hard to join the carriageway. Tyres screech as the back of the car comes round and something thuds beneath, between the car and the road. Nobody has any doubt about what has caused the sickening noise or the sudden jolt of the back wheels as they drive away.

"Nice driving, but watch your speed," Cassie warns. "We don't want to risk another accident."

Cassie is right and Cal heeds her advice, easing his foot back off the accelerator, despite the overwhelming compulsion to floor it. He stays at a fast pace, but not too fast.

"Thank God for that," Lauren mutters in relief.

"We aren't out of this yet. Be ready for more attacks," Cassie cautions, repositioning herself and her rifle.

To reinforce Cassie's words, a shadow comes at the car from the right at the junction ahead. On the left is the hole in the building surrounded by smashed glass where Matt lies. Cal easily swerves around the beast, turning left at the same time to take them onto the main drag leading to the trunk road out of the Arena District, the road where Matt lost control and totalled his police car, the remnants of which will be close by on the right.

Cassie fidgets in her seat and Cal eases back his speed considerably as they approach the location of the accident. He doesn't slow down so that he can rubberneck the crashed police car but because dark figures are streaming into the road just beyond the upturned car.

"What now?" Kim asks fearfully from the back seat, looking around Cal's shoulder.

"We must go left. Find another way out," Cassie says to Cal, ignoring Kim's question.

"I'm not sure there is another way. There's only one way out of this area and it's directly ahead," Cal replies.

"Cassie's right. Go left. I'm sure there's a road that will take us around and back onto this one further along," Lauren offers.

Headlights appear in Cal's rear-view mirror, approaching fast. *What's this idiot doing?* Cal thinks, as the car swerves to overtake. The driver of the mundane family car either doesn't see the horde of undead ahead or doesn't understand what they are driving toward. The car's brake lights suddenly light up as it reaches the pack of creatures blocking the road and the car's horn begins to sound.

Any hopes that the driver has that his horn would move the figures out of the road so that they could pass turn to ruins. Cal has almost come to a stop as the car is swamped by shadows, the poor souls in the car only now understanding what they are dealing with. Their understanding comes too late: shadows consume the family car and it doesn't move again.

Cal is just about to voice his regret about the scene in front of them when bright-yellow light flashes from the other side of the blocked road. A loud metallic ping resonates from the front of the BMW; something has hit their car. Cal's brain takes too long to compute what is happening and it is Cassie who brings him up to speed.

"Drive!" she demands urgently. "Go left. They're opening fire on them!"

All at once Cal understands and plants his foot to the floor. More bullets travel through the horde of undead creatures hitting the road around the car as the assault intensifies. Cal immediately understands Cassie. The battle against the undead outbreak has arrived on the streets around them.

Heavy gunfire brings blinding tracer fire flashing past with it as the sound of the barrage crashes into the air. Every bullet that doesn't hit a target in the melee of undead, or in the doomed car, is a deadly threat. Cal races to reach the road on the left before their car is ripped to shreds by the 'friendly fire'. Bullets hit the rear quarter of the car as it turns for the road and the cover that the buildings there will provide. He panics that Kim will be hit before they reach the cover but all he can do is accelerate as fast as he can to evacuate the combat zone.

With its rear fishtailing, the BMW races to relative safety. Thankfully, the car still seems to be driving as well as it was before, but there is no sound coming from the back.

"Kim, are you okay?" Cal demands. "Are you hit?"

"I don't think so," Kim replies, dazed. "No, I'm okay," she finally confirms.

"Lauren, speak to me," Cal insists.

"LAUREN!" Kim screams. "LAUREN!"

"Keep driving. I'll deal with it," Cassie orders, as she turns in her seat and climbs into the back.

Cal's head is all over the place. He tries to concentrate on driving but the awful commotion behind keeps distracting him. Cassie keeps repeating Lauren's name as she tries to assess her condition and Kim is becoming hysterical. Cal cannot help but keep glancing in his mirror.

"She's unconscious," Cassie announces. "She's been hit in the side."

Kim becomes more hysterical and Cal doesn't know whether to pull over or keep going. Pulling over will do no good, he decides. There is no help to be found on these streets, only more death and trauma. They need to leave the area and find medical assistance.

The road ahead arcs around to the right. It must circle back and rejoin the road where the battle is happening. Cal feels positive that they will emerge beyond the fighting, near the slip road onto the trunk road.

Just as the road straightens out, he sees that the way ahead is blocked yet again by another obstacle. He blinks to make sure that he isn't seeing things, but the massive military tank is still there when he opens his eyes again. The tank's long cannon is pointing straight at them, its tracks eating up the tarmac beneath it. As the BMW approaches, it suddenly brakes to a halt, its hulking body seesawing back and forth as it comes to rest.

Cal looks for a way past the monstrous vehicle, but it spans the entire width of the road, forcing him to also stop a short distance in front of it.

"Get them to move!" Kim shouts into Cal's ear, not caring what is in front of them. "We need to get to a hospital."

"She's right, Cal. We can't afford to stop," Cassie adds.

Easier said than done, Cal thinks, as he debates what to do. Before he decides, troops appear from around the side of the tank, the leading soldier looking like he might be in command of the unit. He comes straight over to the side of the car and Cal winds the window down to meet him.

"Move your vehicle to the side or turn around," the soldier demands.

"I'm Detective Chambers, City Police. We need urgent medical attention. Can you help?" Cal demands.

"No, we can't. We're on a schedule. Move to the side," the soldier growls.

"Then get your... tank to move to the side so that we can continue on our way," Cal counters.

"We haven't time for this. Move your vehicle or we will," the soldier insists.

Cassie leans through the back and across Cal, her identification in her hand.

"Move your vehicle, soldier. I'm Agent Sutton, S.I., on official business," Cassie barks.

"I don't care who..."

"We can either sit here and argue or you can let us past, soldier. But if anyone touches this car they will regret it," Cassie seethes, picking up her rifle from the front seat.

"Just get the tank to move over a bit so that we can slide by," Cal reasons. "We are on official business and have a medical emergency."

Without saying another word, the soldier turns and signals the tank to turn to the side of the road. The tank's massive tracks mount the kerb with barely any issue and why it couldn't have done that in the first place is beyond Cal.

As soon as the tank allows them some room, Cal revs the BMW's engine to warn the troops that he is coming through. They pass the tank with ease, watched by a nervous-looking young men dressed in camouflage and clinging to rifles.

Behind the rumbling tank, a road full of troops is illuminated by the car's headlights. Not one of the men looks like they want to be there, and Cal knows exactly how they feel. As the men part for them to pass, he wants to wind down his window and warn each of them about the danger they are bravely marching toward. There is nothing he can do for them, however. Warning the troops would do nothing but create panic. Cal cannot risk that. The fight has to happen and must be won, here and now.

"We're losing her," Cassie whispers into Cal's ear, bringing him back to reality.

Cal picks up his speed as much as the parting sea of soldiers will allow. City Hospital is the closest for Lauren to be taken to, but that is at least 20 minutes away. Cassie speaks to Lauren to try and keep her conscious whilst an upset Kim does the same, when her crying allows her to. Kim is becoming distraught and, if she loses her sister, she will be inconsolable.

The moment Cal clears the column of troops he floors the BMW. The road winds around a short distance more before it straightens to approach the road from which they escaped the battle. Flashes of gunfire show Cal that the battle is still ongoing, but thankfully they are no longer in the crossfire.

Red brake lights appear on the left of the battle. The queue of cars waiting on the slip road to join the trunk road out of the area sinks Cal's hopes of making the hospital in 20 minutes.

"Head to the back of the battle group!" Cassie insists, when she sees the jammed traffic.

"Let's hope they're more helpful," Cal replies, referring to the troops they have just left behind.

"You leave them to me!" Cassie states.

"We need a hospital," Kim interjects, hysterically.

"The roads are blocked with traffic, Kim," Cal responds, gently. "It will take too long to get to one."

"There'll be a medical trauma team with the battle group," Cassie assures Kim. "This type of injury is what they're trained for."

"Please hurry then, Cal," Kim pleads.

Despite Kim's plea to hurry, Cal takes the decision to slow their approach toward the fighting. He doesn't want to spook a trigger-happy soldier when he drives up to their lines.

Thankfully, Cassie is as correct as ever. At the rear of the battle, there is a green truck with a red cross painted on its side parked up. Cal drives straight at the medical truck. Soldiers covering the rear stand from their positions and hold their hands up for the car to stop. Cal doesn't stop. He winds down his window so that he can lean out to wave the guards out of the way. His move brings the risk of being shot at, a risk he is willing to take in the current circumstances.

Bullets aren't fired at the car. Perhaps the situation hasn't deteriorated that far yet. Cal slips the BMW through the rear-guard, heading straight for the back of the medical truck. He hopes that the vehicle is kitted out as an ambulance would be, or even better, as he slams on the brakes.

Only when he bursts out of the car does Cal fully appreciate the ferocity of the fight escalating around them. Kim emerges from the car at the same time as he does, seemingly unconcerned about the chaos of the battle. Her concern is only for her sister. He looks at her for a moment, immediately seeing how upset and worried she is. The fleeting thought of taking her in his arms and telling her everything is going to be okay overwhelms him. He fights the impulse, however, and bypasses her to run around the car to where Lauren is. He tells himself that he's doing it because

Lauren needs medical help as soon as humanly possible. He must also admit to himself that it's because he cannot tell his wife that everything is going to be okay.

Cassie has already made Lauren's dire condition clear to Cal. His new associate is not one to overdramatise. If Cassie is worried, then there is good cause to be. Cassie emerges from the car through the same door that Kim used. She rushes around the car behind Cal, her urgency reiterating his thoughts.

Pulling open the car door to get to Lauren, Cal is aware that military figures are moving to intercept them. He ignores them completely, his only thought being to help his sister-in-law. Blood glistens in the light from the streetlamps above when he sees an unconscious Lauren slumped in her seat. Cal's eyes follow a trail of blood from halfway down Lauren's side to her thigh, where copious amounts of blood have pooled on the car seat. The horrifying image stuns him for a second.

"Get her out!" Cassie demands, as she arrives at Cal's side.

Cassie's demand snaps Cal into action. He rushes to lean in and take hold of Lauren. One arm slips behind her back while the other forces its way under her legs. A warm wetness soaks against the skin of the arm he pushes under Lauren. Cal barely registers that Lauren's blood is on him. Instead, he concentrates on looking for signs of life as he strains to pull her out of the car.

It is no mean feat to pull an unconscious adult body from the back of a car and into your arms. Cal uses all his strength to achieve his goal. He is as gentle as he can be, but the motion is awkward and there is no reaction from Lauren, which is worrying. Cal tries to put the thought that she may already be dead out of his head when he finally lifts Lauren up in his arms.

"You need to evacuate this area," an authoritative voice demands from behind Cal.

"Get us some help or fuck off," Cassie replies, giving the soldier short shrift.

"Put her on here," a female voice says, as Cal turns away from the car.

Just behind Cassie, three people have appeared. Cal sees the red crosses emblazoned on their armbands immediately on top of their camouflaged military uniforms. *Thank God*, he thinks, when he also sees the raised stretcher bed they are pushing with them.

"Move," Cal demands urgently at all who stand in the way of the bed.

He is relieved to remove the weight from his burning arms but, more importantly, relieved that medical experts can finally attend to Lauren.

Chapter 22

Stepping away from Lauren, Cal lets the medical team move in to do their job. They buzz around her as Cassie informs them of Lauren's injury as best she can. To the side of the commotion around her sister, Kim stands motionless, watching, her eyes wide with shocked disbelief.

Cal notices that the soldiers who had moved to intercept them have sloped away, obviously deciding that their rifles may be of more use elsewhere. He steps beside Kim and puts one of his arms around her, the one that isn't soaked with her sister's blood. Kim trembles against him. At first, Cal thinks she might be sobbing but quickly decides that it could be something more sinister: his wife may be going into shock.

Cal struggles to know what to say. The sisters are extraordinarily close, inseparable in fact. What can he possibly tell Kim to help her cope? He pulls her tighter toward him, hoping some of his body heat might ease her suffering, even if only slightly.

It is obvious from the medical team's urgency, which borders on panic, that Lauren's condition is critical. Cal's body warmth has little effect on Kim; her trembling increases to the point that he becomes worried. He then begins to panic himself. If Lauren dies in front of them, Kim will crumble in his arms.

"Put this around her," Cassie says to Cal, offering a blanket.

Cal has no idea where Cassie acquired the blanket, but he takes it gratefully and puts it around Kim's shoulders. The firefight echoing around them has become secondary to the fight to save Lauren, a fight that Cal knows deep down is tragically being lost.

Gradually, Cal's fears become reality. The medical team's urgency peaks with several rounds of desperately applied CPR to a motionless body. Lauren has passed away. Cal understands that before one of the medical team reluctantly pronounces Lauren's death and they all take a step back from her corpse.

"What's happening? Why have they stopped helping her?" Kim gasps in confusion.

Cal is at a loss as to how to break the news to his wife and he finds that he's unable to speak.

"I'm afraid that your sister has died," Cassie says, seeing that Cal has frozen.

"I don't understand. She can't have died. We found the car and we escaped, didn't we, Cal? Tell them, Cal," Kim sobs in denial.

"A bullet hit Lauren while we were in the car, remember?" Cal replies, finally coming out of his stupor. "It was a tragic accident, Kim. I'm sorry."

"She wasn't hit with a bullet," Kim insists, angrily, peering over to where Lauren lies. "We escaped!"

From below the stretcher bed, one of the medical team reaches for something. Her colleague helps her to unfurl a sheet which is then pulled down on the breeze to cover Lauren's body. The well-practised ritual of covering the body brings the awful realisation home to Kim. Without warning, she breaks away from Cal's embrace and runs toward the body of her sister. She hits the stretcher with a force that threatens to topple the raised contraption over, together with her sister's body. Thankfully, one of the medics sees the accident before it happens and moves forward to steady the stretcher just as Kim arrives.

"Thank you for trying," Cal says subtly to the medical team, as he goes over to try and comfort Kim.

A few minutes pass with Kim weeping and bent over her sister. Cal holds her shoulder in support but nothing he says to his wife is acknowledged by her. He notices Cassie talking to a commanding-looking man dressed in a military uniform who has appeared. The moment they finish their discussion, Cassie looks over to Cal before moving to speak to him.

"We have to leave," she tells Cal. "The fighting is getting worse; they can't guarantee our safety."

"What are we supposed to do?" Cal asks.

Cassie indicates with her head for Cal to come and talk to her, out of earshot of Kim.

"I can't just pull her away!" Cal insists, after he has told Kim that he will be back in a minute.

"That's exactly what you need to do, I'm afraid, Detective. She is in danger here. We all are. There's a battle going on right beside us," Cassie replies, bluntly. "And we have work to do," she adds, sheepishly.

"Work?" Cal asks, even though he knows what work Cassie is referring to.

"This is your investigation now, Cal," Cassie replies, earnestly. "I'm sorry for your and your wife's loss but we must continue. This is just the start. I'm sure you know that as well as me, if not more so. You know this case better than anyone. We have to stop this needless slaughter. Are you with me?"

Cal doesn't answer. Cassie is absolutely right on all counts, but he has something else to consider: his pregnant wife. Kim needs him now more than ever. How can he just abandon her?

"Cal?" Cassie presses.

"I'm going to..." Cal starts, but stops to think again. This time Cassie waits, and doesn't press him.

"I can't leave Kim now, Cassie. I'm sorry," Cal says, reluctantly.

"This is for Kim, Cal, for your unborn baby and for countless others," Cassie pleads. "We need you on this investigation. I need you, Cal."

Cal turns to look at Kim. She hasn't moved from her position of mourning her sister. He can clearly see that she is still shaking from her sobs and trembling through shock. Kim needs him—he cannot leave her to deal with her grief alone—but Cassie's words come back to haunt him.

Can he afford not to help solve this case? What will happen if the disease spreads out of the city? If there are more attacks? Where will it all end? And if he doesn't stand against this evil, then who will? Cal looks at Cassie.

"I will take Kim to her dad's. He lives about a half hour away. Once she is settled, I will see about returning. I can't promise anything, though. You understand that?" Cal offers.

"It sounds like it's the best offer I'm going to get, partner," Cassie replies. Her use of the word 'partner' is not lost on Cal.

"It's the best I can do right now," Cal tells her.

"What about Kim's sister's body?" Cassie asks, carefully.

Cal hadn't even considered Lauren's remains. There are two options, as he sees it. One is to leave it with the medical team, but he quickly discounts that option. He could never forgive himself if the body was lost in the system or, God forbid, buried in a mass grave or incinerated. That is what will happen with the infected. He's seen enough movies to know that it's the only option to help stop the spread of an unknown virus. Kim would also never forgive him, and her father would think even less of him than he already does, so he goes with the second option.

"We will take Lauren with us. Her father would want to bury her properly and we know that she wasn't infected when she died," Cal informs Cassie.

"I'll help you get her into the car," Cassie volunteers.

"What about you? What will you do?" Cal asks.

"Don't worry about me, my friend. I'm a big girl," Cassie replies.

"I know you can look after yourself, Cassie, to say the least. But seriously," Cal presses.

"I'll get picked up and head back to the office at Mercury House to continue the investigation, to keep it going until you return," Cassie smiles.

After some heartbreaking convincing of Kim, Cal manages to part her from her sister's body so that it can be loaded into the BMW. Without asking, one of the medics comforts Kim, while Cal and Cassie, with as much respect as possible, pick up Lauren's body.

After a bit of toing and froing, they manage to place Lauren's body across the car's back seat. Her legs must dangle into the footwell but most of her body fits across the seat. Cal straightens the sheet over Lauren before pulling a seat belt around her. The last thing he wants is for her corpse to roll off the seat while he is driving.

One of the medics offers Cal a black T-shirt to change into, together with a towel and a bottle of water to wash himself down with. He gratefully takes both and cleans himself up before returning to Kim.

"I'll be in touch," Cal tells Cassie, after he has directed a distraught Kim into the passenger seat.

"I'm afraid that I'll be hassling you, Cal. This is too important not to have you on the case," Cassie informs a dubious Cal.

"At least give me a couple of hours to get there and settle Kim in," Cal requests.

"I'll try to," Cassie answers, with a glint in her eye.

Cal rolls his eyes at Cassie's determination. He offers his hand to shake farewell, but Cassie ignores the offer. Instead, she surprises Cal by moving in to embrace him. He awkwardly returns her embrace, saying "Goodbye" as he does.

"Don't become a stranger," Cassie says, as she watches Cal turn toward the BMW.

As Cal takes one last look around before he gets into the car, the sound of gunfire suddenly becomes overpowering once more. The battle rages on and he wonders if the troops are winning as he shuts the car door. Kim looks at him through wet puffy eyes as he settles into his seat, as if she is going to say something, but her words fail her and she turns away, sobbing again.

"I'm sorry, Kim," Cal says, as he starts the car.

Kim doesn't respond to his apology. She continues to sob with her head down and her hair covering her face. Cal understands how upset she must be and doesn't blame her for not wanting to talk to him. He was the one who dragged them from the safety of their apartment. He was the one driving when Lauren was shot. Isn't he ultimately responsible for the death of her sister?

Cal hasn't time to wallow in his guilt. Instead, he must concentrate on getting Kim out of the city. He pulls the car around to head for the queue on the slip road waiting to join the main trunk road. He raises his hand to the medical staff as he passes them and to the surrounding troops, who clear out of the car's way.

In the event, the queue on the slip road has shrunk considerably and they move onto the trunk road with ease. Heavy congestion moving away from the Arena District forces Cal to take the first exit to move onto the back roads. Cal's intimate knowledge of the city allows him to cut out the worst of the traffic. In good time they join the main road that will take them to Kim's father's and, less than twenty minutes later, they reach the outskirts of his neighbourhood.

Kim's head rises slightly as she realises that they are close to her father's house. He lives in an old house at the end of a long winding driveway on the other side of the neighbourhood. Tom moved to the outskirts of the city shortly after his wife, and Kim's mother, died, over five years ago. He told his two girls that he needed a change of lifestyle after his wife's passing and both Kim and Lauren had supported Tom's decision and visited him regularly. They both loved their father dearly and he would do absolutely anything for his two girls.

The poor man is going to be devasted when they arrive and the tragic news is broken to him, a task that will surely fall to Cal. He is not looking forward to their arrival.

All too soon, the BMW's headlights shine onto the entrance to Kim's father's driveway. Kim hasn't uttered a word the entire journey, despite Cal's best efforts. Cal turns onto the gravel track leading up to the house, trying to think what to say to his father-in-law when they arrive. What is there to say? There is no way to dress up such awful news. All he can tell Tom is the truth and then live with the consequences.

As he reaches the top of the driveway, Cal sees homely yellow light illuminating the ground floor of the house. The shadow of a figure is standing in front of one of the windows. Tom has seen the car's headlights approaching and has come outside to greet them.

Tom's shadow disappears when Cal pulls up in front of him, the car's headlights obliterating it. Tom was a young father when he had Lauren and Kim. Even now he is only in his early fifties, and he stands waiting and smiling in anticipation of seeing his two girls.

Cal's stomach churns as he switches off the car's engine, but he leaves the headlights on. Kim turns to get out of the car, to go to her father. Cal wants to say something to her to help her on her way but can think of nothing. Tom's expression changes the moment he sees Kim. Whether he can sense that something is wrong, or he just sees that Kim isn't right, Cal can't say.

Kim runs around the car toward her father and Cal gets out to follow her. Tom spreads his arms to receive Kim as Cal approaches from behind. Kim virtually falls into Tom's arms. Her weeping stuns her father, who appears to go into shock immediately.

"Where is Lauren?" Tom asks Kim, but his daughter is unable to speak. She is too upset.

"Where is my daughter?" Tom asks Cal, his eyes burning.

Cal's eyes well up and his voice cracks as he tells Tom the tragic news. Kim's legs give way with grief and she falls through her father's arms as Cal breaks the news. She lands on the ground at his feet in a heap with Tom too stunned to help her.

Eventually, Tom is able to help Cal move Kim into the house. They place her on a sofa in the kitchen area, where Tom sits with her and takes her in his arms. Neither of them is in any state to try and console the other.

Cal makes hot drinks and generally feels awkward, eventually taking a seat at the kitchen table. Tom sits with Kim, stroking her head whilst trying to keep his own emotions in check. After an inordinate amount of time, Kim cries herself to sleep and Tom gently prises himself from underneath her. He puts a cushion under her head before turning to Cal.

"Tell me again what happened," Tom says, sitting opposite Cal.

Taking Tom, step by step, through how his daughter was killed is tough for both of them. The only details Cal leaves out are those about the severity of Lauren's injuries, but everything else he tells Tom is the whole truth.

When Cal finishes his account, Tom is silent for a moment. Cal thinks the worst when Tom gets up from the table without saying a word and checks on Kim before going to make another drink. Tom will hold Cal responsible. How could he not? Cal waits for his reaction, prepared to suffer whatever Tom's grief brings.

"Thank you, Cal," Tom says, as he puts a steaming mug down in front of Cal before returning to his seat opposite.

"What for?" Cal replies in surprise.

"You have brought both of my daughters back to me, so thank you. I won't forget it," Tom answers.

"I wish I could have saved them both," Cal says, as tears roll down his face.

"I know you do, Cal, and so do I," Tom acknowledges. "I have been watching the horrific events unfold on the news. It was an impossible situation and my only hope was that you were there with them. I knew that you would do anything in your power to get my daughters to safety. I know you did your best, Cal, so I thank you again and beg you not to blame yourself."

"I did do my best, Tom. I promise you that," Cal weeps.

"I know, Cal," Tom assures. "Can I ask you one more thing?"

"Anything," Cal replies.

"Would you help me bring Lauren into the house?"

Kim doesn't wake while Cal and Tom bring Lauren inside. There is no hiding the bloodstained sheet from Tom. To his credit, he manages to hold himself together while they take Lauren inside and lay her on the floor to rest in the family room. Both men stand over the body in respect for a moment before returning to Kim in the kitchen.

Cal's phone begins to vibrate in his pocket as Tom sits on the sofa at Kim's feet. Cassie's name is displayed on the screen and Cal glances at Tom as he wonders whether to answer.

"Work?" Tom asks.

"Yes, but I'm not sure I should answer. I'm needed here," Cal replies.

"I will take care of Kim, Cal. If you are needed to bring an end to this horror, then you should answer," Tom replies, earnestly.

Cal does exactly that.

Supplementary

After a morning of mind-numbingly boring business meetings, Doctor Francis Arnoult ensured that his afternoon was clear. His entire life is a catalogue of one meeting followed by another and every advance in technological communications makes it worse. There is always something to discuss, a problem that needs his attention or a decision that needs to be made in one corner of the globe or another. In the modern era, he is always just a click away from being called upon. He has nobody to blame but himself for this situation, he knows that all too well. His obsessive, controlling nature demands that he is everywhere all at once. He has not built up a multinational pharmaceutical conglomerate by letting other people control his business.

The only time Dr Arnoult feels the least bit relaxed is when he is in his private laboratory doing the thing he was born to do: experimentation and the advancement of mother nature. That is the only time he allows himself to be out of communication. Unless there is an emergency of course. The multibillion-dollar business he presides over is a mere by-product of his passion. Material wealth is of no concern to him, it's simply a means to an end that has given him the freedom required to fulfil his destiny.

As always, his private time in the laboratory zips by in a flash. All too quickly he must wrap his work up, lock the door on it for another day and move on to the next stage of today's itinerary.

Some might think it strange to live at your workplace but Dr Arnoult's living arrangements are unique. Not everyone owns property all over the world as well as science campuses, where the most brilliant minds congregate to further science's understanding of the universal environment. Living in luxuriously designed and custom-built apartments at the pinnacle of the tallest building on his largest campus makes perfect sense to Dr Arnoult.

It is only a short ride up to his sprawling penthouse home from his beloved private laboratory. The penthouse is just as much a workplace for Dr Arnoult as it is a home and he heads straight for his office to proceed with the next order of business.

The next stage of Foundation Day is well underway. Dr Arnoult is sure that if he turned on the television there would be wall-to-wall coverage of the latest stage, which is under evaluation. He has no time to watch ill-informed and censored news coverage of their undertaking. He requires succinct and accurately reported accounts of their work from experts on the ground.

To that end, a scheduled briefing for stakeholders in the endeavour, of whom Dr Arnoult is one, is scheduled for precisely the current time. Dr Arnoult logs onto the secure and encrypted platform, on which the briefing will be given by the endeavour's Director of Operations, codenamed Janus18.

"Greetings, stakeholders," Janus18 begins when the secure platform connects. "I am delighted to report that our work is progressing as planned. The latest stage that we are currently evaluating at City Arena is well underway and is currently on schedule.

"Before I continue with my full report, I'm pleased to say that we have Operative 21 standing by to give a first-hand account of the situation on the ground. They have been in the thick of it at the arena, but they only have a small window of time. So, if there are no objections, I will allow Operative 21 to make their report forthwith."

Nobody objects to Janus18's request and Dr Arnoult sits up in his chair in anticipation of hearing this first-hand account. He is only interested in accurate first-hand reporting and he quickly clicks to check his list of operatives to see who exactly will be reporting. For security reasons, only a select few people involved have access to the list of operatives. As he opens the encrypted file containing the list, a female voice begins to speak.

The spreadsheet opens in front of Dr Arnoult and he scrolls down to find Operative 21. He is unfamiliar with the name displayed but is sure that Agent Cassie Sutton has been carefully selected for her position within the organisation.

TO BE CONTINUED

If you have enjoyed **FOUNDATION DAY**, be sure to leave a review. Amazon reviews only take a minute and are so important in building a buzz for every book.
Many thanks, every review is appreciated!

CAPITAL FALLING – THE SERIES

As Black Smoke Rises, Order Disintegrates...

Former SAS soldier Andy Richards is no stranger to horrors, but no training could ever have prepared him for the nightmare unfolding at home. While a viral epidemic hammers London, Andy finds himself trapped in the epicentre, forced to protect his family. Together with his young daughter, he leads a small group of survivors toward latent refuge, all the while searching for his missing son and infantryman; this is the ultimate game of survival.

With those infected displaying brutal, inhuman behaviour and caught up in a climate of martial law, no one can be trusted. Old connections may help to unravel this mystery virus, but the resultant hellscape means Andy and his group meet danger at every turn.

Stakes are high, and failing means a fate worse than death...

The perfect tale for troubled times, ***CAPITAL FALLING*** delivers dark thrills and surprising sentiment—twisted, cerebral fun. You'll race to the end like your life depends on it...

THE Z SEASON - TRILOGY 1

3 Novels - A #1 Best Seller - 650+ Pages

- Infectious to its Very Core

A trilogy of standalone and unique novels that don't hold back and all with a zombie - undead twist.......
YOU HAVE BEEN WARNED!

KILL TONE

A festival of feverish, exhilarating tension with a rock 'n roll crescendo that unleashes hell itself, this is not for the faint-hearted. KILL TONE proves the perfect blend of decadence and undead carnage, whilst never losing sight of its predominant humanity.

VOODOO SUN

Caribbean Voodoo may have caused this nightmare, and nothing short of a miracle will help Max get out alive.

A tale of undead carnage and mayhem, VOODOO SUN embarks for bliss but lands in true perdition.

CRUEL FIX

CRUEL FIX is a terrifying trip through the labyrinth of loss and lunacy. Bleak and sinister it may be, but spirited humanity retains a twisted shard of hope …. Though all that glitters isn't gold, and all that walks is not alive.

Read these novels in any order, you choose. Each is a tale of its own and completely unique, but be warned they are not for the faint-hearted or easily offended!

Praise for THE Z SEASON TRILOGY

GREAT BOOK ★★★★★

"Just read the Kill Tone what an amazing book. the story had me captivated from start to finish. great author, love his books."

JUST A BRILLIANT AUTHOR ★★★★★

"Another great book by the author Lance brilliant from start to finish kept me on the edge like the others so will have to wait for next one now… hopefully."

ANOTHER GREAT READ ★★★★★

"Action packed from the beginning. So realistic that you could actually imagine this happening! Just wish it didn't end so soon. I would like to see how the virus spreads so roll on the next one."

PAPERBACK – KINDLE & KINDLE UNLIMITED

For more information on Lance Winkless
and future writing see his website.

www.LanceWinkless.com

By Lance Winkless

FOUNDATION DAY

CAPITAL FALLING - THE SERIES

&

THE Z SEASON – TRILOGY

KILL TONE
VOODOO SUN
CRUEL FIX

Visit Amazon Author Pages

Amazon US- Amazon.com/author/lancewinkless
Amazon UK- Amazon.co.uk/Lance-Winkless/e/B07QJV2LR3

Why Not Follow

Facebook LanceWinklessAuthor
Twitter   @LanceWinkless
Instagram @LanceWinkless
Pinterest www.pinterest.com/lancewinkless
BookBub www.bookbub.com/authors/lance-winkless

Printed in Great Britain
by Amazon

87210483R00180